# THE DARING WOMEN OF NEW YORK

A NOVEL

# Gayle Callen

*To Brandon Uy, a wonderful husband to our daughter, Michelle, a loving dad to our grandchildren, and an excellent guide to all things New York City. I feel blessed to have another son.*

**1**

---

## PAMELA
NEW YORK CITY, 2023

Pamela Mosher craned her neck to stare up at the four-story brick building perched on a corner in the Seaport District of Manhattan. As far as she knew, Harbor House was one of the oldest buildings in the city, older than the United States—and it was hers. She clapped a hand to her forehead with a groan.

A small tree blossomed with flowers over the dirt rectangle in the sidewalk in which it was planted, but the sign of early summer didn't make her feel warm. She hugged herself and thought that Harbor House looked as dilapidated and old as she felt. A wooden panel covered the glass-paned restaurant door, and plywood protected the large windows on either side.

It had started life as a tavern in the 1760s, been used as a storefront, a boarding house, a speakeasy, even a stop on the Underground Railroad. During the Covid pandemic shutdown, her family restaurant, Featherstone's, had closed.

Covid had taken her father's life, too. With her husband's death a year ago, Pam was now completely alone, no husband, no kids, no siblings. For a moment, the staggering feeling of despair and loneliness swept over her again, but she'd gotten good at pushing it aside when she needed to.

And she really needed her iron control today. She had scheduled meetings with a real estate developer and a historical preservationist. One wanted her to sell, the other wanted her to restore Harbor House—fat chance of that. It was full of too many memories of her father, including her own feelings of jealousy in her youth. It had taken so much of his time. She'd spent years serving customers in the restaurant when she'd been in high school and college, forgoing sports and hanging with friends. College had been her chance to escape. And then she'd met Will, and a new kind of obsession had grown between them, the drive to succeed at their fledgling business. Was everyone in her family tree obsessed with something?

The building represented so many different emotions for her, and being rid of it would give her peace. She wanted to escape everything in her life. After her husband's death, she'd sold the Long Island insurance brokerage that they had built from the ground up. She was convinced it had killed him in the end. Ambition had been the focus of their lives, and they'd decided against having children because of it. They'd given up travel and close friends.

She'd thought she could now spend the rest of her life traveling, seeing the world that they'd never had time for. She'd spent her fiftieth birthday alone in Thailand. Instead of feeling at peace, knowing she could do whatever she wanted for the rest of her life, perhaps consult and travel, all she'd felt was empty and hopeless.

So she'd come back to Harbor House, telling herself that its fate was hanging over her like a menacing cloud. It was time to be done with it. Maybe then she could find some kind of purpose for her life.

Pam took a step toward the building, head bent as she fumbled for the keys in her purse.

"Look out!"

Pam's head came up just as the front wheel of a bike grazed her leg, sending her reeling backward. The bicyclist fell sideways, collapsing beneath the bike.

"Are you all right?" Pam pulled the bike away from what she could now see was a teenage girl.

For a frozen moment, the girl looked up at her with big brown eyes, her long curly hair caught back in a ponytail beneath a ball cap. Her eyes weren't apologetic or hurt—they were frightened. And was that the start of a bruise on her jaw? The girl looked back over her shoulder, and Pam followed her gaze.

On the next block, a young man wearing an oversized sweatshirt and loose jeans pulled a hat lower on his forehead and quickly stepped inside a store.

The girl got to her feet and took her bike by the handlebars, saying to Pam, "Thanks. Sorry I almost knocked you over. Are you hurt?"

"I'm not the one who landed on my butt on the sidewalk. Are *you* hurt?"

The girl blushed and briefly looked away. "I'm fine. I shouldn't have been riding on the sidewalk. But..."

She stared across the street again, where the young man still hadn't reappeared.

"Do you know that guy?" Pam asked. "Or is he some stranger harassing you? We can call the police."

"No!" the girl hurriedly said. "I know him. He was teasing me, thinking he's funny."

"You don't look amused."

The girl gave a crooked smile. "It'll be okay. I'm sorry to bother you about this." She straightened her jean jacket and glanced down at her clothes.

That's when they both saw the rip in her leggings and the spot of blood on her knee.

"It's fine," the girl quickly said.

"I have a bandage. We could wash your knee."

She smiled nervously. "Here on the street?"

Pam nodded toward her building. "Inside. This is mine."

"The restaurant is closed," the girl said, frowning. "You have an apartment here?"

"Nobody's lived here in a long time. I inherited it last year."

The girl's mouth dropped open. "Wow."

"Yeah, wow."

"Are you going to reopen the restaurant?" Then she winced. "Sorry. Not my business."

"That's okay. Let's go wash your knee."

The girl hung back. "I really shouldn't bother you. And, no offense, I don't know you."

"I'll leave the door wide open so you can run," Pam said dryly. Then she paused. "I don't know you either. If you come in, you should know I have security cameras, as well as alarms that'll ring straight through to the authorities." Well, to the security company, but the girl didn't need to know that. "This place might be old, but I know how to protect it."

The girl lifted her chin. "And I have a phone, and I know how to use it to call those same authorities."

Pam felt a half smile lift her cheek. As she put her key into the solid door, she said, "I'm Pam Mosher. Bring your bike in; don't leave it outside."

"I'm Lucia." But still she hesitated. "I think I remember you. Are you the daughter of the old owner?"

Pam straightened in surprise. "I am."

"I knew him. I worked at Featherstone's for a year before the pandemic, before he—" She broke off with a solemn look. "It was too bad what happened to him. He was a cool guy who hired me even though I never worked in a restaurant before. I was only here a year before Covid hit and closed the place."

Pam swallowed past a sudden lump in her throat. "Lucia.

That name is familiar. I think I remember him mentioning you," she said, surprised that her voice sounded husky. "He loved his restaurant, and when he found a hard worker, he would give me all the details."

In a quiet voice, Lucia said, "That was nice of him."

After stepping inside, Pam punched in the security code next to the door, blocking the girl's view. Lucia rolled her eyes with amusement.

The gloomy interior was only lit by light that found tiny cracks in the protective boards over the windows. Pam found the light switch, but with alternating bulbs burnt out in the wall sconces, it wasn't exactly bright in there.

Lucia looked around with obvious curiosity, and Pam tried to see the old place through her eyes. Tables with upside down chairs on top were stacked along the walls. Past the fireplace, the bar in the back right of the room was overflowing with dusty boxes. One set of double doors led to the kitchen, and the other to the restrooms.

"It could still be a restaurant," Lucia said.

"It's been many different restaurants over two hundred and fifty years. What someone does with it going forward won't be my problem. And I sold the stock of alcohol to Dad's business friends when the restaurant closed," she added pointedly.

Lucia seemed to bite back a smile. "I always liked the vibe here. So historic."

"And historic things need a lot of upkeep," Pam said dryly. "But I've recently had the water turned back on." She gestured toward Lucia's leg. "There's probably a first aid kit behind the bar."

Inside the kit, she found an antiseptic packet and handed it across the bar to Lucia, along with two sizes of bandages. As Pam came around to the front of the bar, Lucia was pulling her leggings up above her knee, bending over to treat the wound. Pam slid a chair behind her.

Lucia looked up and smiled. "Thanks."

She was about to ask if the girl lived around here when someone knocked on the front door and pushed it open, leaving the person backlit by sunlight, framed in the doorway.

Pam saw Lucia tense and found herself stepping in front of the girl, wondering if there was still a baseball bat behind the bar. "Can I help you?" she said coolly.

"Ms. Mosher? I'm Ikeem Trent from Manhattan Seaport Development Partners."

Pam's unease morphed into a smile. "Mr. Trent, please come in."

"Call me Ikeem."

"I'm Pam."

He was a big man with dark skin whose bald head gleamed in the low light, and a tiny diamond twinkled in one ear. As he reached out to shake Pam's hand, Pam noticed Lucia ducking behind him and heading for the door.

Ikeem glanced over his shoulder at the girl as Pam called her name. But Lucia waved without looking back. Pam hadn't even gotten a chance to ask her about herself, or what she remembered about Pam's dad.

When the door was opened again by another person, Lucia started to lead her bike through before stopping abruptly. She sent a worried look over her shoulder at Pam, who wondered if that guy she was afraid of was still loitering about.

"Lucia, you don't have to leave," Pam called.

Lucia hesitated, then brought her bike back inside.

The newcomer was an older woman with short auburn hair framing a round face with glasses. She eyed Lucia before turning to Pam. "Pam Mosher?"

Pam nodded. "You must be Gretchen Smith."

Ikeem frowned. "With the New York City Landmarks Preservation Commission?"

Gretchen grinned. "That's me. And you're..."

"Ikeem Trent from—"

"From Manhattan Seaport Development," Gretchen interrupted. "It seems we know each other by reputation though not in person."

As they shook hands, Pam thought they did not seem pleased to see each other. Both of them turned to look at her, while Lucia stood against the far wall as if she didn't know what to do with herself.

"I thought we had a private meeting, that you were interested in selling Harbor House," Ikeem said, his smile more polite than enthusiastic.

"And I thought you were interested in saving the building that your family has owned for hundreds of years," Gretchen argued. "Designation as a historic property can help preserve your heritage in so many ways."

Ikeem rolled his eyes.

Pam held up both hands in a T for timeout. She planned to sell, but Gretchen had made a hard case for getting her views heard as well. And Pam knew that Ikeem was more interested in the property's location than its historic value. Maybe he could be convinced to keep its historic character—if he was the one to purchase it. "You both want to look at the building, and I don't want to waste anyone's time, including mine. Why should I give the same tour twice? We can certainly have separate discussions afterward." She glanced at Lucia. "Why don't you come along, too?"

The girl straightened and gave a nod.

For a moment, they all stood in the dining room and looked around.

"My father loved this restaurant," Pam said quietly. "I hated working here as a kid. He was so proud that his family had held onto this place since the American Revolution."

Even Ikeem looked impressed.

"Why didn't he apply for the National Register of Historic

Places?" Gretchen asked. "He could have qualified for grants to help repair it."

"My father was a hippie—he didn't believe in registering anything he didn't have to with the government. But he got old, and Hurricane Sandy almost destroyed this place. He was just managing the last of the major repairs in the basement, trying to keep the restaurant going, when Covid hit. It's been closed since 2020." Pam took a deep breath, trying not to think about her strong dad withering away on a ventilator.

Ikeem and Gretchen didn't say anything—what was there to say? They just glanced at each other in obvious discomfort. But Lucia's dark eyes glistened with sympathy. Pam didn't know a lot about teenagers, but suspected Lucia had known her share of grief.

Pam took a deep breath and donned her professional demeanor. "You're not here for a history lecture. Let's get on with the tour."

"I do love history," Gretchen said.

Ikeem rolled his eyes again, but a smile tugged on his lips.

Pam clapped her hands together. "Okay, then here we go. You're in the restaurant dining room. My father had an apartment on one of the upper floors the last few years of his life."

"How much was he able to repair after the hurricane?" Ikeem asked.

There was no point in being evasive. "To be honest, not enough. Some electrical and plumbing in the basement was updated. But there was so much to do, and I was so busy with our brokerage, I didn't realize—" She stopped herself. "The entire basement was under water after the hurricane. After major repair work, it looks a lot better than it used to."

"Grants could help you repair the damage," Gretchen said. "The National Register—"

"Please stop," Pam interrupted. "Will the National Register offer millions of dollars in grants?"

"Um...probably not."

"That's what it's going to take. I'm not about to risk everything I have for my retirement on this place."

"And why should you do all that work?" Ikeem asked. "The amount of money you could receive for Harbor House would set you up for life."

"Her family has been here for hundreds of years," Gretchen pointed out between gritted teeth.

Pam groaned. "You two are like the devil and angel on my shoulders, trying to tell me what to do."

"I'm not sure I know which of us is which," Ikeem said dryly.

Gretchen lowered her shoulders and gave a reluctant smile. "Me neither. I guess we should keep it that way."

"I promise we'll discuss everything," Pam said. "Can we finish the tour?"

They moved into the industrial kitchen and beyond to the hallway that led out the side entrance.

"Deliveries are made here," Pam said, "and it leads to the upper floors where there are offices and storage and apartments. This was also the entrance to the speakeasy."

Gretchen smiled and rubbed her hands together. "History! Let's go check it out."

As they walked down the stairs, Pam pointed out that all the walls had been ripped out to the studs due to water damage. There were boxes stacked here and there, and a shiny new furnace and water heater in a back room. It didn't look like a place where revelers partied every night.

"Dad really meant to bring this old building back to life," Pam said wistfully. "There is so much history—family history —here. My great grandfather got caught up with mob and went to jail, leaving my great aunt, a young flapper, to keep the place going to support the rest of the family." She glanced at Lucia. "Flappers were what they called young single women in those days who dressed and behaved how they wanted."

"I've seen pictures," she said. "Cool dresses."

When they ascended to the second floor, doorways led into rooms piled with more stuff—Pam had no idea what. "My dad used these rooms as offices and storage for the restaurant. His apartment was up above. But if you want another historical fact, my ancestors were forced to quarter British officers in these rooms during the American Revolution, back when Featherstone Tavern was also an inn."

Gretchen's eyes were wide with excitement, while Ikeem just heaved a sigh, as if this didn't look good for him.

"Don't worry, Ikeem," Pam said, patting his arm. "I'm going to sell the building." She *had* to sell.

"Even with all this incredible family history?" Gretchen asked.

"It's just...history," Pam said, "and the occasional relic. What does that really matter? I have no kids to leave it to. Here, you'll see what I mean. I think Dad kept it in his office."

She turned on the light in the first room off the staircase.

"Aha!" She brought out a metal tankard and blew the dust off it.

Ikeem sneezed. Lucia's forehead wrinkled with disappointment.

"Not much to look at," Pam said as if she could hear the girl's thoughts. "But this was passed down in my family. I'm told it was used in the tavern during the 1700s."

"Shouldn't that be in a museum?" Ikeem asked.

Gretchen elbowed him. "It's her family property—its history!"

Pam shrugged and set the tankard down on the floor next to the stairs. "I know what it is and what it represents—I just don't want to be under the weight of it anymore. I can't afford to. Let's continue the tour."

The third floor was her father's shabby apartment. It brought back a wave of longing for the man himself, but not Harbor House. She remembered him selling their home in Queens after her mom died because he'd rather live with his family's ghosts than the memories of his beloved wife. Pam always suspected he felt guilty for the hours he put into the restaurant, evening hours that kept him away from his wife and daughter.

"You said you're not staying here," Ikeem said, forehead wrinkled as he looked around.

"No. I've rented an Airbnb nearby and I own a house on Long Island."

Should she be speaking so openly in front of a teenager she didn't know? Maybe not, but although the place looked abandoned, she had plenty of security.

"This place can be made habitable without too much effort." Pam's spirits sank as she looked around. There were so many boxes, so many unopened drawers. "I've thought about moving to Manhattan, but I don't know."

"You don't want that," Ikeem said. "City living is a pain."

"I love my apartment in the East Village," Gretchen said.

The two eyed each other combatively.

Pam sighed. In college, all she had wanted was to graduate and move to the city, to start her life. Then she'd met Will and fallen in love. He'd wanted Long Island where he'd grown up, where he thought he could use his family contacts in their insurance brokerage. She'd put her dreams of city-living out of her mind.

And now here she was, in the city, in a multi-million-dollar rundown building she owned. And it wasn't anything she'd wanted it to be. She was alone, making her own decisions.

Gretchen and Ikeem were watching her with curiosity.

Pam turned to Lucia. "What about you? Don't you want to weigh in on where I live, too?"

The girl opened her mouth, hesitated, then said, "You should live where you want."

"That's not much help."

Lucia slowly grinned. "I love the city."

Gretchen shot Ikeem a smug smile.

They toured the fourth-floor apartment without any more bickering. This space had basically become her dad's attic after he sold the Queens house. They didn't linger long, but went up the stairs to the roof.

A half wall guarded them on three sides, and the fourth side hugged the taller building next door. There was nothing here—but a spectacular view of the East River and the Brooklyn Bridge, awash in the fading light of the sinking sun.

Gretchen gasped. Ikeem frowned, as if even he thought this would be too much temptation for Pam to resist.

Lucia spun in a circle, eyes wide with wonder. "You could hang lights and make this really special."

"No thanks." Pam led them all back down the staircase to the side entrance. Out on the sidewalk, Gretchen and Ikeem tried to jockey over who could schedule a one-on-one with her, but Pam wasn't in the mood to decide immediately, and told them so.

Ikeem shrugged with good humor. "I'll be waiting for your call. Good meeting you, Pam. Gretchen." He nodded to his opponent and strolled away.

When Gretchen opened her mouth to speak, Pam held up a hand. "I don't remember the last time I visited Harbor House, and now I'm feeling sad and overwhelmed. We'll talk when I schedule an appointment."

Gretchen nodded. "I understand. Take care, Pam. And remember—memories are a good thing. It just might take you some time to realize it." She spoke as if she understood but didn't elaborate on her own experiences.

Pam was grateful. As Gretchen left, she turned to find Lucia standing in the doorway.

"I guess I'll go, too," Lucia said, turning to go back through the kitchen.

Pam locked the side door and followed her back to the dining room.

Lucia retrieved her bike by the door, and Pam opened it for her, looking out both ways up and down the block.

"The coast is clear," Pam said.

Lucia smiled. "Thanks for your help, and for reminding me how happy I was working here."

Though Pam didn't feel the same, she nodded. "I hope you stop by again. I'd love to hear your memories about my dad."

Lucia nodded, climbed onto her bike, and rode away, leaving Pam to lock the door behind her. She should just shut off all the lights and leave, but she found herself wandering back upstairs again, as if she hoped to see the ghost of her father.

"How do I find happiness again, Daddy?" she whispered aloud. "Did I ever even have it?"

No ghostly voice spoke to her, but she did see the glimmer of the colonial tankard on the floor near the stairs.

She picked it up, carrying it as she checked that all the lights were off and the door to the roof was locked. Back down in the dining room, she put the tankard on the bar where it seemed to belong, turned off the last lights, and shut the door.

# 2

## ABIGAIL
### JULY 16TH, 1780

The scarlet-clad British soldier slammed the tankard down on Abigail Featherstone's tray harder than he needed to, almost making her stagger, but she only nodded and kept walking to the bar located in the rear of the taproom. She was used to the arrogance, the entitlement, the derision. New York City had been occupied by the British for four years now, and since they hadn't defeated the colonies as quickly or as easily as they'd hoped, they often took out their frustration on the citizens they were supposed to be protecting. She didn't want to be their next victim. Over the years, her overwhelming fear had sunk to simmering, ready to boil back to the surface if a soldier looked at her too closely.

But for the moment, in her tavern, they were just men, gambling over cards or playing ninepins in the alley nearby and drinking too much rum, bolstering themselves for battle or commiserating over the loss of a comrade.

Abigail had once been a staunch Loyalist, but it seemed a lifetime ago. Her late husband Edmund had been with the Sons of Liberty, where they'd gone from shouting mottos like "No taxation without representation" against the Stamp Act to stockpiling arms and gunpowder for war. They orchestrated crowds to burn effigies but were also guilty of censorship and destruction of property in the name of freedom.

She'd been appalled, but nothing she said to him had mattered. He'd died in the Battle of Long Island trying to defend Manhattan near the start of the war, leaving her to mother their two children while operating their tavern and renting out the lodgings above. His death had been pointless, for the Continental army had to retreat, and the British had swarmed back into New York City. They'd declared martial law, shutting down the courts and leaving New Yorkers without rights.

The British government ignored its citizens, leaving a quarter of the city a blackened mass of disease after the great fire. They took all the food stores and firewood for themselves. Prisoners died in filthy inhuman conditions on prison ships moored in the harbor. All of this had turned Abigail into a woman who denied her British citizenship—privately. She had to support her children, and she served whoever wanted food and drink.

As she set the tray on the bar, her barkeep and man of all work, Henry Barlow, gave her a concerned frown. Henry was a free man of color who'd fought at her husband's side in Brooklyn. Some northern armies integrated, but in the South, they wouldn't arm slaves, yet had no problem sending free Blacks to serve in the place of wealthy White men. Henry had returned with both her husband's body and an injury that soon took his leg below the knee, causing him to limp with a peg leg. He was nearly forty, with touches of white in his close-cropped hair, and a thin, wiry body that was sturdier than it looked. His wife, Pearl, was Abigail's cook and companion, a second mother to her children. Abigail didn't know what she would have done without them these last four years.

They'd stayed with her even when the British insisted on

taking over the tavern lodgings, relegating Henry and Pearl into a storage room behind the kitchen, forcing Abigail and her two children to share the smallest room on the third floor. At least the soldiers were paying for the privilege.

But the Redcoats being nearby had sometimes worked to her advantage...

Abigail gave Henry a reassuring smile as she joined him behind the bar to double-check that the cash box was locked. She never let anyone see the doubts that plagued her into the night, the fears that war would touch her children even more than it already had. She projected calm competence and unflappability. After all, she was a woman running a man's business. She'd always done the bookkeeping and overseen the domestic side of the lodgings, and now she was doing that on behalf of her son, who'd legally inherited two-thirds of his father's property. Abigail was keeping her widow's third afloat and ensuring her son's future.

But since the war had unfolded the way it had, the British showing their cruelty and excess, guilt often invaded her dreams over how she'd disagreed with her husband, Edmund —and how he'd been right all along. She'd spent her entire life believing in the Crown, and it had only tarnished itself with every cruelty inflicted on innocent citizens and helpless prisoners of war.

She'd never had the chance to apologize to him, had watched him go off to a war she hadn't supported, and he'd never come back. He'd died for what he believed in. Even before he'd joined the army, he'd been so brave, keeping the tavern going when the Loyalists had streamed out in 1775 as Patriots took over the city, and then the reverse, when all the Loyalists came back in 1776 as the British occupied the city. She thought they'd be safer with the king's soldiers and the king's laws. It hadn't been so.

The door to the kitchen opened behind Abigail, stirring her

from her thoughts. Her ten-year-old son, Andrew, was walking slowly, carrying a tray of clean glasses. Every time she saw him, he reminded her anew of his father. For a while, it had hurt like a vise squeezing her heart, but now it made her soften with love at the memories. He had the same auburn hair as Edmund, the same intelligent brown eyes, the freckles—she swallowed hard to ease the lump in her throat. Someday she'd forget the guilt that she'd disapproved of her husband's choices.

Henry took the glasses and tousled Andrew's hair, which he would have ducked away from if his mother had done it. But Andrew looked up to Henry and wanted to please him.

"How are your studies progressing, Andrew?" she asked.

Two men at the bar looked at him curiously, the red ribbons in their hats proclaiming them loyalists.

Andrew swallowed. "Fine. Lottie needs to work on her printing."

His sister Charlotte, whom they called Lottie, could never live up to his high standards. She might only be eight, but he expected her to be as educated as he was. It caused friction between them, but Pearl, who often oversaw their work when Abigail couldn't, had a way of soothing them both.

Henry and Pearl had been able to read and write when they'd come to work for her, but they'd hidden it for many months. Abigail hadn't blamed them for the fear. They didn't know how Abigail would react to their education—some took it poorly, fearing that an educated Negro caused trouble. That was absurd. They, too, had once supported the British, who offered slaves freedom if they joined the British army. They weren't slaves but understood the dilemma. Like Abigail, they, too, watched the British behavior in New York and revised their opinion.

As Andrew retreated into the kitchen, Abigail said another prayer that she'd done the right thing, keeping her children with her during the war.

The door had barely swung closed when Pearl emerged with another tray, bearing a bowl of lamb stew—which hid how scrawny the lamb had been—and slices of her fresh-baked bread with apple butter. With a nervous smile, she handed Abigail the tray and retreated into the kitchen as fast as she could. Pearl had never been well-treated by White men and had ample reason for her fear of them. She was younger than Henry, closer to Abigail's age, with lighter skin and delicate features, things that lured male gazes. She kept her mob cap on to cover her dark hair, her eyes lowered. She wore the plainest gowns made of broadcloth, no matter how Abigail encouraged her to try the lighter chintz or calico muslin during the humid summer. No lace at her neckline or trimmed on the edges of the fichu gathered around her shoulders. Pearl wanted to be plain and unnoticed, and kept to her kitchen as much as possible.

Abigail took a deep breath and turned around, looking for the customer who'd ordered the lamb stew. She saw him on the bench near the bare hearth, beneath a lantern that lit the dark corner. With a nod, she placed the bowl and plate of bread before him. When she saw he'd left his payment—British coins instead of Continentals—she gathered it quickly before he could change his mind. The British had done their best to make Continentals almost worthless and had mostly succeeded.

Letting her empty tray hang to her side, she turned back toward the bar and then came to a sudden stop. A man stepped through the open front door and stopped to survey the tavern interior. The mullioned windows silhouetted him, briefly obscuring his face, but Abigail recognized him immediately. It was Benjamin G., her contact with the Culper spy ring. She wasn't allowed to know his last name—and it bothered her that he knew hers because of the tavern name, Featherstone's. He pulled off his tricorn hat, revealing black hair laced with silver at the temples, tied back into a queue. There was several days' growth of scruffy beard on his face, and his eyes were heavy-lidded with wariness and exhaustion.

And inside her rose the wall she'd carefully constructed to keep herself free of any emotional entanglement.

Ben glanced around the taproom as if looking for a table, his gaze passing right over her as if they didn't know each other.

And they weren't supposed to. Just his appearance meant she was to prepare for his return tonight after she'd closed the tavern.

Abigail went past the bar and into the kitchen, her stomach tight with dread. It had been months since General Washington had wanted information from their spy network, months where she'd begun to feel normal—as normal as one could feel when one's city was under occupation during a war.

At least she'd assumed they'd been unneeded. Once the British fleet had left New York City last December, then took Charleston, South Carolina, back in May, all the focus seemed to be moving to the south. But General Clinton had recently returned to the city after his "victorious" southern campaign and would be overseeing the war from his northern base. Or so all her customers discussed. Did General Washington have something planned?

Initially when Ben had approached her—he'd known her husband in the Sons of Liberty—she'd been willing to contribute what she could, as if she could make up for not supporting her husband. It had been easy to listen in on the conversations among soldiers, and occasionally to talk to officers at the parties thrown by her sister, Rebecca, who was married to a Loyalist turned British officer.

But then she'd drawn the suspicion of Lieutenant Rutherford, a junior officer looking to make a name for himself by meeting the right people at the party. He'd almost caught her eavesdropping, and although she'd been able to avoid the worst of his attention, he'd continued to be suspicious, and she'd left before anything else could happen.

"Abigail?"

The concerned voice brought Abigail out of her worried musings. She forced a smile. "Yes, Pearl?"

Pearl studied her closely, then glanced at Lottie, whose little head was bent over her slate as she worked at a corner table.

Abigail opened her mouth to whisper about Ben, when there was a knock at the side door.

"Sorry," Pearl said, "our regulars have arrived. Would you answer the door while I prepare the food?"

Abigail opened the door to find it just as Pearl had said—three little children with ragged clothes and dirty faces stood looking up at her eagerly. Her wary heart melted. So many families scrabbled for a meager living in Canvas Town, the burned neighborhood on the other side of Broadway. Open cellars were filled with water. For shelter, people tied canvas to chimneys that rose like sentinels guarding the memory of the homes that once stood there. They lived under those makeshift tents, and their children roamed the streets, looking for anything that dropped off wagons, from sticks of wood to heads of cabbage. And those were just the legal avenues to feed themselves.

Their young visitors looked up at her with equal parts hope and wariness, as if they expected to be disappointed.

Abigail smiled and stepped back. "Do come in and share a meal with us."

Like a litter of cats, they entered close together, and the boy took off his cap after one of the girls elbowed him.

"Lottie?"

Without needing to be reminded, her daughter wore a welcoming smile as she skirted closer to the wall to make more room at the little table. The war had certainly made her children realize that other children were not as fortunate as they.

Andrew and Lottie might have lost their father, but they had adults to protect them, and a home to shelter them—even if they shared it with guests, both welcome and unwelcome.

For the next half hour, Abigail kept an eye on the taproom out front and talked to her young guests in the kitchen. When their visits had first started, they ate silently, quickly, and fled. But now they were used to Abigail's questions, and she was convinced showing interest in their lives helped them understand that they weren't forgotten.

After she sent the children on their way with packages of sausage, apples, and bread for their families, Abigail and Pearl exchanged a glance.

"Lottie," Abigail said, "please fetch your brother and head upstairs for your afternoon reading. Remember to—"

"Lock the door," Lottie said impishly. "You've been saying that for years. I don't forget."

The war had been going on for much of her daughter's life. At Lottie's age, Abigail would have been playing with her friends, roaming from house to house when she was finished with her chores. Poor Lottie and Andrew had never known such freedom.

When Lottie had gone, Pearl turned to regard Abigail with worry. "What's wrong?"

Abigail sighed. "I saw Ben in the taproom."

Pearl winced. "Which means he will be back tonight."

"I assume so. I was hoping we were no longer needed."

"But the war isn't over, even if many of the soldiers have gone south."

"I'd sworn to myself not to put my children and the two of you at risk."

"We're all at risk until this war is over, if that makes you feel any better."

Abigail gave her a wry smile. "It doesn't. But it reminds me of what's at stake. I'll meet him and see what he has to say."

"I can stay with the children while they sleep."

Abigail put her hand on her friend's arm, then whispered, "Thank you."

~oOo~

After midnight, Abigail sat alone in the tavern kitchen, examining the day's ledger and writing about her daily tasks in her journal. After Pearl had gone upstairs, Abigail sent Henry to bed—and since their bedroom was just off the kitchen, he didn't protest too much about leaving her alone.

The quiet knock on the side door startled her, even though she was expecting it. Taking a deep breath, she waited for the second solitary knock. When it came, she opened the door.

Ben was a few steps lower than her, and their eyes met on an even level. His were sober, intent, and she wondered if he could see any fear in hers. She hoped not, and had been told before that her expressions often hid her emotions. Such a skill had come in very handy during the war.

"Good evening, Abigail," he said quietly.

With a nod, she stepped back. "Please come in."

He came through the door, and she closed it behind him.

"Would you join me in a cup of cider?" she asked, always the tavernkeeper.

When he nodded, she poured from a pitcher into two pewter mugs on the worktable. It was of a height for standing and preparing food, so she pulled a stool out from beneath it and he did the same, right next to her. It was inconvenient for a conversation where one wanted to look into the eyes of a person giving life or death instructions, but made clear to anyone who entered that they might be courting, stealing time away from children or customers. A British officer staying in her rooms had once or twice come down to steal a late-night meal, and such an intimate tableau might seem less suspicious.

Abigail took a small sip of the cool, sweet cider, then folded her hands and waited.

Ben swallowed, set down his mug, and spoke softly. "Were you surprised to see me this afternoon? I could not tell."

"Yes and no. I had hoped, with the war moving south…" She let her voice trail off.

"But New York is still the British headquarters, and probably always will be. General Clinton knows it's one of our major ports, located as it is between the northern and southern colonies. He's not about to abandon it. And where he is, there is news that will interest our friends."

"I have thought something might be afoot," she said.

He inhaled sharply. "Why?"

"The city seems more crowded with troops. I hear ship-of-the-line captains grumble about an embargo."

He nodded. "It is so on Long Island as well. Troops have been called in from Lloyd's Neck and many other distant posts."

"It sounds like they might be headed south," she said.

"We suspect they are going to make a diversion upriver, that this has to do with the expected French fleet."

It was her turn to give a sharp inhale. "More help is finally arriving?"

"If they can get here," Ben replied. "We believe the French are sending an even larger fleet this time, filled with munitions and troops."

"It will mean all the difference," she said, afraid to hope, afraid to remember what it felt like to be free of fear for her children.

"General Washington needs to know if the British are aware of the impending arrival of the French fleet and planning a counterattack, or if they are merely preparing for a move southward. And if they intend to confront the French, what are their plans?"

"He doesn't want much, does he?" she asked dryly.

"We only have three or four days at most. Washington needs to plan how best to position our army."

"Days?" she echoed, shocked. "What can we possibly accomplish in such a short time?"

He shrugged. "He needs to know the troop movement on Long Island, whether they're confined to the port at Brooklyn or if they have men posted elsewhere, and the size of those detachments. Basically, anything worth their notice."

Abigail's thoughts raced. She couldn't imagine how she could set things in motion in such a short time, certainly not for that amount of intelligence. "I don't know if I can be of help," she said at last.

Ben took another drink of cider. "You are not a soldier. This has always been your decision."

"*You* are not a soldier," she countered.

"Because I was deemed more valuable as a false Loyalist. This is the only way I can help."

She heard the words as if he spoke them—*this is the only way* you *can help.*

"I'll be back tomorrow afternoon," he said. "Signal your answer."

They had so many signals, for so many eventualities. But that would not help her if in her haste to find answers, she was captured. What would become of her children, their livelihood?

She thought Ben would depart while she brooded, but he didn't, lingering over his cider. She noticed he was almost finished and topped off his mug without asking. He raised an eyebrow but didn't protest.

"What worries you now, that didn't before?" he asked quietly.

Abigail let out a sigh. "I didn't mention it before, but I was almost caught eavesdropping by a British officer. I think he might remain suspicious of me."

"There are many other officers."

"But besides the tavern, my main source of officers is at my sister's home, where he is often invited."

Ben nodded, then hesitated. "It must be difficult to be on opposite sides of the war with your family."

"Don't so many of us have that problem?" she asked bitterly. "I was raised on a farm in Westchester county after my parents brought my sister and me from England. We were grateful to the king for our good fortune. My parents and my sister still are. Early in the war, they kept demanding that I leave my husband for the relative safety of the farm. They were so... dismissive about his beliefs. But I couldn't leave my husband and the business we'd worked so hard to build. They offered to keep my children safe, away from the city, but I was—and still am—worried they'd turn them against me, against their father's memory. And I still think I can keep them safer, just by being their mother. But am I wrong? Am I selfish?" She sounded defensive even to herself. She took a deep breath. "Please ignore that outburst."

"I won't. I asked you a question and you answered. It is not easy to be in your situation."

He was meeting her gaze with an honesty that compelled her to keep talking, even though a voice inside warned that it would be a mistake to learn personal details.

"And now you know even more about me," she said. "And I know nothing about you."

He shrugged and looked back at the cider. "There's not very much to tell. "I'm a silversmith in a world where metal is being melted into bullets. Few need what I do right now—or can afford it."

"I imagine British officers and Loyalists might still be patronizing your shop."

He gave a crooked smile. "True. It can be useful—as you know." He tapped his mug to hers.

She met his gaze for a long moment, then turned away. Sometimes it was too easy to forget he should only be her conduit to spies and not a person—a man.

This was a war, and there was no time to think of him as anything other than a fellow Patriot.

As if Ben, too, wanted to avoid whatever had flashed between them, he said, "Your tavern seems as busy as ever. You've certainly succeeded in what some would term a man's occupation."

She snorted a laugh. "After my husband's death, there were many who thought me incapable because of my sex. A man tried to claim he was my husband's business partner, bringing accounts I could prove were false—as if I would be stupid enough not to counter him. Another merchant kept trying to loan me money, though I knew what he'd demand in return. A third has asked me to marry him every three months since Edmund's death, as if I am an appointment on his calendar."

It was Ben's turn to laugh. "You own a prosperous tavern with lodgings. I'm not surprised that some would do whatever they could to take control of it."

There was a long moment's silence as he finished his cider. Abigail stood up and went to bank the fire, piling ashes over the hot coals to keep until morning. Not that morning was far off.

Ben rose and picked up his tricorn hat. "Thank you for the cider. I'll be back tomorrow afternoon for your answer. I hope you'll help us."

He didn't try to convince her, just went out the door, put on his hat, and walked down the dark street.

**3**

---

# ABIGAIL

1780

Not five hours later, Abigail was adding wood to the fire, still giving thanks that she was able to purchase any at all after the previous disastrous winter, when every tree on the island had been cut down by the British. The cold had been so bad the people dragged sleds across the frozen Hudson to bring fuel back.

Henry emerged from their room, carrying a basin. He gave her a weary smile, then limped outside to dump the dirty water. As he returned, Pearl entered the kitchen, tying on her apron before adjusting her mob cap.

"Good morning," Abigail said to them with a smile.

Henry nodded gravely and the married couple both studied her, obviously awaiting her report on Ben.

Abigail sighed. "Yes, Ben would like our help." After checking that no one was outside either kitchen door, she whispered the details.

Pearl's dark eyes were narrowed in sympathy. "What will you do?"

"I spent a mostly restless night debating the answer he needs today. Gathering intelligence didn't seem so dangerous when I began last year, but I wanted to help the war effort, partially out of guilt."

They both nodded with understanding.

"But when I was almost discovered, and I realized how that would affect my children..." She trailed off, hugging herself as if a chill wind had swept through the room.

"But isn't the war already affecting the children?" Henry asked quietly, his deep voice somber.

Abigail didn't know how to answer.

~oOo~

Henry's words proved prophetic, when not an hour later, he staggered back into the kitchen through the side entrance, carrying Andrew, who hung limply in his arms. Both of them were spattered in blood.

For a frozen moment, Abigail covered her mouth against a scream. This was her worst fear come to life. The war had taken her husband—would it take her son?

But even as Henry fell back into a chair steadied by Pearl, Andrew moaned, lifted his head briefly, then let it drop to Henry's shoulder.

Abigail rushed forward and put her arms around her son, helping to hold him up. She wanted to press him to her bosom as she had when he was a babe, but she knew he considered himself too old for that. One of his eyes was swollen shut, and a bruise marred cheek.

"It's my fault," Henry said. Blood leaked from his cut lip. His face was darkened with bruises.

Pearl quickly dipped a cloth in a water bucket and dabbed his mouth. "Don't talk. You're making no sense."

Seeing how he was trembling, Abigail slid another chair next to him and took her son's upper body across her lap.

Andrew's good eye, damp and bloodshot, blinked at her. "It wasn't right, Mama."

Her heart gave a squeeze at the name he used to call her when he toddled around her legs. "Andrew, don't talk. Where does it hurt?"

When Pearl pressed another wet cloth into her hands, she used it on her boy's face.

He grimaced and tried to turn away. "The things they said about Henry—they were evil!"

Helplessly, Abigail turned to Henry.

Tears ran down his battered face. "It's my fault," he mumbled again, setting his swollen lip bleeding anew. "Those Redcoats—British soldiers," he amended, obviously remembering how she tried to keep her children away from the ugly words of war. "They were just lashing out. I should have hustled away immediately, but—"

"We were getting water from the well," Andrew said, sitting up straighter in her lap. "It wasn't right for them to stop us. And then they hit Henry, when he was doing nothing to them."

Henry patted Andrew's leg, where it still trailed across his lap. "Next time, let *me* deal with soldiers."

Andrew stared at him, a tear spilling from his good eye. "I made things worse, didn't I?"

Abigail hugged him closer. "Defending your friend isn't making things worse. But in these times, it's wisest to do as Henry wishes. Those soldiers could have been even more cruel, and no one would have stopped them or held them accountable. I've tried to explain how we must live until this war is over, Andrew. We must not antagonize the people who have power over us. Our soldiers are working to defend us on the battlefield, and we must be patient."

But Abigail's patience was at an end. War had been dragging on for several years now, and without French help, the battle for independence could be lost. She lived in a perpetual state of fear, soldiers quartered above their tavern, existing side by side with her children. The Patriots needed to be the victors. If she could help make it happen, she owed it to herself and her family to do so.

Though Pearl was bustling about the kitchen, fetching cloth bandages and heating water, she kept glancing at Abigail with speculation. They didn't speak, only worked together to help Andrew take a quick bath before the fire. He asked them to put up the screen for privacy and retreated behind it, but not before she saw more bruises on his thin chest. What kind of monsters beat children for defending their friends?

Pearl helped Henry retreat into their small bedroom to change. When she emerged a few minutes later, Abigail was already preparing the morning meal for the soldiers quartered in her tavern—bread, stewed pumpkin mixed with milk, and tea made from strawberry leaves. She wanted to tend to her son, but at ten he felt himself too old for his mother.

Pearl came to her side and spoke quietly. "What do you intend to do?"

"Tell Ben he can count on my help," Abigail said grimly as she continued to knead the risen bread.

Pearl pushed open the door to the taproom and peered through, before coming back to the worktable. "Henry is well enough to hide in his usual place."

A storage closet on the third-floor hall had a secret compartment in the back that they'd created to spy on British soldiers housed in the next room. It had proven useful occasionally, but since higher-ranking officers seldom stayed in her tavern rooms, discussions were not usually full of military plans.

"That is good of him to offer," Abigail said, "and if there's time, he can try, but Ben told me we only have three or four days to figure out what's going on."

"What is your plan and how can I help?"

Abigail nudged Pearl's shoulder with her own. "You know Captain Stanton, who comes for dinner every day?"

Pearl looked at her with dark, concerned eyes. "He follows you with his gaze."

Abigail sighed. "It is very annoying. But I think it will come in handy now. He is newly assigned to General Clinton's staff."

"Ohhh." Pearl drew out the word, frowning. "But what can you do? You cannot endanger yourself."

"I don't plan to." Abigail divided the dough into two round loafs, covered them with a cloth and placed them near the hearth to rise again. "But a man who is flattered often speaks foolishly. He asks me to join him for the meal every day. Today I will accept."

It was either that or approach her sister Rebecca for access to another Loyalist dinner party. But she remembered how she'd crept along the hall outside the drawing room, eavesdropping so intently she hadn't heard Lieutenant Rutherford approach. She could still remember the shock of hearing his voice in her ear, his breath on her bare neck, his hand on her arm as he demanded to know what she was doing. She'd had a ready lie, claiming to be checking if it was time for the women to join the men. But he'd watched her with veiled suspicion for the rest of the evening. Could she risk moving in his circles again?

They suddenly heard boots clumping down the stairs in the taproom. Andrew gave a little gasp behind the screen and emerged with his breeches on, holding his bloodstained shirt. Pearl draped one of Henry's around him, and after insisting he didn't need help, he limped up the back staircase.

Abigail watched him go, her frown making her head ache. With a sigh, she said to Pearl, "How is Henry?"

"Stiff, achy, embarrassed. But he'll be ready to work soon."

"He should rest."

"He won't rest, knowing Ben will return, along with Captain Stanton."

The two women exchanged a long glance before continuing breakfast preparation.

~oOo~

As luck would have it, both Ben and Captain Stanton came for their midday meal at the same time. She greeted the officer with a smile and ignored Ben.

"Captain Stanton, how good to see you on this fine day," she said, wiping her wet hands on a cloth as she approached him.

He briefly doffed his hat and bowed, showing a bald spot on the crown of his head above the queue of his plaited hair. "It's begun to rain, Mistress Featherstone, and the humidity will surround us, but your company for my meal would make it all bearable."

He waited, eyebrows raised, smile wide with encouragement. His red uniform made her feel faintly nauseated. He was probably her father's age, with a little belly that showed he enjoyed the finer life of an officer without hard training for the battlefield.

"That is a kind invitation, Captain. I do believe I have some time to spare today."

He blinked in surprise, then his smile somehow became wider. "Then do show me to your best table."

"Perhaps one by the window where we can feel the breeze." She gestured to an empty table with two wooden chairs. "I'll join you in a moment. Henry," she called as she headed back toward the bar, where the barkeep waited, his eyes bloodshot as they regarded her, "please prepare a tankard of beer and a mug of cider."

As she passed Ben who was sitting at the bar, she deliberately tripped on the leg of his stool.

"Do forgive me, sir," she said with a smile, then continued into the kitchen.

That agreed-upon maneuver would tell Ben she was in. Maybe he already knew by her welcome to the captain.

In the kitchen, Pearl was basting a turkey where it hung on a spit over the fire. The room was hot, and the open windows helped only a bit. Pearl's face glowed with perspiration as she stepped away from the hearth.

"Lottie is in the keeping room, reading," Pearl said. "When Andrew comes down, I'll have them study there together."

"Thank you." Taking a deep breath, Abigail removed her mob cap. "Is my hair in place?"

Pearl nodded, her brow furrowed in worry. "Be careful."

Discarding her apron, Abigail nodded. "I plan to."

She sailed back into the taproom, speaking briefly with all the customers she knew—which was the majority of the fifteen people seated at tables or the bar. She held mail for some of these men, held court sessions before the war, hosted parties for dancing. Her tavern had always been a central gathering place—and that hadn't changed with the war.

She knew Captain Stanton watched her, and she made a concerted effort to appear carefree and comfortable. It wasn't difficult. She'd always been able to playact, to hide her own emotions and project what she wanted others to see. Besides, customers wouldn't return if she didn't put them at ease, and her family certainly needed the money in these uncertain times. She didn't want anyone to assume something bad because she shared a table with a British captain—they all had to do business with the enemy to survive the occupation.

Stanton rose to his feet as she approached, and she smiled as she took her seat. As if on cue, Henry approached with their drinks.

Stanton took a deep pull of his beer, swallowed, then eyed

Henry, who still waited at their table. "Are you well, man? Those bruises look fresh."

"An unavoidable accident, Captain. What would you like for dinner?"

Stanton turned back to Abigail. "Your recommendation, Mistress Abigail?"

"I think the leg mutton and pickles are very good today."

"Then we'll take two servings," he said to Henry.

When Stanton turned his attention back to her, Abigail decided to take over the conversation. "You seem in a pleasant mood, Captain."

"I'm sitting here with you, am I not?"

She smiled demurely. "I can't be the only reason."

"Things are going well, eh? We sit comfortably in New York City, protecting our dependents such as yourself." He gave her a superior smile.

"And we're so glad of it, of course."

"Not all of you," he pointed out dryly.

"The intelligent among us."

"But you would say that, of course."

She kept her composure, maintaining her flirtatious smile. "If I didn't believe in the Crown, surely I would have fled New York City long ago. But now I hear rumors that the French might be bearing down upon us once again."

His smile lessened faintly.

She continued as if she didn't notice. "People say that all the time, and I don't know if I should believe it. But if it's true, what can you do to keep us all safe?"

He put his hand on top of hers. "My dear, you need not fear such things, nor dwell upon them. We will take care of the French."

Just as she opened her mouth to reply, she heard something drop with a hollow thud. Instinctively she turned, only to see Andrew, a pewter tankard at his feet, staring at her with one eye wide, the other painfully swollen, his expression so betrayed it nearly rent a tear in her heart.

Pearl came bustling out from the kitchen and put an arm around Andrew. He tried to shrug it off, not taking his gaze off his mother.

Abigail rose to her feet.

"Where are you going?" Captain Stanton asked.

"My son needs me. Please excuse me."

She threaded between tables where customers ate and drank as if nothing had happened—but a boy had lost faith in his mother.

Andrew started to back away as she approached, and although Pearl tried to restrain him, in the end she had to let him go. He ran up the main staircase before Abigail could say anything.

But what *could* she say?

**4**

———

# PAMELA

2023

As Pam was tiredly sorting junk in the boxes behind the bar, she heard a knock at the front door. At the peephole she'd drilled through the wood protecting the glass door, she could see Lucia, the young woman who'd once worked at Featherstone's Restaurant. Pam was surprised to feel a small surge of interest. That so seldom happened lately.

She opened the door to find Lucia looking a bit red, as if she was embarrassed, and once again holding her bike at her side.

"Hi, Lucia," Pam said.

"Hi, Mrs. Mosher."

"Please, Pam's fine."

Lucia's smile became a little less tense.

"When we met last week," Pam continued, "I didn't get your last name—we were too busy being suspicious of each other."

Lucia's smile got a little wider. "Alvarez."

"Good to know. Come on in."

Lucia seemed relieved, but not the *I'm scared of someone else* relieved like before.

"Can I get you something to drink after your bike ride?"

"Water's fine, thanks."

Pam went behind the bar, grabbed two bottles out of the fridge, and returned. Lucia was resting her bike against one of the stacked tables along the wall. She came forward, pulling off her cross-body bag and slinging it on the back of a chair.

"I promise not to steal anything," Pam said.

Lucia chuckled. "A girl has to be careful."

They sat down, opened their bottles, and had a sip. Lucia's gaze swept the room.

"I know, I know," Pam said, "it doesn't look that different."

"You said you're selling it, so maybe you don't care?"

"I care. I'm definitely selling. I just don't know if I want to sell to someone who'll appreciate the history, or someone who wants to tear it down. I've been doing some research into the real estate development company he represents. We had a meeting, and he made an offer, but...I don't know why I'm hesitating."

Lucia eyed her. "So you're still planning to do some work around here before selling?"

"I am. I just don't know if I could let it go to someone who won't care about it. I feel like my dad would curse me from above."

"Any chance you would be hiring someone to help?"

Pam frowned. "I haven't even thought that far."

"What about me? I'm a hard worker and I certainly know the building—the first floor and basement, anyway. I'm trying to save up some money for college textbooks this fall. I'm serving at a restaurant, but I can only pick up a few shifts a week."

"Where are you off to?"

"Syracuse University."

"Congratulations. That's a good school."

Lucia lowered her eyes, a faint blush staining her cheeks. "Thanks."

"Your parents must be proud."

Another hesitation. "I hope so. They died a few years ago. Car accident."

Pam drew in a sharp breath. "I'm so sorry to hear that. How terrible for you." And here she was dwelling on her parents' deaths when they'd lived well into their seventies and eighties. She'd had their counsel, their support, and the knowledge that was never alone. She remembered how her dad had praised Lucia, and before she knew it, she was saying, "I can find some hours for you here and there. You've had the tour—you've seen what a few years of neglect have done, so I can certainly use some help."

Lucia's brown eyes widened with excitement. "Thanks! I could start whenever you want."

"Don't thank me yet. It'll probably be hard work. Come back tomorrow at ten and we'll put in a few hours. I'm thinking maybe ten to fifteen hours a week?"

"Awesome. And if you need more, I'm fine with that. Does your job let you set your own hours?"

"I'm retired."

"Cool."

Pam looked away. "Not that cool. I'll probably start consulting at some point, but for now, I'm trying to remember how much I loved the city, and preparing the building to be sold."

"I'm kind of surprised you didn't hire a cleaning service."

"Yeah, me, too. But everything I touch holds a memory. I'm trying to decide what to keep for myself or what to get rid of. I don't have any kids to leave it to, but I have some cousins who might want the memories."

"That's good of you to think of them."

"Stop buttering up the boss—you're not even on the job yet."

Over the next couple days, Pam couldn't decide if Lucia truly was flattering her as an employer or was actually interested in the building's history. Pam found herself answering question after question, even when she sent Lucia to another room to give herself a break from talking. Lucia wanted to know what she knew about her ancestors, how long the speakeasy had stayed open, how the Underground Railroad might have worked. But when she heard that Pam's distant ancestor wrote a novel set during the American Revolution, and that Pam had a copy, it was as if Lucia's awe radiated out from her excited expression.

"Can I see it?" she asked.

Pam eyed her over a stack of boxes that separated them in the third-floor apartment. "There has to be something wrong with you. Why does an eighteen-year-old kid care about a musty old book written in the early eighteen hundreds?"

"Didn't I tell you—I'm majoring in history at SU."

"History?" Pam echoed in disbelief.

"I know, I know, go ahead and tell me that's impractical, but I don't care. I love learning how people used to live. Is the book right here?" she asked eagerly.

"It's upstairs."

"Let's go!"

"I—"

But Lucia was already out of the room. With a sigh, Pam stepped over a collection of old chipped china, around several boxes, and found her waiting in the hall.

"Lead the way," Lucia said with a grin.

"I'm not sure I can find it easily."

"I can help. If I had an ancestor who was a famous author—"

"I don't know how famous—"

"I'd be bragging about it all the time."

"It's written in a very old style. It was hard to read."

Lucia came to a stop, fists on her hips. "You didn't read it?"

To her surprise, Pam felt herself reddening. "I was busy

with school, and working here, of course. I just never got through it."

"Can I read it? To know someone who lived in this building wrote a book about such an important time in our history—"

"Let me guess—you want to teach American history."

Lucia grinned. "Is it that obvious? I'd really like to go for my PhD and write history books while teaching college, but that probably won't work out."

Her brow furrowed and she turned away. Though Pam was curious, it wasn't right to interrogate an employee on her third day on the job.

In the end, locating the book was easier than she'd expected. It was right next to her dad's desk, in a box marked "Important books."

When Pam unearthed the slim, maroon, leather-bound book, its corners ragged, the leather scarred, Lucia emitted an actual gasp.

Pam rolled her eyes. "You are like no other teenager I know."

"May I hold it?" she asked reverently. Once it was in her hands, she opened it up and inhaled deeply. "Old book smell."

Pam laughed aloud.

Lucia sent her a mock frown. "I like the title: *One Woman's Story During the War of Independence*. Seems pretty cool that a man would focus on a woman. Could I read it? I won't take it out of the building. I could read for an hour when I'm done with my work—if it's okay with your schedule, of course."

"Sure, that would be fine."

"And he's a great-great-something grandfather?"

"Yep. Many greats, going back two hundred years. There's an old family tree around here somewhere. The book was written a couple decades after the Revolution, about a spy plot when New York City was occupied by the British."

Lucia frowned. "Is it history or fiction?"

"Fiction."

"I know spies helped General Washington win. New York City history has always been my favorite."

"I guess my ancestor was inspired."

"What's his name?"

Pam looked at the spine of the book. "A.E. Featherstone. I think that stood for Andrew." She turned to the copyright page and found his entire name, Andrew Edward, and the publication date of 1823 by a publisher right there in New York. Which made sense.

She looked at the book for a long moment. This was her family history, connected to her across the centuries. It had been exactly two hundred years since the book was published.

Lucia clasped her hands together. "It's the book's anniversary!"

"Or birthday," Pam added, bemused. "What a coincidence. But my dad always told me he didn't believe in coincidences."

"Your dad was smart."

Pam smiled and had to speak through a tight throat. "He made sure I didn't forget my family heritage. When I was a kid, he walked me through the building, pointing out anything historical. I would whine about being bored. He continued to patiently explain that this would all be important to me someday."

Then she gave herself a mental shake. She was still selling Harbor House. Every day that she cleaned and unearthed more problems to be fixed was more proof that she didn't want to sink everything she had into it. She had to stand on her own and make sound financial decisions.

Lucia gave a wistful sigh. "That kind of family history is rare. I'd love to know those details. I plan to do some searching on Ancestry.com when I get older."

"Good for you." Pam closed the book gently and tried to imagine what it was like to lose your parents at such a young age. Had Lucia felt like she'd lost her identity? Surely her grandparents or aunts and uncles helped her feel connected to her past. Pam's few aunts and uncles were gone, and her cousins lived other places in the country. She wanted to warn Lucia not to lose track of family but didn't want to sound preachy. A girl who'd lost her parents already knew that lesson.

"Did you make an appointment with Gretchen, the preservationist?" Lucia asked.

Pam winced. "No." At Lucia's concerned look, she added, "Not yet."

"She could help you preserve the history of this place, even if you plan to sell."

"I do plan to sell."

"I know, I know."

So Pam did make an appointment, and Gretchen sounded thrilled over the phone, even though Pam warned her she was just interested in info about the National Historic Register, to present the building as an investment in New York's history when she sold.

That evening, Pam took *One Woman's Story* back to her Airbnb, a studio apartment in the East Village. The apartment didn't have a balcony, and the view was of another building— yet it still cost thousands of dollars per month. It was hard to justify staying there when she not only had a home on Long Island, but a building just blocks away. If she focused on her dad's apartment for the next week or so, it would be livable.

Temporarily.

With that plan in mind, she curled up on the couch and opened her Grandpa Featherstone's book. The formal style was not nearly as off-putting as it had been when she was a teenager, especially since she'd devoured Jane Austen's books after falling in love with Colin Firth in the *Pride and Prejudice* miniseries.

When she realized the book was set in a tavern in the

Seaport district, she couldn't wait to tell Lucia. She almost texted her but thought, maybe it's not cool for a fifty-year-old boss to text her teenage employee outside work hours. But there was something about the young woman that made Pam think they could be friends, even with their age difference.

~oOo~

Pam waited until the end of Lucia's workday to tell her about the book's setting. Lucia's mouth dropped open. She grabbed the book and sank onto the apartment couch by the window.

And she didn't move. Not for hours. Pam ordered in some Vietnamese food, set a bowl of pho beside Lucia, then watched in amusement as the girl tried to eat her noodles with chopsticks while still reading a hardcover.

"I'm not getting anything on the book, I promise," she said after swallowing.

"I can see that." Pam bit her lip to hide her laugh and returned to scrubbing the windows.

A couple hours later, Pam looked out the newly clean window at what she could see of the setting sun between tall buildings. The teenager was now lying back on the couch, the book resting on her stomach as she read.

"Lucia, it's getting dark. Didn't you ride your bike here? How far do you have to go to get home?"

Lucia slowly stirred, looking up at Pam with growing awareness as if emerging from a deep pond.

"I take it the book is good," Pam said.

"It really is. And I know I should go, but...wait a minute." She carefully placed her bookmark—one of Dad's old postcards—in the right spot, set the book down, and headed for the hall outside the apartment.

Curious, Pam followed, only to find her opening the hall

storage closet and pulling on the string attached to a bare bulb. Shoulder to shoulder, they stood looking inside. Cleaning products were jammed onto the shelves on each side. Pam made a mental note to add the closet to her cleaning list. Against the back wall, mops and brooms and old vacuums slumped against each other.

"I have a weird hunch," Lucia murmured, hands on her hips. "Can you go back inside and listen for my knock?"

"On the door?"

"On the closet wall." Before Pam could open her mouth, Lucia rushed on. "I promise I'll explain everything."

Sighing good-naturedly, Pam went back into the apartment. The hall storage closet jutted into the room, and beside it was the apartment coat closet next to the front door.

A moment later, she heard a knock, but something struck her as wrong. It seemed...muffled, distant. When Lucia knocked again, Pam knocked back.

"I knew it!" Lucia yelled.

Pam hurried back to the hallway.

"It has a false back!" Lucia exclaimed, doing a little dance as if she couldn't contain herself.

"What?"

"I could barely hear your knock—you could barely hear mine, right?"

"Well, I heard it, but it seemed pretty far away."

"Exactly." She gripped Pam's hands in hers. "In the book, they talk about the rooms above the tavern, and mention that one of the closets has a false back, so they could spy on British soldiers. Maybe some of the book could be based on a real story? They lived here above the tavern, right, even during the occupation?"

"I don't know," Pam said slowly. "My dad was always more excited that an author lived here, but your idea does make sense."

"I love history—I would have been nagging my parents endlessly about our family. I just never got the chance."

Pam felt foolish. "Well, what about your grandparents or your aunts and uncles?"

"I don't have any," Lucia said, turning back to the closet. "Would you mind if we try to remove that extra wall?"

"Wait." Pam touched her shoulder until Lucia turned back around. "Do you have any relatives at all?"

Lucia winced. "I didn't mean to bring it up. I'm fine."

"You didn't answer my question."

She sighed. "No, my parents were only children."

"Do you have siblings?"

Lucia shook her head.

"Who do you live with?"

"Until a couple months ago, I lived with my foster parents."

Pam blinked in surprise. "Foster parents?"

Lucia rolled her eyes. "Really, it's been no big deal. I was one of the lucky ones. My foster parents are older than you and were never able to have kids. We clicked immediately, and I will always consider them my family."

"I sense a 'but' coming."

"They were ready to move to South Carolina, where they have parents who are pretty elderly. My foster parents hung on here in the city just long enough for me to finish high school and get ready for college. They knew I didn't want to move south. New York is my home, and I never plan to leave it, except for college. My foster mom's dad suddenly got worse a couple months ago, and I insisted they go. I'm grown up now. They've done more than enough for me. I'm in a supportive housing program, so my foster parents don't have to worry." She took a deep breath and pasted on a smile. "So what about the fake wall?"

It was obvious that Lucia was done talking about herself,

and Pam wanted to respect her wishes. But she kept remembering that boy who scared Lucia the first day they met.

"So there's no one waiting for you to come home," Pam said. She looked out the window. The lights of the city were shoving back the darkness, but it was still there. "I think you should stay with me tonight."

"Pam, you don't need to worry. I've been on my own for a couple months. I'm used to the city—more than you are," she added, smiling.

"I let you read too long, and now there's this closet. We'll look at it a bit, then head to my apartment or crash here. Okay?"

Lucia hesitated, looking out the window, then released a sigh. "Okay."

The teenager's shoulders seemed to droop a bit as they walked back into the hall, but the closet perked her up. The two of them pulled out everything against the back wall, then realized even the shelves would have to come down—they'd obviously been added well after the eighteenth century.

"There were probably pegs in the walls," Lucia said confidently. "Did you know that's how people hung their daily clothes? No clothes hangers then."

"I see," Pam said, hiding her amusement.

They filled several boxes with dubious bottles of cleaning solutions that would have to be disposed of later.

When the closet was bare, Pam said, "Let's examine the back wall before we go tearing everything down."

Pam brought in a flashlight from her dad's apartment— "More powerful than our phones"—then aimed it at the back wall, crowding behind Lucia. They examined every inch of the wooden wall from floor to ceiling, murmuring repeated "excuse mes" and trying not to breathe on each other.

Lucia traced her fingers along every edge of the wall, top to bottom, side to side, until at last she gave a little gasp. "There's a depression here. I think I can get my fingers into it."

It was above eye level, on the right side.

Lucia grunted. "I don't know if it's meant to be pulled out, but I can't tell with the shelves in the way."

"Then let's tear them out."

"Are you sure?" Lucia asked. "I could be totally wrong."

"It's not like they're original to the house—they're just nailed in place. I'll go find a hammer and crowbar."

A half hour later, after removing the shelves and prying, they pulled open the back wall like a door that had rusted hinges. Inside was nothing but a tiny room, barely big enough for one person to sit or stand. It was full of dust and cobwebs— and one little square of wood nailed at eye level.

"It's how they spied on the British!" Lucia said triumphantly.

"This is pretty amazing." Pam touched the wall, as if she could feel the history. Her dad would have been so excited. "I wish there were a way we could prove it."

"Maybe we can. I'll keep reading."

By ten o'clock that night, Pam was stretched out on her dad's old bed, and Lucia had taken the couch.

In the morning, after they brought back bagels for breakfast and were eating in the apartment kitchen, Lucia was strangely quiet, eyes downcast.

"Spill," Pam said, spreading plain cream cheese on her Everything bagel.

"I didn't realize this place was pretty livable now."

"If you don't mind spiders and dust and years of accumulated dirt."

"And you're moving in?"

"Probably this week. Why?"

"Any chance I can rent a room from you?"

Pam chewed her bagel and studied Lucia thoughtfully. Ever

since she'd heard that Lucia had no relatives, and her foster parents had gone, she'd wondered about her living situation. She'd given her address as the housing project in the Two Bridges neighborhood. Pam thought about that boy who'd frightened her the first day they met.

"Sure," Pam said.

Lucia's eyes grew shiny with tears she tried to pretend weren't there. "Thanks. The foster care system has been helping me, so I promise I'll be able to make the rent."

"I'm not worried. I'll just work you harder."

Lucia giggled. "And college starts in a few months, so this is just temporary."

Lucia finished her bagel with a new gusto and, suddenly, Pam had a thought—the baby she'd miscarried in college would be older than Lucia.

Whoa, where was she going with these old memories? She hadn't been around a teenager regularly in a long time. She'd forgotten what it was like to see the world as a fresh new place, where the future could be so much brighter than the past.

"If this is too nosy," Lucia said, "just tell me to stop, but I was wondering if you've ever been married."

"My husband died last year."

Lucia's eyes widened. "Oh, I'm so sorry."

"Thanks. Keeping busy is helping me recover, but I really don't need to talk about it."

"Sure."

As they worked on cleaning the apartment for the rest of the morning, Pam thought about how she'd felt when Lucia had brought up her husband. She'd felt tense and ill-at-ease— and had that been anger, deep inside? Still? Will was dead; she had to let her regrets go. But it was easy to say that, and much harder to believe it.

**5**

───────

# PAMELA

2023

Over the next week, Pam worked on the list Gretchen had given her to submit Harbor House for the National Register of Historic Places. It wasn't as if you could just say, "My building is over two hundred years old," and that was it. She had to prove it had cultural significance, or an important person had lived there, or important history had happened there—Lucia was positive they could prove this last one, but Pam wasn't sure how.

It was Lucia who found boxes marked "Attic" that had come from Pam's parents' house in Queens after it had been sold. Between scrubbing floors, buying new bedding and towels, and saying hello to the occasional neighbor who stopped in with nosy curiosity, they sorted through old photo albums looking for pictures of the building. Pam found one very old photo from the late 19th century, showing the storefront as a dry goods store. But that didn't exactly mean it was historically important. Lucia was undaunted and intended to keep searching.

At the end of the week, they moved into Dad's third floor apartment, with its two small bedrooms that overlooked the cobblestone street, galley kitchen, bathroom, and living/dining room. Lucia said she didn't need help with her stuff, but Pam drove to the apartment complex to load the boxes. Lucia was obviously embarrassed by the garbage in the corridors, but Pam knew there were far worse places she could have lived. Her little studio apartment was neatly kept, and except for two old-fashioned suitcases, she only had a few garbage bags with the rest of her belongings.

As they made two trips to the car, Pam asked, "Is any of the furniture yours?"

Lucia shook her head. "They helped me find a furnished place."

Pam nodded. "What about stuff from your parents' home?"

"Since they were renters, there were only a few things to sell. None of it was worth much. The money helped me buy my bike and whatever clothes I needed."

Is that what she told herself to get over the pain of having little from her parents?

"I know what you're thinking," Lucia said, sending her a grin over her shoulder. "I have some stuff that my foster parents put in storage for me. Mom's photo albums, her wedding dress, some of my toys and stuff from when I was a baby. She liked to crochet, so I have some blankets, stuff like that."

"What about your dad?"

"He liked the theater. I have his collection of ticket stubs and programs. I have his lacrosse stick, too. He played in college."

Pam put a hand on Lucia's shoulder when they set down their stuff by the car. "I'm glad."

"Memories are the most important. I've written down what I can remember in a journal, so I can always remind myself."

Pam blinked back tears. "You are just too smart."

Lucia rolled her eyes and slung her bags into the backseat.

Back at the apartment, Lucia hesitated in the door to the

small bedroom she'd been assigned. "I'll only be here a couple months. I could keep my stuff in my suitcase."

"You're renting this, so it's your space. Do what you want, but that dresser is empty—you scrubbed it. I'll only be here a couple months too, but I'm still unpacking."

Pam left her alone but peeked into the open door occasionally and saw the teenager's clothes spread out on the bed as she decided how to place them in the drawers. Pam felt a warm satisfaction as if she was nesting.

No, this was temporary, as she and Lucia knew. They were helping each other out. Both of them probably enjoyed not being alone.

That first night, Lucia went to bed hoping for ghosts, but Pam found herself lying awake, listening to the old building's faint creaking noises, as well as the muted sounds of city traffic. If you didn't count hotels, she hadn't slept in the same building with another person in a year, and it was strangely comforting. This building had housed members of her family for over two hundred years. Surely any ghosts would be friendly. Although they'd rented out rooms here and there so maybe Lucia would be in luck.

Lucia made her own luck a couple days later while exploring the basement. She ran up to their apartment, where Pam was regrouting the shower tiles.

"Pam!"

Pam jumped, bumping her shoulder on the faucet. "Ow."

"Sorry. But I think I found something scratched on the basement wall about the Underground Railroad!"

Though skeptical, Pam washed up and followed her down the narrow staircase into the basement. "My dad was told by his grandpa that we were a stop on the railroad, being so close to the seaport, but I never heard there was any proof."

Lucia led her into a storeroom off the main bar area. It was full of old-fashioned crates with cardboard boxes on top, but

Pam could see that a lot of the wallboard had been ripped off the walls after the flooding from Hurricane Sandy, revealing a stone foundation. It smelled damp and earthy. Pam touched it in wonder, knowing it had been laid over two hundred and fifty years ago.

Lucia gave her a knowing smirk. "Look at you."

It was Pam's turn to do a teenage eyeroll.

Lucia knelt down beside a group of wooden crates that mostly blocked her way. "Check this out."

Pam used the flashlight on her phone, but she had to admit it just looked like random scratches to her, no ghostly faces etched as she'd read about at other Underground Railroad sites.

"Let's make some room," Lucia said, obviously not ready to give up.

The uneven stack of crates had signs of water damage and were grimy to the touch. The stack was high enough that the tallest crate was at Pam's eye level, and when she tried to awkwardly lift it, something crashed to the floor behind it.

"Uh oh," Lucia said, guilt morphing into a worried frown.

"Don't worry. We'll clean it up in a minute." Pam squatted and trained the phone's flashlight on the wall. "What do you think?"

Lucia crouched down next to her, and they both examined the uneven stone foundation. There were definitely scratches on the wall—but that's all they looked like to Pam. And there were other scratches, too, here and there. There was no attempt to communicate or leave something behind.

Lucia sighed. "Okay, maybe I was wrong."

Pam patted her shoulder. "Good try, Professor Alvarez. Hey, I like the sound of that."

Lucia's smile was tentative and almost shy. "Me, too." Then she rose and went to the crates. "Let's see what I damaged."

She squatted down and reached behind the crates. Her

frown cleared as she pulled out a picture frame, the glass cracked.

They stepped beneath the ceiling light bulb for a better look. It was a black-and-white photo of a crowded nightclub or bar. A stunning young woman stood near a slightly raised stage, wearing a sleek drop-waisted gown with draped fringe about her knees, her bobbed hair peeking out beneath a bell-shaped hat that fit close to her head. Just behind her, a quartet of Black musicians played for a dancing crowd.

"That's our speakeasy," Pam said in wonder.

"Wow!" Lucia took the photo out into the main room and held it up in better light.

Pam remembered where the carved mahogany bar had been on the right-side wall before flooding had destroyed it. The bandstand was still against the far wall.

Pointing to it, Pam said, "I'd never realized it was a stage."

"Look at how beautiful the bar was," Lucia said wistfully, holding the photo closer to examine it.

Pam sighed. "I remember it well. One of my jobs as a kid was to dust it occasionally, all the intricate carvings and shelves. I didn't understand why, since we didn't use it, but my dad hoped to open this room again someday—until the hurricane. When he had to tear down the water-damaged bar, I know he grieved." At the time, she'd had been so distracted by the brokerage that she hadn't bothered to understand his emotional attachment. But looking at this photo, she knew he'd considered the bar a lost tie to his family, to his past.

"Do you know who the young woman was?" Lucia asked.

"My great-aunt ran the speakeasy during the twenties, so I assume it's her."

"What was her name?"

"Lillian."

# 6

# LILLIAN
## UNIVERSITY OF PENNSYLVANIA, 1926

"Darling, this petting party is the cat's meow!"

Lillian Featherstone clinked glasses with her friend Dorothy, a fellow English major at the University of Pennsylvania. "We know how to entertain. Now pour me another glass of that grape juice wine you made. It's delicious."

They looked at each other giddily. The parties held at Lillian's apartment were becoming legendary. Everyone who was anyone on campus crowded into her parlor, spilling over into the kitchen and the two bedrooms. Louis Armstrong played on the Victrola and several couples danced the Black Bottom where the carpet had been rolled away.

Dorothy leaned closer, her headband flower brushing Lillian's face. "Did your daddy send your hush money?"

Lillian kept a smile on her face as she shook her head. "Not yet. I'm sure it's coming."

This was the first time her monthly allowance had been late. Perhaps Papa's accountant was too busy.

But she wouldn't complain. Not every girl was lucky enough to drive a Chrysler Roadster and go to college—her father had progressive ideas. She loved books, and since she wasn't a gifted writer, thought a career in publishing the next best thing. Her mother was scandalized, and the only way Lillian got her approval for college was promising that when she married, she'd quit her job.

Lillian didn't plan to marry any time soon—if ever. Life was too exciting for flappers. Let old ladies like her mother sit on their porches and wait for men to come calling like it was still the 1890s; Lillian was a woman of the world and would do what she wanted, date whom she wanted, party where she wanted. The Great War and the Spanish Flu had shown everyone that you had to live life to the fullest right now because there was no guarantee how many years you could enjoy, let alone find a husband.

And then Johnny Coleridge stepped through the apartment door, sweeping off his fedora with an easy elegance. Dorothy gasped, but Lillian leaned against the wall, showing off her figure, especially where her short skirt almost showed her stockinged knees. With one bare arm, she waved languidly at Johnny.

"He's such a cake-eater," Dorothy said, her voice dreamy.

"He doesn't have *that* many girlfriends."

"Oh, I don't particularly care. If he looked at me the way he looks at you, I would forget all the rumors."

And there were so many rumors, Lillian thought, even as Johnny threaded between dancers toward them. He wore his dark hair slicked back and parted in the middle, with the smallest mustache gracing his upper lip. His jacket followed the lines of his body, narrowing to his waist. His waistcoat had a dashing pattern different than his jacket. When he smiled and took her hand to kiss the back, Lillian felt a flush heat her skin, but she kept her own smile lazy and confident.

"Hello, Johnny," she said.

"Hello to you, Lillian." He nodded to her friend. "And to Dorothy, of course."

"Of course," Dorothy said demurely. "Did you bring something to share, Johnny?"

He pulled a flask out of his coat pocket. "I always do my part."

"Good boy." Dorothy took a step away from them. "I see Marian across the room. You two have fun."

And with a wink, she sauntered away, the fringes of her skirt swishing.

Johnny kept his gaze on Lillian, and she felt a thrill of awareness. He wasn't just good-looking and athletic—he was smart, studying for a degree in engineering, something she, as a woman, wasn't permitted to do at Penn. Luckily, it wasn't what she wanted. She loved her New York City life, and publishing was an exciting career.

"I hear you were almost raided at your last party," Johnny said.

"Someone said that just to make this party sound more attractive." Lillian batted her lashes at him.

"You shouldn't go denying the rumors. You might lose your title of most exciting girl on campus."

She held up her glass as if in toast. "Most exciting woman, you mean."

He took a step closer. "Something wrong with being a girl?" he asked, his tone low and intimate.

"A girl is still immature and without plans. A woman knows herself and sees her future path."

He cocked an eyebrow. "And what do you see?"

"New York City publishing."

"A lot of girls—women—here are just looking for a husband."

"Not me," she said firmly. "At least not any time soon. Are you just here looking for a wife?"

"I'm not ready to be handcuffed either."

"Then don't assume it about me." She lifted her chin, feeling defiant and far too attracted to him, as if he had power over her.

She wouldn't give any man that kind of power.

The song changed, and he said, "Want to dance?"

"I would love to."

Soon, they were laughing and perspiring as they danced the Charleston, and she felt his arms as he held her. It was so good to be a woman with her whole life ahead of her.

A short while later, when Johnny was staring down as if he meant to kiss her, Lillian heard her name being called.

"Ignore it," Johnny said, taking her by the hand and trying to lead her into a dark corner.

Looking over her shoulder, she saw Dorothy holding the telephone in both hands, the receiver lifted toward Lillian, her forehead wrinkled in worry.

"I can't," Lillian said. "I'll be right back." She took a deep, even breath as she wove between dancers. To Dorothy, she said, "Who is it? If someone can't find the party, just give them directions."

"It's your mother," Dorothy whispered, holding the receiver against her shoulder to muffle their voices.

Lillian stared at the clock on the mantel. "It's ten o'clock."

Dorothy nodded. "Just answer it instead of worrying."

Lillian wanted to deny any worry, but her friend knew her too well. She took the telephone and leaned toward the mouthpiece, bringing the receiver to her ear. "Hello, Mother, aren't you up late," she said cheerfully—too cheerfully, because Dorothy winced.

Though there was static on the line, her mother's voice came through forcefully. "Lillian, you need to drive home first thing tomorrow."

"But Mother, I can't come home tomorrow." She and

Dorothy stared at each other with wide eyes. "I have an exam in the morning."

"It will have to wait. I need you immediately. I'll explain everything when you get here."

And the line went dead.

~oOo~

Lillian drove her roadster from Philadelphia to Manhattan, only stopping once for a flat tire. A farmer was kind enough to help her. She tried to concentrate on the rural beauty of New Jersey, with autumn colors spreading out on both sides like a woven blanket, but her thoughts were going too fast. Why had her mother sent for her? Didn't her parents care that failing an exam might mean retaking the class? Luckily, her professor had been in his office this morning, and when she'd explained the emergency, he'd offered to let her take the exam next week.

But would she be back next week? There was something in her mother's voice that made Lillian uncertain and uneasy, all balled up.

But no—she was in her third year. Her father would never permit interference this late. Mother had tried everything to keep Lillian at home sitting dutifully in the parlor awaiting callers.

And then her thoughts circled back to the central question —what was so important that her mother wouldn't discuss it, just issued orders?

Back in Manhattan, the traffic slowed, and Lillian drove up Fifth Avenue to the Upper East Side, hoping that the traffic towers would keep cars moving faster. She found a place to park on 62$^{nd}$ and grabbed her small suitcase for the short walk to the family townhouse on 61$^{st}$.

Though her mother's roses had faded in the little garden

near the kitchen entrance, potted chrysanthemums at the end of each stone step guided her up to the main entrance.

The front door was unlocked, and Lillian went in, where the polished wood paneling smelled of lemon oil, and the stained-glass window colored the beam of sunlight.

"Mother?" Lillian tossed her jacket onto the coat rack and left her suitcase near the carved wood staircase.

"Lilly!"

The cry came from her fifteen-year-old sister Viola, who raced down the stairs, blond ringlets flying, and almost knocked Lillian over with a powerful hug, sobbing into her shoulder.

Lillian held her sister tight for a moment. Viola was usually a happy, cheerful girl. For her to cry like this…"Dearest, whatever is wrong? It cannot be so tragic."

"It is," Viola sobbed. "It truly is. Papa is in jail."

The shock of those words seemed to slow time, as if everything around Lillian was moving away, leaving her frozen. Papa was the center of their family, the jovial parent to their mother's sternness, the one who saw that since women now had the vote, they should be able to determine their own careers, their own lives. But along with idealism, he had a strict sense of honor that would never permit lawbreaking. There was some kind of mistake. He had traffic tickets he'd forgotten about, or there'd been a misidentification.

Their mother stepped in from the parlor, and her blanched complexion and red eyes confirmed the news. Deep inside, Lillian's renewed certainty in her father's plight took its first blow.

"Viola, keep your voice down," Mother said sternly. "Your younger brother does not need to hear the details."

There were details children shouldn't hear? Lillian swallowed. "Where is Julian?"

"In the nursery with his governess."

"Then we need to talk right now," Lillian said.

When she tried to disentangle Viola, it was as if her sister had become a clinging vine.

Viola stomped her foot. "I'm coming, too. I'm almost an adult—you can't keep the truth from me. How do you think I will feel wondering what the truth is? I'll fall behind on my studies, my teachers will ask why—"

To Lillian's shock, her mother's lower lip quivered.

"Oh, do stop." Mother gestured to the parlor door behind her.

Viola slipped her hand into Lillian's and looked up at her with plaintive damp eyes. Lillian tried to give her a reassuring smile, but it was truly a grimace.

When they filed past, Mother closed the glass-paneled sliding doors. Lillian sat down on the patterned silk divan, and Viola wedged herself in closely at her side. Most girls would cling to their mother, but their mother had never been the emotional, sweet-natured center of the family. Mother had never encouraged that sort of intimacy, believing it was her duty to lead her daughters by guarding her place in society.

But did Mother worry that would be over now?

No, there was a reason for all of this, Lillian reminded herself.

Mother took the upholstered chair opposite the sofa and turned her head briefly toward the bare hearth with its carved columns. Lillian kept a rein on her impatience.

Mother took a deep breath. "Your father's lawyer was here to explain things but...I just don't understand it all yet."

"Then start at the beginning," Lillian said.

Mother nodded and seemed to pick a thread from her old-fashioned dress. But her fingers were trembling. "Mr. Webster arrived without calling ahead. I was taken aback, of course, because his name was unfamiliar, but I greeted him here."

Lillian frowned. "What do you mean, unfamiliar?"

"Your father has used the services of a lawyer before, but not this man."

A new lawyer? Lillian thought, uneasy but not certain why. Her mother continued to talk.

"Without any niceties, he just announced the news that your father is—is—incarcerated."

Lillian bit her lip to keep herself from impatiently demanding more. She focused on Viola's damp palm in hers.

"The worst of it is," Mother whispered, "he's not planning to fight this at all. He's pleading…guilty."

The last word rang in Lillian's ears. She and Viola stared at each other, and Lillian distantly wondered if her eyes looked as wild as her sister's.

"Guilty?" Lillian echoed. "Of what? Unpaid traffic tickets?"

Mother shook her head. To Lillian's growing alarm, two tears tracked down her mother's cheeks.

"Manslaughter."

That word hung in the air like the specter of a demon, something to shrink away from with fear. Viola buried her face in her hands and sobbed again, falling across Lillian's lap. Lillian put her arm around her sister as if she could protect her from the world.

*Manslaughter.* It couldn't be true—not Papa!

"You—you misunderstood his words," Lillian said at last.

Mother shook her head. "I did not. Apparently, your father caused a man's death."

For a long minute, there was no sound in the room but the ticking of the grandfather clock and Viola's deep breathing as her shoulders shook. Then Lillian realized it was she who was breathing too fast as panic rose inside to swell her throat.

*Who had died?*

She pushed the panic back down and drew in a slow

inhalation. She would not give in to helplessness. This could not be true—it was *not* true.

"What did the lawyer say happened?" Lillian asked.

Twisting a handkerchief between her fingers, Mother said, "There was something about a mobster threatening your father—"

"That's self-defense!" Lillian insisted.

"I said the same, but Mr. Webster said he was only threatening to ruin our restaurant or-or some such nonsense, when your father wouldn't pay for protection." Mother dabbed at the tears on her face.

Lillian had read about mobsters rising in prominence ever since Prohibition became the law, making alcohol a lucrative product, but why would a mobster threaten a restaurant owner? Papa didn't serve alcohol.

"This doesn't make sense," Lillian said. "There has to be more to the story. The truth will come out at the trial."

"Didn't you hear me?" Mother said shrilly. "He's pleading guilty. There will be no trial."

The three of them said nothing for a long while. Lillian could hear the faint drift of music from the nursery up above.

Someone tapped on the door, and without looking, Mother called for their entrance. Bonny, their Scottish maid with red hair tucked behind a ruffled headband, slid the door open, then reached for the tea tray she'd set on the hall table.

"Beggin' yer pardon, Mrs. Featherstone, but Mrs. Vickers said after a long drive, Miss Lillian would be hungry."

"Trust our housekeeper to only think of Lillian at a time like this," Mother muttered.

Bonny acted as if she hadn't heard, but Viola said, "She knows we're all hungry—there are plenty of sandwiches."

Lillian watched her mother, who just tiredly shook her head. It was an open secret that the children could come to

Mrs. Vickers whenever they needed something. Mother believed the housekeeper coddled them.

"Thank Mrs. Vickers for us," Lillian said, smiling at the maid, who poured them each a cup of tea, prepared as they liked it, and departed, closing the door behind her.

They all stared at the food on the little table, but no one moved toward it. Lillian was certain her stomach would revolt if she tried to eat. But her mother already looked hollow-cheeked with worry, so Lillian lifted her teacup. Viola took a polite sip and set it down, while Mother tried to hold her cup and saucer. They rattled together precariously.

"Oh bother," Mother said and set them down.

"You really should eat or drink something," Lillian said.

"I am your mother—you don't need to tell me what to do, young lady."

Lillian set her own tea back on the tray without trying it. "What is our plan?"

"Plan?" her mother echoed.

"He's pleading guilty—we know that can't be right."

"The crime was already in the morning's papers."

"But not Papa's name," Viola said.

"'A suspect in custody' were the words used. That will change by tomorrow," Mother said bitterly.

"I don't care about any of that," Lillian said. "I care about Papa."

"Mr. Webster said we should not go to your father's jail cell. He was quite clear that your father wanted none of us near... those kinds of people."

"So we just trust this lawyer? Have you met him before?"

Mother shook her head. "But I will be calling to speak to your father. Surely they will allow that."

"Good," Lillian said, letting out the breath she didn't realize she'd been holding.

"And you will not go running off to the jail willy nilly."

Lillian blinked in surprise, but that was probably what she'd do. Her mother knew her too well. "Once you speak to Papa, we'll see about visiting him. We aren't going to abandon him."

"Of course not!" Viola cried, then burst into tears and fell dramatically across Lillian's lap again.

Mother rolled her eyes with exasperation. "Come, girl, get control of yourself. Hysterics will help nothing."

Viola scowled. "At least I have some feelings for Papa."

Lillian drew a sharp breath, glancing at her mother and waiting for an explosion.

It didn't happen. Two more tears fell down Mother's cheeks as she bit her lip to control the quivering.

Viola sagged, sobbing again. "I'm sorry. That wasn't fair. It's just—it's just—"

"We always think of you as so strong, Mother," Lillian said. "Isn't that right, Viola?"

Viola nodded, face buried in her arms.

"We all have to be strong." Mother wiped her cheeks with a handkerchief. "I'll try to talk to Papa and find out what—what he intends."

"And I'll see to the restaurant," Lillian said.

"What?" Her mother blinked in astonishment.

"I've been to college. I can put my education to use and talk with Papa's manager. They might not know what's going on, and I certainly won't explain all our personal problems," she added, seeing Mother start to protest. "But they should know Papa won't be in any time soon. And we need to know about our finances and make sure everything continues to run smoothly. Mother, perhaps you can visit the bank after you telephone the jail."

"But, your studies," Viola said, her gaze worriedly meeting Lillian's.

"It'll be fine."

Lillian looked from her dazed mother to Viola, whose face was drained of color as she took a shaky sip of her tea. Lillian knew she was making the right decision—but deep inside, she felt like the life she'd always wanted was slipping away, and it was easier to blame her mother than her father.

But what had Papa done to himself, to their family—to another man?

7

———

# LILLIAN

1926

An hour later, after changing into a fresh dress and donning her favorite red cloth coat against the autumn chill, Lillian drove her roadster down to lower Manhattan and Harbor House, the four-story building housing Featherstone's, her family's restaurant, on the first floor. She found a side street to park on only a couple of blocks away. On her walk there, more than one man tipped his hat to her, and she smiled and winked and tried to pretend nothing had changed, when everything had.

Harbor House was still an elegant maroon clapboard building, with large glass windows on either side of the door, luring dinner guests inside. The third and fourth floor apartments weren't open to the public but lent to friends of the family. More than once, Lillian had asked Papa if she could live there when she graduated from Penn and had an exciting career downtown, but he always put her off—Mother's doing, Lillian assumed.

Tears suddenly pricked her eyes. *Oh Papa,* she thought with disbelief and confusion. She prayed her mother learned something to explain what was going on. But until then, it was

Lillian's job to discover what was happening at the restaurant, even though she'd done nothing but eat there in the past. And what was she supposed to say to the manager, when she didn't know how long it would take to straighten out her father's legal problems? She assumed they could handle things without her father's daily input, but she didn't really know.

Taking a deep breath, she opened the heavy, glass-paned door and stepped inside. Though the dinner hour hadn't started, she inhaled the scents of food preparation, onions and garlic sautéing. White cloth-covered tables gleamed with silver, scattered between the columns supporting the second floor. A hearth with a decorative fire screen took up much of one wall, and on the mantel in a place of honor sat a pewter tankard Papa swore was from his ancestors almost one hundred and fifty years before.

A patterned tin ceiling reflected the sun that shone through the windows as several waiters set out place settings. When they saw her, two of them looked at each other, then one sighed and came toward her, wearing white shirt sleeves over black trousers, a white apron at his waist.

"We aren't open until four o'clock, miss."

"My name is Lillian Featherstone, Samuel's daughter. I don't believe we've met." She put out her hand like a businessman, like a career woman.

The young man blinked at her, then slowly reached to shake her hand. "Herbert Tanner, Miss Featherstone. I...um..." His face reddened, and he looked over his shoulder at the other waiter, who shrugged. "If you're looking for your father—"

"I'm not. I'm here to see the manager."

He looked relieved. "Then right this way."

He led her back through the swinging door to the kitchen, where several men in white aprons and hats stood at a long wooden table chopping vegetables. Cast-iron gas ranges lined one wall. And there were even several electric refrigerators, newly purchased by her excited father. She struggled to keep her emotions under control.

The cooks glanced at her, one even boldly letting his gaze take in her silk drop-waisted dress beneath her open coat, but she was used to the attention of men. She gave a nod and kept following Herbert through the next set of doors into a hall where produce crates were stacked. A door to the outside occupied one wall, and another closed door beneath the staircase led to the basement. She remembered playing down there when she was a child, while her father was cataloguing the restaurant inventory. Herbert led her to the staircase and up to the second floor, where there were offices and more restaurant storage rooms. The first office was her father's, and since the door was open, she looked in with a pang of sorrow. For a moment, she wanted to curl up in his swivel chair and wait for him to come upstairs with a treat from the kitchen.

Herbert knocked on the second door, and a man's voice called for them to enter.

When Herbert opened the door, cigarette smoke drifted past him. "Miss Featherstone to see you, Mr. Dabrowski."

Lillian stepped into the room, which was lined with shelves of catalogues and ledgers. From behind his desk, Mr. Dabrowski rose to his feet, stubbing out his cigarette in an overflowing glass ashtray. She reached to shake his hand, and he took it. He was a middle-aged man with a receding hairline, glasses perched on his nose.

"Mr. Dabrowski, I'm Lillian Featherstone."

"Daughter of Samuel, I assume."

His smile seemed hesitant, and he shot Herbert such an unreadable look that Lillian knew at once that she wouldn't have to explain her father's troubles to Mr. Dabrowski.

Lillian glanced at the waiter. "Thank you for your help, Herbert."

Mr. Dabrowski nodded, and Herbert left, closing the door

behind him. Mr. Dabrowski gestured to the chair across from his desk, and she sat down.

"I assume you have heard about my father's circumstances," Lillian began.

"It happened just a block away on the street," Mr. Dabrowski said soberly.

Lillian inhaled sharply. "Then you know more than I do. Please explain it to me."

"It's not a tale for an innocent young lady," he said.

"I can't afford to be innocent, sir, not with my father in jail, and his lawyer telling us he intends to plead guilty to manslaughter."

Mr. Dabrowski's eyes went wide behind his glasses, and he reached for another cigarette. When he offered her one, she shook her head.

After he lit up and gave a deep inhale then exhalation of smoke, he let out a faint whistle. "Pleading guilty. Why would he do that?"

"If you tell me what you know, maybe you can help me make sense of it."

"I wasn't there, so I don't know everything. Samuel got a call two nights ago as we were closing up, and he went racing out of here. Not an hour later, the police were here, searching the place after arresting him. They said a man died."

Lillian shuddered. It still didn't seem real.

"And then I saw the article in the paper today," he continued, "that the dead man was known for his mob connections, and that someone was arrested. Frankly, it was a pretty small article and not on the front page. But then this is New York," he added with sarcasm. "There are bigger fish to fry."

"And you've heard nothing else?" she asked.

"I was hoping he'd be out on bail. But you've said he's pleading guilty."

She nodded. "And his lawyer isn't adequately explaining why. Mother is going to call the jail today."

"I hope she can find out what's going on. Samuel is not the type of man to—well, you know."

"There's a mistake—there must be. We will discover the truth. But until then..." She trailed off, looking around the office at the ledgers on shelves. "Do you think we can keep the restaurant open?"

"Of course, as long as Samuel's problems don't dissuade customers. He's a well-known man in the community."

"Then people must know that he would never do something so horrible."

"Then why would he plead guilty?" Mr. Dabrowski asked gently.

His tone brought tears to Lillian's eyes. "I don't know," she whispered, then cleared her throat. "I'll find out. Until then, how has business been lately?"

"The restaurant business?" he asked.

She blinked in surprise. "Of course. What else could I mean?"

"Fine," he said immediately. "Well, we're...okay. Without being able to sell alcohol, it's been difficult to survive these last few years."

She hadn't known—she'd never asked. She felt guilt creep in, but she banished it. She had asked how her father was doing, and he always said everything was fine. Apparently, he'd been so good at misleading people that she'd never questioned him further.

"We hired a new chef," Mr. Dabrowski continued, "and the improvement in our menu began to bring a new, more decerning clientele, and that has helped."

Relief made her lean back in her chair.

"But..." He moved aside his ash tray and opened a ledger. "We are getting by, but it isn't what we'd hoped. We have some different...revenue streams to help, but every week's end, we skirt the edge of having to let someone go."

"Let someone go," she echoed, wide-eyed. "You mean we can't hire someone to help out in Papa's place?"

"You mean a general manager? No. I'm the assistant manager, and I'll do my best."

She nodded, feeling more and more like college was disappearing into her past. Guilt about her selfishness made her refocus on the restaurant. She latched onto Mr. Dabrowski's earlier hesitation. "You said revenue streams?"

"Well, we do have apartments on the third and fourth floor. Your father was very generous to his friends, letting people stay when they were in town. I always thought renting them out would bring a steady income, but Samuel didn't want to impose by turning out friends."

"Then let's impose."

Mr. Dabrowski put his cigarette in the ashtray and gave her a kind smile. "Miss Featherstone, I don't manage the building, just the restaurant."

She blinked at him in bewilderment, feeling her eyes sting with tears and hating such a weakness.

He sighed. "I'll see what I can do. One of the apartments is open, and I can let the other occupant know to expect a rental agreement or he'll need to vacate."

Lillian knew she should feel sorry for this unknown person, but she didn't. Her father had granted him a favor, but now it had to be over. She had siblings to protect, a home to keep.

"I can't thank you enough for your help," she said. "And as soon as possible, you'll need a raise."

He looked down at the accounting ledger and said dryly, "That might be awhile."

"Can you show me the books? I've taken a business class. I want to understand and be able to explain things to my mother when she asks."

He turned the ledger toward her and came around the desk to stand shoulder-to-shoulder with her as they bent over the accounts. She saw the deductions for wages, food, repairs. She saw cash listed as income for the restaurant, but scattered throughout was another designation for cash, but without any explanation.

She pointed to one of those lines. "Mr. Dabrowski, where does this cash come from?"

"The restaurant," he said quickly—too quickly.

She straightened and tried to meet his gaze sternly. "I know I'm only Samuel Featherstone's daughter, but I'm the family's representative. I have to understand what is going on."

He eyed her for a long moment. "Samuel didn't want the family to know."

"To know what?" she demanded, nerves like bugs beating against her stomach.

"Let me be more specific—he was concerned that his wife should not know the details of how we've been able to keep the restaurant open for the last few years."

"Are we talking about the mob?" she asked faintly.

"No, we've been lucky there. Somehow, your father avoided having to pay protection to keep us safe."

She opened her mouth, but he raised both hands.

"Don't ask me how because he wouldn't tell me."

This sounded worse and worse.

He took a deep breath, then seemed to come to a decision. "You're a young woman in college, am I right?"

She nodded.

"Then this might not seem so shocking to you." He gave a long sigh. "It might be easier to show you." He gestured for her to follow him.

Confused, trying not to feel even more panicked than she already was, Lillian followed Mr. Dabrowski out into the hall and down the stairs. When they reached the hall on the first floor where crates of food were stored, she expected to head back into the restaurant kitchen, but the manager opened the door to the basement.

He shot her an encouraging smile over his shoulder as he descended, with her trailing behind.

Instead of restaurant storage, she saw a wide-open space scattered with plain wooden tables and chairs and the most beautiful carved bar along the right-hand wall. It sparked a feeling of familiarity, and she suddenly realized that it had graced the dining room upstairs before Prohibition. A raised platform at the far end sported an upright piano. The walls were hung with draperies that disguised the stone foundation.

"This is a speakeasy," Lillian said breathlessly.

Mr. Dabrowski's smile was cautious. "It is. We call it The Underground."

"Why didn't Papa ever tell us?"

"Perhaps because it's illegal?"

"But—"

"He was concerned your mother wouldn't put up with it."

"Oh, that could be true. She's a teetotaler." Lillian walked toward the bar, where bottles of forbidden alcohol lined shelves backed by a mirror. "This is how Papa netted a profit."

He nodded. "Not that it's been easy. But we've only been raided once, and after that we figured out how to have someone man the windows on the second floor and ring a bell if they saw the cops. Then the alcohol is hidden beneath the coal chute."

She thought of the "protection" her father hadn't paid for but didn't want to bring that up. "What are the hours?"

"Midnight to five a.m. It's a steady group of customers, and our piano player keeps them happy."

"I'll return tonight and see for myself."

A male voice intruded. "No, you will not."

They turned to see a man emerge from a door near the bar.

He was short, with a belly hanging over skinny legs. He wore his dark hair parted in the center and slicked back, and a cigar was caught between his teeth.

"This is Mr. Weinstein," Mr. Dabrowski said. "He's the manager of The Underground. This is Miss Featherstone."

Mr. Weinstein looked her up and down with indifference and spoke around the cigar. "You're Sam's little girl?"

She nodded.

"Not so little anymore."

He elbowed Mr. Dabrowski, who responded with a cool stare. Mr. Weinstein didn't seem to care.

"You don't need to be here," Mr. Weinstein told her. "This is your father's club, you're not the Big Cheese, and you'll just be in the way."

He turned his back on her, and she felt the dismissal of certain men everywhere when women tried to involve themselves where they weren't "wanted."

Mr. Dabrowski gave her a reassuring nod. "Until Samuel is back, Miss Featherstone is representing her family's interests."

"Samuel coming back?" Mr. Weinstein said in disbelief. "Didn't you hear what happened?"

Lillian's eyes flooded with tears, and she hated showing such weakness in front of him.

"We've all heard," Mr. Dabrowski said between clenched teeth. "Show some compassion."

Mr. Weinstein barely spared her a glance as he moved the cigar from one side of his mouth to the other. "This is New York City—we don't got time for compassion." He disappeared back through the door.

Lillian realized her hands were clenched into fists at her sides, as she glared at where the manager had disappeared.

"Miss Featherstone," Mr. Dabrowski began hesitantly.

"I'm fine," she said. "But I'm returning tonight."

~oOo~

Mother didn't join Lillian and Viola until supper, then waited until Mrs. Vickers and Bonny had set down individual bowls and were leaving before asking them to slide the dining room doors closed. In the momentary silence, Lillian stared at the gleaming carved panels on the wall, then the crystal chandelier, anything rather than think about what came next. She saw her mother sip from her soup spoon and realized that she, too, was hungry.

Viola asked, "Did you speak with Papa?"

Mother, who had a spoonful of soup halfway to her mouth, finished her sip before speaking. "It has been a long day. We're going to eat our meal before discussing this dreadful business."

"This dreadful business" was how she referred to Papa? Lillian thought angrily. But Lillian took a deep breath, squeezed Viola's hand beneath the table, and tried to eat. She was hungrier than she'd imagined, having forgotten to eat at midday.

A half hour later, the dishes had been cleared, and Lillian reluctantly admitted to herself that their mother had been right —she felt steadier.

Still, Mother didn't meet their anxious gazes, just folded and refolded the linen napkin she'd left on the table.

"Mother?" Lillian said, striving to sound pleasant but firm. "How was your telephone call with the jail?"

"They would not let me speak to your father."

Both Lillian and Viola slumped back in their seats, deflated.

"But how will we know if he is well?" Viola asked plaintively.

"They said he hasn't been arraigned yet. A date will be set with a judge to accept his plea."

Lillian hugged herself, feeling bewildered and afraid. She wanted to cry, but since Viola was already doing so, she'd only make everything worse by joining in. "Then we just wait?"

"That's what the lawyer told me yesterday. He said he would call with news."

Lillian sighed. "What about the bank?"

"We are all right for now."

"What does that mean?"

"Although we have some investments," she said vaguely, "it means the restaurant needs to continue to be successful."

Nerves prickled in Lillian's stomach. Her mother didn't know about the speakeasy; she might not condone what Papa had done to keep the restaurant afloat—to keep their *family* afloat. And if she insisted it be shut down, they might lose everything.

What Mother didn't know couldn't hurt her.

"The restaurant is doing well enough," Lillian said. "I spoke at length with Mr. Dabrowski, the manager, and although he is concerned that what has happened to Papa might make customers shy away, he's hoping that is not the case. I think we can trust him. He's the real McCoy."

Mother's chin dropped to her chest as she whispered, "Then we will pray that as long as their meal is excellent, customers will keep returning."

Lillian didn't think the speakeasy customers, so used to being outside of the law, would care a bit about Papa's troubles. At least that was a silver lining. But she wouldn't know about this clientele until she mingled with them herself.

~oOo~

Lillian had plenty of experience sneaking out of the townhouse. Her mother always retired to her room early. A half hour before midnight, Lillian donned a long coat over her beaded evening dress and headed down the main staircase. A small lamp illuminated enough of the staircase for her to see and another shone in the front window.

Just as she reached the front door, a quiet voice said, "Miss Lillian, what are you about?"

She winced, recognizing their housekeeper, Mrs. Vickers. She turned to see the older Black woman, who was wearing a flannel robe, her hair wrapped in a scarf, her glasses reflecting the lamplight.

"Hello, Mrs. Vickers," Lillian whispered. "I'm off to see a friend."

"You're not at college, where I can't keep an eye on your comings and goings, Miss Lillian. You live in this house, and I worry about you."

Mrs. Vickers came closer, and Lillian realized there were new lines in her forehead, and her cheeks sagged a bit more in the lamp's shadow. She hadn't noticed that earlier today.

Lillian gave her a hug. "How I've missed you."

Mrs. Vickers patted her back. "And you know how I feel about you, honey. So where are you going, now that you're all grown up?"

"Back to the restaurant. I need to see how they're managing this evening."

Mrs. Vickers tsked, shaking her head. "Your papa has done it this time, making his women worry like this. But isn't the restaurant closed?"

Lillian sighed, knowing she had to offer the truth. "Please don't tell Mother, but the way Papa has kept us going is by serving people after hours."

"Serving people—you mean a speakeasy?"

Lillian put a finger to her lips, glancing up the stairs.

Mrs. Vickers sat down heavily on a bench beneath the stained-glass window, drawing Lillian with her. "I'm not surprised," Mrs. Vickers said. "A man has to support his family."

"I hope you don't think less of him," Lillian said.

"It being against the law," the housekeeper added dryly. "He's not the first, nor will he be the last. Them teetotalers never thought about what would happen when they got their way."

"And I can't just assume that the club is functioning. I have to see for myself. I saw the accounting books, and we break even more than earn profits lately. I've been to many successful places—I mean I've heard about them—and maybe I can offer some advice."

Mrs. Vickers harrumphed, but she was obviously hiding a smile. "You young people think the world is meant for partying."

"There's nothing wrong with an evening's entertainment. And if we can lure more customers, then it's all the better for our family." Lillian leaned closer to repeat herself. "Please promise you won't tell Mother. There's no one else to take care of things, and I don't want to get in a perpetual argument with her."

Mrs. Vickers nodded. "I'll keep quiet, unless I think it's in your best interests to speak up."

"But—"

Mrs. Vickers lifted a hand. "I've vowed to protect you, and I will, but I know you can handle more than your mama thinks you can. But promise me you'll be careful. It's still a man's world."

Lillian stiffened. "Not anymore. Things are different. We women will have careers and influence business. We can vote!"

Mrs. Vicker's arched a brow. "Women been saying something like that for generations. Every group of young people coming of age thinks they'll change the world. But I'm old enough to see how slowly things change. My people thought the end of slavery would make us equal. Did it? No. But things are better, and I hope womenfolk can someday say the same."

Lillian had never thought to equate the plight of women with that of Negroes; White women certainly had it better. But not as good as White men.

She now regarded Mrs. Vickers solemnly, ashamed she'd never asked about her ancestors. "Did you have family from the south who were slaves?"

The old woman nodded. "Cousins. My parents moved north when they were freed after their owner's death. I was lucky to be born and raised free. My cousins were not so lucky. Ever since the Civil War, they've farmed the land they could never afford to own, not able to put anythin' by for their children, treated barely better than slaves."

Lillian bit her lip, unable to meet the gaze of a woman who'd taken such good care of her all her life. She knew Mrs. Vickers had never had children of her own, had lavished her love on the Featherstones.

"I hope we've always shown you how much we love and appreciate you," Lillian said, kissing Mrs. Vickers' cheek.

The old woman chuckled. "The older you get, the better you get at showin' good sense."

Lillian couldn't solve the world's problems, but she hugged Mrs. Vickers tightly and hoped that she could solve Featherstone problems—and keep Mrs. Vickers employed.

**8**

---

## ABIGAIL
1780

Abigail stood in front of her sister's home on Broadway at midafternoon, staring up at the fashionable townhouse, a Georgian home of stone and brick, decorated with wrought-iron scroll work. She told herself that maybe for once, Rebecca would not mention that Abigail was *employed*, as if she scrubbed floors for a living rather than owning her own business. But then Rebecca had followed their parents' wishes, marrying a lawyer who'd been an officer in the British army and had promptly re-enlisted when the war began. Abigail had married a tavern-owner with radical ideas, but one who always made her feel like the center of his life.

She took a deep breath and blinked away the wetness in her eyes. Her husband Edmund would be proud of her for helping the American cause, even though she was using her sister. She hadn't wanted to abuse her sister's trust again after her near unmasking at an earlier party. But after Andrew's reaction to his mother flirting with a Redcoat in their own tavern, Abigail had realized that imposing on Rebecca had less consequences for her children.

When the maid showed Abigail into the parlor, guilt settled

like a dark cloud around her heart as Rebecca's face lit up with joy.

"My dear Abigail!" she cried, rushing forward to embrace her older sister, holding on a little too tightly. "I haven't seen you in weeks—I've been so worried!"

When Abigail could finally step back, she gave her sister a genuinely fond smile. "Why worry about me? I'm safe here under British control, am I not?"

"Of course you are."

Rebecca didn't hear the subtle sarcasm, which was just as well.

To the maid who hovered at the door, Rebecca said, "Emily, please bring us a tea tray."

Abigail bit her lip to withhold a comment about her sister's use of British tea—it would not be well-received, and she didn't want to argue. They'd done enough of that early in the war. But after Edmund's death, Rebecca had never wanted to discuss politics, as if Abigail's status as a widow and the mother of young children made her fragile. Abigail had appreciated the concern and the way Rebecca was a loving aunt to her nephew and niece, so far not having been blessed with children of her own.

And Abigail was once again going to repay her sister's innocent kindness with betrayal of the cause Rebecca's husband stood for.

She couldn't think about it now. She sat down opposite her sister in a damask-upholstered chair next to a carved console displaying fine china. Abigail knew this was where Rebecca oversaw the household in the morning and entertained her close friends in the afternoons. It was a cozy, feminine room that should have relaxed Abigail. But it didn't.

Rebecca poured tea with the grace of an aristocratic lady. She had the same dark hair as Abigail, but without the threads of gray that had begun to weave through. Rebecca's hands were white and soft, her hair artfully pulled to her nape, with an occasional curl styled to lie on her neck and shoulders. Her pale green silk dress had a pink bow at her bodice and a matching ribbon tied at her waist, as if she'd known she was having guests.

And then it dawned on Abigail. "Oh, dear, did I come at an inconvenient time?"

"My husband and I are having a dinner party. Do say you'll stay. I wasn't certain if you wished to be invited, due to various...reasons, but it is as if God sent you to me!"

For a moment, Abigail stirred her tea, watching the cream lighten the color, even as her mind raced fervently. Her sister entertained frequently—she'd hoped for just such a fortuitous outcome when she'd left the tavern, having been firmly ignored by her son since her failed attempt at a meal with Captain Stanton.

Then she looked down at her gown, sewn with modest calico muslin. "But Rebecca, I am not wearing appropriate clothing. I should walk home and change."

As if Rebecca suspected this was a means to avoid the party —far from it—her sister hurriedly said, "Please borrow something of mine. I have so many garments due to my husband's generosity. He would be pleased that I could help my widowed sister."

Abigail briefly closed her eyes as she took a deep breath. It was sometimes difficult to tell if Rebecca was innocent or sly when her words seemed to cut in a way that left no scars— visible ones.

But Rebecca had never been sly. She had just always been rewarded with everything she'd ever wanted. Things came easily to her, and she simply wanted to share that with her family.

"Very well," Abigail said, drawing out her response as if she hesitated.

Rebecca clapped her hands together. "I am so happy! It's been too long since we enjoyed ourselves."

"There is a war," Abigail said, then wished she could bite back the words. She shouldn't risk antagonizing her sister.

But Rebecca sighed. "I know that. My own dear husband risks his life every day."

He was advising General Clinton's cabinet on legal matters—he was hardly on the front lines.

But was that just Abigail's jealousy talking? Wouldn't she have given anything if Edmund had been safe for the duration of the war? It wasn't Rebecca's fault what her husband did, any more than Abigail had been able to persuade Edmund to caution. She wouldn't wish a lonely life of widowhood and its responsibilities on anyone.

Rebecca rose to her feet, having barely touched her tea. "I am too excited to introduce you to some new friends. Let's retire to my rooms and see what gown would suit your complexion and figure best."

~oOo~

The gown Abigail borrowed was light blue, with a fitted bodice and lace-draped sleeves. An embroidered satin overskirt was stylishly drawn back to reveal a delicate lawn and lace underskirt. She felt like a different person, as if she was wearing a disguise.

When she followed Rebecca down the staircase into the foyer, her brother-in-law's eyebrows rose before dropping ominously as he turned to his wife. Abigail knew that Lieutenant Thomas Chambers considered her husband a traitor to the British empire, and was not overly fond of her either.

Through gritted teeth, he said quietly, "I thought I made my wishes clear."

Abigail held her breath. This evening might be her only chance to quickly overhear news to help the American cause.

If her brother-in-law knew, he'd call *her* the traitor now.

Rebecca glided between her husband and Abigail. "She is my sister, Thomas," she said in a calm, firm voice. "And she is a widow. I have not seen her in some time."

Thomas eyed Abigail as if she were old vegetables tossed at a passing army. She gave him a faint smile and didn't have to pretend nervousness to appease him.

"Very well." To Abigail, he said, "Please do nothing to antagonize our guests."

Before Abigail could speak, Rebecca said, "She was raised as I was, and we are loyal to the Crown. Not all women are lucky enough to marry a man like you."

Abigail felt a pang deep in her heart, knowing she was lying to her sister and forcing Rebecca into lying on her behalf to her beloved husband. Much as Abigail disagreed with Thomas's choices, she remembered his ardent courting of Rebecca, and knew he'd not once blamed her for their lack of children. They were not yet thirty—surely God would grant their dearest wish.

Thomas let out his breath in a sigh and began to move past them.

"Ahem." Rebecca gave him a sweet smile.

He leaned down and kissed her cheek before entering the dining room to immediately question the servants as they prepared for the meal.

Rebecca grinned at Abigail, who returned it.

"You are quite the stern wife," Abigail whispered. "I am impressed."

"A woman has to be honest and determined with her opinions," Rebecca said. "Who wants to be married to a meek little mouse?"

"Many men," Abigail said dryly. "I seem to meet them all. If one more man professes shock and disapproval that I own and operate the tavern myself..."

Rebecca took her arm and eyed her with interest, seeming about to say something that she soon thought better of. "Perhaps those are the kinds of men who frequent taverns."

"All men frequent taverns—where else would they discuss their concerns with other men?"

"They could try discussing them with their wives."

Abigail barely withheld a snort.

"You are very cynical these days," Rebecca teased.

And then both of them sobered as they realized "these days" were during a war. One could only be cynical when the country that ruled them, where men represented the people in Parliament, would not allow the colonies the same rights, as if they were not full citizens. She thought of Henry and Pearl, denied rights by the same men who wanted their own freedom from England and did not see the hypocrisy. She felt suddenly so very tired. But she knew only by hastening the end of war could they as a country heal other divisions, right other wrongs.

"Cynical? Me?" Abigail said, putting a hand to her chest with exaggeration.

"You are the eldest. It must be your many years."

"I am an ancient, or at least I feel that way."

"Then tonight you will forget your cares. We will forget this war. We will be two ladies who dazzle our friends with our wit and good humor."

*Your friends,* Abigail thought before she could stop herself. But she only smiled, determined to make her sister happy even as she was betraying her.

Then there was a knock on the door, and Rebecca gave an innocent squeal of excitement. The maid Emily emerged from the corridor leading to the kitchen.

"Let us await them in the drawing room," Rebecca said, pulling Abigail with her.

They found Thomas pouring a glass of punch. He offered it to his wife, then poured another for Abigail. She thanked him and stepped back, allowing them to begin playing their part as hosts.

She looked about the room, at the upholstered chairs and sofas, the wall tapestries for keeping out a winter draft, the elaborate paintings of Thomas's ancestors. Thomas had done well for himself and now moved within circles of power on Clinton's staff. If the American army drove the British out, would Thomas wish to remain behind and rebuild his life and practice? Would he even have a practice if Patriots and Loyalists could not forget or forgive the past? It was something she didn't usually allow herself to contemplate—she didn't want to imagine her sister leaving her for England, perhaps never to see one another again. Already, Abigail wanted to cry, and none of this had even happened.

She took a deep breath and instead watched the couple greet their guests. Rebecca and Thomas were handsome, successful, and generous, and it was no surprise that others wanted to bask in such a reflection, even including officers on Clinton's staff.

Abigail found herself holding her glass of punch too tightly and loosened her grip. Each man who came through the open doors in a scarlet uniform brought another bead of sweat to her already heated brow. But Lieutenant Rutherford, the officer who'd been suspicious of her months before, did not put in an appearance.

Although she wanted to remain in a corner with two spinster sisters, she knew her purpose here and could not put it off. As the guests conversed before dinner, she moved from group to group and tried to listen in on conversations among British officers where she could. It was difficult, because other ladies spoke to her, and she had to converse politely.

More than once, she stood just outside a group of men, and

then giggled and blushed when she was noticed. She'd never been the best at flirtation, but she focused on making the men feel respected and admired. Occasionally, Rebecca caught her eye, and though she didn't interrupt, she did frown her confusion at Abigail's behavior.

Abigail took a moment for herself at the tall windows, letting the night air bathe her perspiring face. An overgrown fern partially blocked her from guests in the corner of the drawing room, and she closed her eyes and tried to pretend she was alone, listening to the evening birds at twilight, which seldom happened since she shared a single small bedroom with her children.

She realized she could hear the conversation of two men she couldn't see on the other side of the fern. They weren't exactly being quiet, but their voices were lowered and stern.

"What do you mean the *Raisonnable* has gone to sea?" said a deep voice with a British accent. "I would have heard."

A Scotsman answered dryly, "I believe ye're hearin' it from me. I don't know the orders; it's all been kept quiet."

"Are other ships receiving new orders?"

But before she could hear the answer, a male voice right behind her said, "Good evening, Mistress Featherstone."

She jumped and almost spilled her punch.

"Do forgive me for startling you."

She immediately recognized the voice she'd been dreading even as she turned around. Lieutenant Rutherford was smiling at her, but amusement did not reach his eyes. He was near her age, tall and thin, with a scar on his chin and powdered hair tied back in a queue on his neck. She remembered feeling as if he followed her from room to room at another dinner party last winter after he caught her standing alone in a corridor outside a parlor full of British officers.

She returned his smile. "Lieutenant Rutherford, what a pleasure to see you. It's been far too long."

"You've kept yourself scarce from your sister's circle of friends."

She saw two men leave the corner of the drawing room, and knew she'd lost her chance to hear more about the British navy.

"I've been quite busy."

"You own a tavern, I believe?" he asked.

She knew she'd never told him, so he must have asked someone about her.

"I do, closer to the wharves."

He nodded. "Another officer in my regiment rents a room from you."

She almost flinched, as if he had a man spying on her.

But she was doing the same to him, wasn't she?

The lieutenant stepped beside her, as if he, too, was looking out the window at the gardens. Several lanterns were hung among the trees, softening the growing darkness.

In a quieter voice, the lieutenant said, "He says you have young children and that you've been widowed. I offer my condolences."

She felt a chill as she murmured, "Thank you."

"How did your husband die?"

Before she could answer, from across the room, Rebecca called, "Dinner is served, my friends. Do follow me."

Abigail nodded at the lieutenant and ducked past him. But she could not escape. Because of her last-minute invitation, place settings were tighter, and she found herself perched on her sister's left at one end of the table—and Lieutenant Rutherford on Rebecca's right. Not close enough to have any kind of real conversation as they ate their duck and sweet potatoes, but his watchful eyes always seemed to be upon her when she glanced his way. It made her feel uncomfortable. Her nervousness and fear might soon become a beacon to him if she wasn't careful. It didn't help that although the windows were open, no breeze flowed through to provide a measure of comfort to the perspiring guests. Abigail couldn't imagine how the bewigged older gentlemen felt, with perspiration tracing down some of their faces.

Rebecca talked to Lieutenant Rutherford, while Abigail turned to the corporal on her left. It soon became clear that he was unmarried, fresh from the Carolinas, and ready to seek relaxation and amusement in New York City. He described the plays the soldiers were re-enacting, the fox hunt he'd attended on Long Island, and the next day's concert at Bowling Green. He was so free with his words, Abigail wondered if he might be able to offer some kind of clue to help her cause. But there was so little time—how to befriend him quickly so that he might boast to her of things she shouldn't know?

After dinner, when the men had had their fill of brandy and cigars by themselves in the dining room, they rejoined the ladies in the drawing room. Abigail tried to remain in the background, letting the conversation flow among people who knew each other well and had imbibed enough to relax their guard. She heard about supplies arriving from England and a victory near Waxhaws, South Carolina. Whenever anyone spoke to her, she kept up the blushing and the giggling and the awed interest, until she thought her mouth would freeze in an inane smile.

Lieutenant Rutherford didn't approach her again until the guests were taking their leave. Abigail inhaled deeply to calm herself as he approached.

"I hope you enjoyed your evening, Lieutenant," she said.

"I did. Your sister is a gracious hostess." He paused. "Will you be joining us at Bowling Green tomorrow?"

"I don't know," she said truthfully. "It will depend upon my children's needs."

"You are obviously a good mother in your concern for them. Do be careful to shield them in this time of war. Sadly, it is always the innocents who suffer the most."

Her mouth suddenly dry, she managed a smile as he departed, the last guest out the door. As Thomas sighed, leaning his back against the door to look upon his wife with fond satisfaction, Abigail found her mind whirling, contradictory thoughts chasing each other about. Had Lieutenant Rutherford been threatening her? Or was he truly concerned about the effects of war on children? She didn't know what to think.

In both public rooms, the servants could be heard cleaning away evidence of the party, and she let the sound draw her away from pointless worrying. As he'd said, this was war, and she was doing what she had to to protect her children.

Thomas clapped his hands together. "A successful evening, my dear," he said to Rebecca, then kissed her cheek. He almost seemed surprised to see Abigail still there. With a frown, he asked, "Are you spending the night?"

Rebecca opened her mouth, but Abigail spoke first. "I am not, but thank you for your kindness," she said, as if he'd extended an invitation. "I do believe Henry is waiting to accompany me home. My children would worry if I weren't there when they awoke."

"Then I'll retire for the night," he said, giving a pointed glance to his wife.

"I'll join you after I say good night to my sister," Rebecca answered.

With a sigh, Thomas ascended the stairs, and Rebecca watched him until he disappeared into the corridor. Only when a distant door closed did she take Abigail by the arm and lead her back to the small parlor on the far side of the foyer.

"Abigail, I did not know what to make of your behavior tonight," Rebecca began.

Abigail felt the evening's tension rise up to tighten her shoulders. If her sister had noticed something unusual, what had Abigail betrayed to the officers—and could Rebecca have trouble because of it? "What do you mean?" she asked, trying to portray confusion rather than fear.

"Don't be such an innocent, Abigail Featherstone. I know exactly what is happening."

Abigail held her breath.

Then Rebecca laughed and took both of Abigail's hands in hers. "Why didn't you tell me you were ready for marriage again?"

Abigail's lips parted, but she didn't know what to say, so great was her relief. Rebecca pulled her in for a hug and then let her go.

"Courtship is such a dance these days," Rebecca continued, "as men leave for weeks at a time and then return, expecting that a lady is just waiting on them alone."

They were leaving for battle, one they might not survive, but Rebecca was so sheltered she treated war like a courtship imposition that had to be tolerated. It was as if she'd deliberately forgotten that Abigail's husband had died in this war that the British had forced upon them, as if she and her sister lived in two different worlds.

Rebecca threw up both hands. "Men can be so arrogant! But I can help you—you know I can. When you met Edmund, I was too young, but now I'm in a better position. Lean on me; let me introduce you to men who will suit you."

So Edmund hadn't suited Abigail? No, she was letting her anger alter Rebecca's sentiment. Her sister truly wanted to help.

Rebecca rushed on. "I know kind and good bachelors who would be honored to meet a woman of your hardworking and generous disposition. They would support you and you'd never have to work in that tavern again."

Abigail stiffened.

"We'll go to the Garrison Assembly. They hold it twice a month and you'll meet all the junior officers. I'm certain Lieutenant Rutherford will attend—I noticed you trying to make him jealous at dinner."

"Make him jealous?" Abigail said, finally managing to speak.

Rebecca chuckled. "Oh, you hid it well, but I know you."

*Do you?* Abigail thought sadly. *Or have I been changed so much by war and heartache that I no longer am the person you once knew?*

"I was not trying to make him jealous." Abigail suddenly felt very tired. She couldn't explain the real reason she had intruded on her sister, and she shouldn't blame Rebecca for living the life she'd been raised to expect. "And I don't need to marry for the sake of marrying. I am in no hurry."

"Hmm," was all Rebecca said, looking thoughtful, as if she had plans in mind. "Protest all you like. But you are still coming to the concert tomorrow afternoon."

Abigail knew she couldn't refuse. "I promised, didn't I?"

"Good." Rebecca leaned forward and kissed her cheek.

"I should leave," Abigail said. "Henry is waiting. I'll try not to disturb your husband while I change into my own clothing."

Rebecca tried to insist that Abigail keep the gown, but it seemed too much. Abigail was using her sister, and would continue doing so, even knowing it was a betrayal that Rebecca might never forgive.

After changing and wishing her sister goodnight, Abigail found Henry in the kitchen, sitting on a bench beside the back door. He stood up to greet her.

"It was good of you to come," Abigail said, "but you know the tavern is only a few streets away."

"And night has fallen, with soldiers roaming the streets."

"You have a point," she murmured, as he held the door open.

Though the walk home was uneventful, they were both

startled upon entering the kitchen door of the tavern when a man stepped forward out of the shadows.

9

---

# ABIGAIL

1780

Henry tried to push Abigail aside as if to protect her from an intruder, but she patted his arm.

"It's Ben," she said. It was still so strange that she didn't know his last name.

Henry let out his breath.

Now that lantern light touched his face, she could see Ben wince.

"Forgive me for startling you," he murmured. "Pearl said I could wait here for you."

"Of course." Abigail turned to Henry. "I won't keep you from your bed. Thank you for the thoughtful escort."

"Jacob should be closing down the taproom as we speak."

"Thank you."

Their part-time barkeep, who'd lost an eye in the war, was thorough, quiet, and good at the job.

"I wish you both a good night." Henry nodded to her and Ben, opened the door to the small room he shared with his wife, and disappeared inside.

Abigail turned to Ben and saw that there was a mug on the table next to him. "May I refresh your drink?"

"I'm fine." He hesitated. "That was a late evening for you."

"It is not even an hour past dusk," she said mildly. "Are you keeping track of my movements?"

"No," he said quickly. "I was simply...worried."

She didn't want him worried about her—that wasn't his place. "You knew what I'd need to do to get the information you require."

"It doesn't mean I don't worry."

The quiet sincerity in Ben's voice made her feel something she refused to think about. "Please sit down. Let me pour myself a cider and I'll join you."

She removed her shawl and bonnet and hung them on a peg beside the rear door.

They met at the scarred worktable, perched on stools across from each other. The fire burned low beside them, necessary for food preparation, but making it uncomfortably warm. She wished they could be outside, walking beside the wharves, her favorite place when she'd needed a moment to think in the evenings. The sound of birds calling, water lapping, the faint groan of timber swaying had all been so peaceful, but since the war broke out, that feeling along the East River was gone. British ships of the line, two and three stories high, bristling with cannons, crowded the harbor, filled with the enemy.

Ben's hands circled his mug, and he met her gaze. "Pearl said you went to your sister's. I'm sorry you had to be put in that position."

"You're not sorry," she said, with a trace of tired bitterness. "My connection to her is useful."

"But I'm still sorry it weighs on you."

"Why?" she demanded irritably. "I'm completing my assignment, doing what you and others are doing. Why care how it makes me feel as long as we have something that will help General Washington?"

His gaze didn't leave her. "I don't know. I just do."

She wanted to look away as an uncomfortable tension grew, but that would be cowardly. She wasn't going to continue this line of conversation. "I went to speak to my sister, to ingratiate myself again, but luckily, she was hosting a dinner party and invited me to attend, against her husband's wishes. I am an embarrassment to him after Edmund's stand as a Patriot, but Thomas obviously loves my sister."

"Who was in attendance?"

She listed the officers from General Clinton's staff. "And Lieutenant Rutherford," she added.

Ben frowned. "You were concerned he'd realized you were eavesdropping a few months ago."

She nodded. "He made a point of talking to me. I can't decide if he is suspicious or just interested in me personally."

Ben arched one dark brow. "I don't want you to do anything that risks your safety."

"I won't. My children need me just as much as my country does."

"They need you more."

"Good of you to say so, but I don't think others would agree. Regardless, the lieutenant was not helpful in terms of information. I did hear that the *Raisonnable* is heading out to sea in some mysterious manner. I didn't get the chance to hear more details."

"And I heard that the *Europa* is doing the same."

She lowered her voice. "Do you think they intend to confront the French fleet?"

"I don't have confirmation of that."

"But isn't it *some* kind of confirmation?"

"We don't even know if the British have intelligence that the French fleet is arriving. Putting ships to sea could just be routine."

"The officers I overheard didn't seem to think so." She sighed. "We need more. I'll be attending a concert with my sister tomorrow afternoon at Bowling Green. I'm sure more of her friends—and their Loyalist husbands—will be there."

Before he could answer, the sound of light feet bounding down the stairs alerted Abigail. Andrew appeared, still wearing his daytime breeches and shirt, and carrying a pitcher. He came up short when he saw them.

Abigail wanted to hold him to her as if he were still a little boy instead of a ten-year-old. Instead, she gave him a tired smile. "Does Pearl know you're wandering about? You know who we're housing."

Andrew gave an exaggerated roll of the eyes. "You remind me every day, as if I cannot see them with my own eyes."

Ben took a sip of cider, and Abigail knew he was hiding a smile.

Andrew glanced at Ben quickly, then put his head down.

"You can speak in front of my friend Ben," Abigail said. "He is no fan of the British."

"Me neither." Andrew lowered his voice. "But I don't like being afraid of them."

"I'm sometimes afraid," Ben said. "This is war."

"They killed my father. They hurt me and Henry. I know what kind of people they are."

Abigail winced. "War makes people do things they regret. And not all of them are our enemy—they're obeying their king."

"Well, we don't want their king."

"No, we don't," Ben agreed.

"Mother, is that why you were talking to that British soldier today?"

Abigail felt her throat close up with suppressed tears, but at least he was speaking with her about it. That had to be a good sign.

Andrew sighed. "I know we have to let them be here, that

we have no choice, and maybe someday, if we win this war, we'll be able to say no when we want to, right?"

Nodding, Abigail stood up, put her arms around him, and kissed his brow that smelled of chalk dust and firewood. "You are growing up too fast. Where did my little boy go?"

He shrugged off her hug, looking uncomfortable as he glanced at Ben. She knew she was embarrassing her son, but she couldn't help it.

"I hope all these thoughts weren't keeping you from sleeping," Abigail said.

Andrew bit his lip before speaking. "Lottie was thirsty, and the pitcher was empty. It had been my chore to fill it today, but I forgot."

Abigail briefly touched his cheek. "A lot has happened. Your forgetfulness was understandable. Fetch Lottie some water and then both of you should be abed."

He filled his pitcher and, after a glance at Ben, went back upstairs.

Abigail sank down on her stool and found herself staring blankly at the fire.

"You have raised a fine boy," Ben said.

"Thank you." She'd almost forgotten he was there. That wasn't a good sign. "Are you married?" And then she realized how that sounded. "I'm sorry—we're not supposed to know about each other. This is dangerous, what we do, and I don't even know anything about you except that you're a silversmith, and yet we sit here and talk like we have a friendship."

"I feel like we're friends," Ben said quietly. "You might be the only woman I've ever talked to so easily."

She wasn't going to take that personally. "Then you're not married."

He shook his head.

"Why not?" She stiffened. "You don't have to answer. It is certainly not my business."

He gave a half smile. "We're friends, remember?"

"This war has made me do—and say—things I never would have before." She knew she was blushing, and hoped the flickering firelight hid it. She was an adult, a widow and mother. Blushing seemed like something from the charade she played in the presence of British soldiers.

Ben gave a sigh and looked toward the fire, which shone in his green eyes. "I was engaged to be married when I was twenty years old. We were young and in love and thoughtless. She was with child before we married, and when her parents found out, instead of just letting us marry, they forbid us from seeing one another, saying that I had abused their trust. While my parents were still trying to settle the agreement between us, she died in childbirth, along with the babe."

Abigail stared at him, her eyes wide and wet with tears. "Oh, Ben," she whispered, reaching out instinctively before pulling her hand back.

"It was over twenty years ago. The pain has dulled with time. She was a sweet girl who didn't deserve to spend her final painful hours filled with grief at our separation. I used to brood on what I should have done differently, but all that did was keep me alone in my sorrow and anger for many years. I left our village and came to New York City to apprentice myself to a silversmith and start a new life, but I didn't let go of the past for a long, long time. It made the thought of marriage and the possibility of failing another trusting woman too difficult to contemplate."

They sat in silence for several minutes. The embers in the fire ticked softly, booted feet plodded on floorboards overhead.

"I know well of what you speak," Abigail finally said, meeting his sad eyes. "It's hard to forgive myself for wishing my husband hadn't supported the Patriot cause early in the war. I thought he was foolish—how could we defeat the greatest empire in the world? And then he gave his life for his beliefs, leaving me with my grief and my shame for not supporting him enough."

"He wouldn't want you to feel like that," Ben said.

"And I'm sure someone said the same to you."

He nodded, his lips quirked in a faint smile. "Very true. But you have forged your own life, kept the tavern open—"

"The British helped with that," she said dryly.

"Don't make light of your accomplishments. Your children are a testament to your strength. And now you're playing your own part in this war, danger be damned. I admire you very much."

She stiffened with discomfort, but he didn't seem to notice as he finished the last of his cider and stood up.

"I should go," he said, lifting his tricorn hat from the wall peg.

She found herself wanting to delay him, and that scared her as much as any lurking British soldier. "You'll come back tomorrow night? For my report?" she added quickly.

"I will. Take care."

And then he limped out the door and disappeared into the darkness.

Abigail put away any thoughts of Ben as she washed their mugs. She heard the Barlows' bedroom door open, and Henry emerged.

"I'm so sorry we kept you awake," Abigail said.

"You didn't."

Henry limped stiffly into the kitchen and sat down with a sigh on a stool, stretching out his maimed leg. Andrew was recovering from their shared beating far more quickly, but then Henry had borne the brunt of British brutality, losing his leg during battle as well as protecting her son.

"How are you feeling?" Abigail asked. "I wish you hadn't had to accompany me home tonight. You need your rest."

"I'll rest when the war is done." He lowered his voice. "I

wanted to tell you that I spent some time today eavesdropping on our *guests*." He emphasized the last word dryly.

She put her hand on his arm. "That must have hurt, but I appreciate your dedication. Why didn't you come out and tell Ben what you heard?"

"I didn't want to interrupt." He arched a brow at her and smiled.

"Nothing to interrupt," she said briskly, "and certainly any news that might help would be good to know."

"I have little that helps. I only overheard two of them talking about sudden orders to ship out. They don't know why, so I thought it wouldn't be much use to you. No need to interrupt," he added again.

Abigail found herself smiling. "Now stop that. And yes, it isn't much, but it confirms what Ben and I both heard today— that some of the fleet is putting out to sea, but no one knows where."

"And you need more information."

She nodded and told him about the concert.

"I'll go with you. People talk around servants, especially Negros, as if we're not there."

"I wish I could say that I don't need you, that you should rest and recover."

He shrugged and winced. "I'll go rest now. It'll be enough. Take care, Abigail—I'm with you."

**10**

---

## LILLIAN

1926

Her car was parked down the block, but Lillian never felt uneasy walking in her Manhattan neighborhood at night. The streetlights were lit and couples walked arm in arm, furs wrapped around women's shoulders against the autumn chill, jewels glittering in their headbands and at their throats. The men wore black coats and tails, top hats tilted jauntily. It represented everything she loved about the city, people living freely, enjoying themselves in the present, when they couldn't know the future.

She winced, remembering that Mrs. Vickers had said young people thought the world was meant for partying. Maybe that was true, because Lillian had always felt there would be plenty of time for adult responsibilities, but that had caught up with her.

Once in her roadster, she raced down Second Avenue with the top down, her neck scarf whipping in the wind. The further south she went, the more the streets narrowed. But as usual in the city, there was always traffic and people out for a good time, even after midnight.

It took her some circling to find a place to park, but soon

she was walking up to the side door of Featherstone's. Luckily, a man and woman drunkenly linked arm in arm arrived just before her, and after knocking and getting a look-over from a large employee, they were all allowed inside.

The small hallway where restaurant supplies were unloaded looked different at night, with lamps with round glass shades at different levels scattered about. The stairwell itself was lit at the top and bottom, and Lillian felt the rise of warm air and cigarette smoke, and heard the tinkling of a piano.

Entering into the club was not what she expected. Instead of people dancing and carousing and enjoying themselves, it seemed almost like a cave, with low lighting and a few people scattered at wooden tables, more standing at the bar, some talking, others just staring into their glasses as if only forbidden alcohol would solve all their problems. The solitary piano player had his back to the room and played without enthusiasm. This was nothing like the places she and her friends went to in Harlem, where there was dancing and excitement, full bands, and live shows. She had to be the youngest person in the room by more than ten years.

She took a menu off the bar, and the high prices for single malt scotch didn't surprise her. If a customer wanted something that was illegal, he had to pay for the privilege. It was that way everywhere she went. Speakeasies had to be prepared to pay large "fines" to police who looked the other way. And there was no food on the menu, just some mixed peanuts and almonds in bowls scattered down the bar. She was deciding what drink to order when a belligerent male voice spoke behind her.

"What are you doing here? You need to beat it."

She turned to see Mr. Weinstein, hands on his hips in a way that thrust his belly forward, cigar between his teeth.

"I am here to see my father's business," she said, lifting her chin.

He took her arm and propelled her into a side room that

was obviously his office. The water heater and furnace were there too, although he'd tried to hide them with a folding screen.

Lillian shook his hand off her arm.

"Girl—"

"My name is Miss Featherstone, and I am the person making the decisions on behalf of the family right now. You had best remember that before manhandling me again."

He arched a brow and sat down in a squeaky chair, amusement mixed with disdain in his expression. "Miss Featherstone," he said, dragging out the name, "you'd best remember that I am keeping this club profitable so you and your mommy can live on the Upper East Side."

She ignored the provocation of his words, knowing that he wasn't lying. "And I believe you're being paid a decent salary to do so. I've already examined the books."

His face reddened, but all he said was, "Then what's your problem?"

"This!" She gestured behind her. "You call this a club? Where is the entertainment? All this is is a place to get drunk, and only desperate people come to such a place."

"And you with all your experience know better," he said with sarcasm.

"Apparently, I do, for I have been to places with bands and dancers and abundant menus. Female customers want to be there, and believe me, they spend as much as men—or men spend more on them. If you're going to pay off the police, at least let's make it more profitable."

He said nothing for a long minute, chomping that cigar in a manner she found revolting.

"I will discuss this with Dabrowski," he said coolly.

"Thank you. I will discuss this with my father as well."

He arched one dark eyebrow. "Have you seen him?"

"Not yet, but I will."

During the drive home, Lillian ruminated over the frustrations of the evening. She'd never had to stand up to strangers, particularly in the business world. Mr. Weinstein was deliberately trying to make her feel unneeded and useless, a woman who should be home dealing with her own small feminine concerns. Her father had raised her to believe she could do anything, and a college degree was supposed to help, but perhaps she'd been too naïve where the rest of male society was concerned.

She felt incredibly isolated and powerless. The only thing giving her any authority was the weight of her father's name. It was time for her to visit him, even if he didn't want his family to see him in jail.

~oOo~

Mother was persuadable when Lillian asked to see her father, as if she was relieved she didn't have to go herself. Mother was still waiting anxiously for Papa's name to appear in the newspaper and dreading what would happen to their social standing.

Or was Lillian being unfair? Maybe Mother just couldn't take seeing her husband brought low—or maybe she blamed him for everything that had happened. Lillian didn't have the time to figure out the woman's motives. So far, they'd been able to keep the truth from their little brother Julian, and Viola was distracting him since Mother wouldn't send him to school.

With the backlog in cases at the police department, they still hadn't arraigned him, so he was in City Prison on Centre Street. Even she had heard its nickname—the Tombs. When she approached it mid-morning, the conical gray pointed roof at each end rose over ten stories. The walls were gray stone, with lines of barred windows stacked on top of each other. The endless gray blended into the clouds threatening rain. Lillian felt small and inconsequential going in the front entrance, although she was not the only woman.

A clerk told her where to sign in and a matron searched her purse. She was led into a room where men and women representing every class of society waited their turn to visit. She saw slick lawyers in nice suits and humbly dressed women holding on tightly to small children. A distant gong rang, a door at the far end opened, and visitors began to stream into the prison itself. When Lillian stepped through the doors, the smell of men and urine and filth made her pause and fumble for a handkerchief to cover her nose and mouth. She looked up into the prison, with an open courtyard all the way to the roof, cells surrounding it, and walkways spanning open air on every floor. When she realized she would have to meet him through the bars of his cell, where anyone could eavesdrop, she turned to the first uniformed man she saw.

"Excuse me, officer, I am Lillian Featherstone. And you are..."

"Officer Riley."

He had short gray hair beneath his cap, and glasses that reflected the lights.

"Officer Riley, how do I arrange to meet my father in a private room?"

He paused when two people began arguing at shrill levels at a nearby cell. She jumped when someone banged something against metal.

Officer Riley said quietly, "So you want to see your pop alone? It's usually only lawyers who get that treatment."

She glanced uneasily at the courtyard beyond him. "I would appreciate your help in arranging it."

He said nothing, just continued to look at her with expectation.

And she stared back.

He gave a dramatic sigh and put out his hand, palm up. "This will go easier if you're generous."

Wincing at her ignorance, she opened her purse and handed him a five-dollar bill.

He grimaced. "You'll want to bring more next time, little girl."

*More?* That would buy her several meals and a new dress!

"And you could bring your pop some food or money—it's not like we feed him well inside, and he's not ordering from restaurants like some of the others. But that would be another fee, of course."

She pressed her lips together and followed him down another hall where he opened a door. The small room had two chairs facing each other, divided by a wall of bars.

"Wait here," Officer Riley said, pulling the door shut behind him.

Lillian looked at the chair, then sat in it hesitantly, as if it might break under her. While the minutes dragged by, she worried about her father, who'd only been incarcerated for two days. She remembered the screaming in the prison courtyard and her mind raced with fears of what might have happened to him when faced with true criminals.

When the far door opened, she jumped to her feet, purse dropping to the floor, and gripped the bars as if she could pull them apart. Officer Riley led in her father, who was wearing a black-and-white-striped prison uniform. His face seemed haggard to her, but then she'd never seen him with stubble. His gray hair looked dull instead of shiny with pomade.

When he saw her, he scowled. "Lillian, what are you doing here? I told Webster I didn't want any of my family to visit such a terrible place."

Lillian hadn't intended to cry, but tears now slid down her face.

"Sit," the officer said, steering her father into the other chair by his elbow. "If my daughter wanted to see me, I'd be grateful if I was you." He glanced back at Lillian. "You got twenty minutes."

That didn't seem nearly long enough, but all she did was nod.

"I'll be right outside the door watching," the officer said. "No touching."

And then he clanged the metal door shut behind him. There was a small grate at eye level. He didn't look through, but she knew he was listening.

"Papa?" she whispered.

When he raised his head to attempt another scowl, she saw tears glistening in his eyes.

"You shouldn't have come," he whispered hoarsely.

"But I needed to see you." She reached through the bars for him, not caring what the officer thought.

With a glance at the door, Papa stood up and came to her, taking both her hands in his. He bent and kissed her knuckles, and Lillian bit back a sob.

After a long minute of watching her father's shoulders silently shake, Lillian heard the officer yell, "That's enough! Sit down."

She reluctantly released him, and they both backed up and sat down. She lifted her purse and clutched it in her lap, feeling the cold cement walls pressing in on her.

Papa cleared his throat. "How are your mother and the other children?"

"Just as you'd expect—the same as me. Confused and frightened. What happened?"

"It's too much to go into. But no need to be worried for me. The jail is crowded, so there is a man sharing my cell, but he's tolerable."

"Too much to go into?" she cried. "Your lawyer says you plan to plead guilty to manslaughter! You're admitting to killing someone, even if it was accidental. As I left home, I saw that the newspapers finally published your name. And all of that is too much to go into?"

She hadn't realized how loud and shrill her voice had gotten until she shut her mouth, and the small room echoed with her last words.

Papa's head was bowed, as if the weight of the Tombs pressed on him. With a sigh, he asked, "How is your mother taking the thought of gossip?"

"I don't know. I came here before she left her room. But Bonny always brings a copy of the newspaper while she has her breakfast, so she must have seen it."

"I have let all of you down," he said gravely, still not meeting her gaze.

Her shoulders stiffened. "I don't believe that."

Now he looked at her. "Believe it."

She reared back in her chair as if he'd hit her. "Papa, I won't accept this. There is surely something I can do to help. What about your lawyer? He must have ideas."

"No. He came well-recommended as a man who does what his client wants. And this is what I want."

"What about your old friend, Mr. Russo? His family is well-connected and powerful. Maybe they can get to the bottom of this."

She knew what "well-connected and powerful" meant. Her father had once explained to her that in his youth, he'd become fast friends with "Big Jim" Russo, never realizing that his father was a mobster until they were adults. Papa had distanced himself from that family, he explained, because criminals always hurt the people around them, even if it was accidental. But she knew his old friend Jim came to dinner at Feather-stone's a few times a year.

"No!" He leaned forward, face frighteningly serious. "The

Russos cannot help and will only make things worse. Do not involve them. Promise me."

"I promise," she said, knowing she was lying, knowing she'd do whatever it took to help her father. To distract him, she said, "You could have told me about"—she dropped her voice to whisper—"The Underground."

With a sigh, he rubbed his hands down his face and gave her a wry smile. "I thought it would take your mother longer to find out about it."

"Oh, she doesn't know. She put me in charge of coordinating with Mr. Dabrowski at the restaurant. I noticed the cash entries in the books, and he reluctantly showed me around."

Papa's laugh sounded rusty. "You are too smart, my girl."

"I don't plan to tell Mother. She might make us close it down, and I know the restaurant won't be enough to support us. When did you open the speakeasy?"

"During the first year of Prohibition, Featherstone's wasn't going to survive. Weinstein was one of my assistant managers— he brought it up and agreed to manage it. Have you met him?"

"I've met him," she said dryly.

Papa's face creased in the ghost of a smile. "He's not an easy man, but he gets the work done."

"Does he? I was not impressed."

Papa stared at her in surprise. "Lillian—"

"I've been to college, Papa. I didn't just study. I've visited many such clubs in Philadelphia and New York City. I know what makes them successful. Entertainment, good food. We need to do the same. I told Mr. Weinstein I'd be discussing it with you."

"You shouldn't involve yourself," Papa said sadly, "your studies—"

"You think I can go back to college?" She tried to stifle her bitterness as the awareness of her fate finally closed its grip. "I will be here for my siblings, for Mother—for you. I will make the club a success, so you don't have to worry about us."

To her shock, another tear fell down his cheek. "My girl," he whispered, then cleared his throat. "These should be the best years of your life. And I've ruined them." He trailed off, shoulders sagging.

Though she was uncertain of her words, she spoke them forcefully. "I always wanted to have a career, Papa. This might not be publishing, but it is our family business—I will continue its success. And when you get out, I'll go back to college."

Officer Riley banged open the door, and she and Papa jumped.

"Time's up." The officer grabbed Papa's elbow and pulled him to his feet.

"No, please," Lillian said, rising swiftly to reach through the bars.

"Wait there," Officer Riley said to her. "I'll escort you out."

As Papa was led out of the room, Lillian cried, "Don't plead guilty! I know you're innocent!"

But he didn't answer.

Her eyes ached with so many tears. She hugged herself, head drooping. There hadn't been enough time to figure out what had happened to Papa, why he wouldn't speak of it. What had he really done?

**11**

———

# LILLIAN

1926

When Lillian arrived home, pandemonium reigned because the newspapers had published their father's story. Viola was sobbing in the parlor, Mrs. Vickers was cuddling eight-year-old Julian who cried despondently. Mother was nowhere to be seen.

Mrs. Vickers gave Lillian a tired smile and spoke over the sounds of sorrow. "How was your father?"

As if by magic, the sobs quieted, and Viola emerged into the hall, splotchy red face full of hope.

Lillian took her sister's hand and gave it a squeeze before facing Mrs. Vickers and Julian. "He is well enough, and he sends you all his love."

Viola searched her gaze as if she could find another truth, then she rubbed her eyes.

Julian's mouth dropped open in a howl. "I want Papa!"

Lillian sat down beside them on the bench and reached for her brother, who flung himself around her neck like a monkey. He suddenly seemed so small and vulnerable. And she felt the weight of responsibility as if it too, hung around her neck.

"Papa can't come home any time soon, Julian," she said softly. "Crying won't make it any better."

"I—I can't stop," he said with a hiccup.

So she patted his back and let him cry. Viola sank down on the bench next to Mrs. Vickers, and the four of them wallowed in their sorrow.

"There now," Mrs. Vickers said. "I have your dinner waiting. Eating will make us all feel better."

They ate in the kitchen instead of the dining room, and Lillian realized the simple but delicious beef stew actually made her feel better. Julian and Viola had stopped crying at least, although she thought Mrs. Vickers seemed a bit more stooped. Maybe the weight of the world was on her, too. They were Mrs. Vickers' family, and their sorrow was hers, or so Lillian had always thought.

Viola solemnly pulled apart a piece of bread. "Pansy sent word I couldn't come visit today."

"I'm so sorry." Lillian had been expecting this, but it still stung. She thought about her friend, Grace, a married woman with her own household. Surely she'd never abandon Lillian. But suddenly, all she wanted to do was confide her fears in her compassionate best friend.

Viola's eyes were wet with desperation. "Will she ever speak to me again? Will anyone?"

"They will," Lillian said firmly. "None of this is our fault, and people will realize that." *Some people.* "But it might take time, so we must be patient."

"Papa was going to take me to the horse races this weekend," Julian said.

"I'm sorry that he won't be able to. Maybe the Blackwells are attending. I'll ask if they can take you."

He didn't look convinced, only picked at the tablecloth.

Lillian's heart ached for her little brother, and she had no answers for him. "Has Mother been down?"

Mrs. Vickers, stirring a pot on the stove, spoke over her shoulder. "For a bit. She took the mail and went back upstairs. I don't think she liked the looks of them envelopes."

Lillian wanted to wince, but she just nodded. She forced herself to take several spoonfuls of stew for Mrs. Vickers' sake, then said, "I'll go up to see Mother."

But that didn't go well. As Lillian had suspected, Mother, too, had received several rescinded invitations, and she went on and on in self-pity from her collapsed pose across a mound of pillows on her bed. And it was very true that they might have lost most of their friends. Lillian tried to tell herself that they obviously weren't very good friends, but inside was the nagging fear of how she'd feel if Grace abandoned her.

When at last Mother seemed to run out of complaints, Lillian said, "You haven't asked me about Papa."

Mother inhaled deeply and let it out in a rush before bursting into tears.

Lillian sank down on the edge of the bed and put her arm around her mother.

"How is he?" Mother whispered. "I should have gone, too."

"You can go another time. It's...not a pleasant place."

"You're a brave girl."

"Thank you, but it's not brave to need my father."

Mother patted Lillian's leg, looking toward the window, trembling lips pressed together.

Lillian sighed. "He's as fine as is possible in jail, where he has to share his tiny cell."

"You saw it?"

"No, but I can imagine. It's a far cry from here." She looked around her parents' bedroom, with its floral-patterned walls and delicately carved furniture. Much more a woman's room than a man's, but Papa had always wanted Mother to be happy and comfortable.

"Did he tell you why this happened?" Mother asked.

Lillian shook her head. "He didn't want to discuss it."

Mother stiffly turned her head to gape at Lillian.

"That was my reaction, too, but I didn't have enough time to persuade him. He was worried about us and wanted to know about the restaurant."

"He cared more about *his business* than us?"

"He was concerned his problems would impact the restaurant—which would impact us," Lillian pointed out.

Mother sagged back into her pillows as if regretting her words.

"Though he doesn't want us to come," Lillian continued, "I think it would be good for him to see you. You'll have to give five dollars to the guard to be alone with Papa—"

"What?"

"It's how things are done. And bring Papa some food. He looks thin. I don't know if he can have more visitors in one day, so go tomorrow."

"It's not as if I have anything else to do," Mother said bitterly, gesturing to the opened mail scattered across the diamond-patterned bedspread.

When Lillian didn't answer, Mother added, "That was uncalled for. Forgive me."

Lillian patted her shoulder and climbed off the bed. "Of course. This has been hard on all of us. I'm off to visit Grace before I go back to the restaurant this evening."

"How do you know she'll see you?"

"I don't. But I have to try."

~oOo~

Lillian took a deep breath and lifted the knocker on the brownstone that faced Central Park. When the white-bearded butler opened the door, she had a sudden fear that Grace might have instructed the servants to politely say she wasn't at home.

But Davidson simply nodded his head. "Miss Lillian, do come in. Mrs. Nash will be pleased to see you."

Feeling as if she'd passed a test, Lillian gave him a relieved smile and entered the foyer with its gleaming marble floors and carved paneling. The butler ascended the stairs, leaving her alone.

Grace's husband William was a banker, from a family of bankers, and the home had been decorated with understated but obvious wealth. Whereas Lillian had gone to college, Grace had married, the traditional path for their friends. They'd gone to school together, traded their favorite books, giggled about boys, and dreamed of what their adult lives would be. Lillian had always imagined the exciting path of a career in publishing, but Grace had wanted her own home, and a husband and children to care for. Lillian wanted those things too, but *after* she experienced life for a while.

Whenever Lillian was away at college, they wrote to each other, and it was fun for each of them to experience through letters the opposite paths they'd chosen.

But this new path Lillian was on was something neither of them had imagined. Once, Lillian had persuaded Grace to join her at the 21 Club, and although Grace had looked around with wide eyes, tapped her toes and clapped along with the music, she'd never wanted to visit again. Grace hadn't blamed William but Lillian often wondered. He had never made much of an attempt to get to know Lillian, and Grace always said he was too busy furthering his career when he let himself be monopolized by the other men at parties. How would he feel about what Lillian's father had been accused of?

But before Lillian could work herself back into nervousness, Grace came skimming down the stairs, her dress flowing over her pregnant belly.

"Lillian!" she cried, and at the bottom of the curving staircase, flung her arms around her friend.

Lillian closed her eyes in relief and held on a moment before backing away. "I don't want to hug you too hard in your condition."

Grace waved her concern away, threaded her arm through Lillian's, and pulled her into the small drawing room with sunny windows facing Central Park. "No worries! Even the morning nausea has gone. I feel like I could take on the world—and my world is preparing the nursery," she added, smiling.

Grace was petite in stature, her hair a subtle shade of auburn, her nose covered with freckles she'd had no luck hiding. There was Irish in her ancestry, though her parents never admitted it.

Once they were seated facing each other across a tea table complete with little cakes, Grace instructed the maid to close the door behind her, then turned to face Lillian, her smile fading into concern.

Lillian sank back into the cushions, her stomach too full of nerves to eat. "You read the newspaper."

Grace nodded. "I am so worried for your entire family. How is your mother?"

"Not well, as you can imagine. We're all very worried about Papa, and the household is full of crying children."

"Surely your father is innocent and will return home soon."

Lillian hesitated. She usually told Grace everything, but how could she say her father planned to plead guilty? With a soft voice, she murmured, "I hope so."

Grace leaned forward to cover Lillian's hand with her own. "You don't sound convinced, dear friend."

The kind words made Lillian's eyes sting, but she blinked back tears, trying to smile. "I am worried for him, trapped in jail with..."

"Murderers." Grace gave a shudder.

Lillian found it difficult to swallow, but Grace seemed not to remember what Lillian's father had been accused of. Or else Grace didn't imagine it was possibly true, and Lillian silently blessed her friend.

Grace continued speaking. "I cannot imagine how I would react if my own father were in such straits. Your whole family is very brave."

"Not really. We're doing what we have to do." She paused. "I saw Papa today."

"He's home? Or—oh, Lillian, you went to visit him?" Her voice ended on a squeak. "You cannot deny your bravery to me."

Lillian shrugged. "Not bravery. Desperation and fear. But for now, he is well enough. I will have to trust in his lawyer." *Whom I don't know.*

"The world is changing, and not in a pleasant way," Grace said solemnly. "Mobsters roam freely about town, laws are being broken—"

Lillian winced, thinking about The Underground.

"—who knows what can happen when a good and decent man like your father ends up in jail?"

Lillian bit her lip, words drying up in her mouth. She'd wanted to confide everything in Grace, but from the moment she arrived, she'd held her tongue on one detail after another.

"Will the restaurant continue to operate?" Grace asked.

"Yes, that's my focus," Lillian said, "to keep the restaurant running smoothly." Not a lie, but not the whole truth.

Grace studied her for a long moment. "What about college?"

She let out her breath, relieved at the change in topic. "It will have to wait. I'll go back when I'm able. But right now, Mother needs me. I'm going to oversee the restaurant in my father's place."

"You are so smart and capable," Grace said.

Her friend's voice was filled with a quiet awe that discomfited Lillian. She wondered what Grace would think if she knew Lillian was keeping an illegal enterprise going. But right now, all she could do was bask in her relief that her friend had not abandoned her.

**12**

———

# PAMELA

2023

While they had dinner that evening at the little Formica-topped table next to the galley kitchen in her father's old apartment, Pam stared at the broken photo frame she'd propped up against the wall between Lucia and herself. Great-Aunt Lillian stared back at her, her expression mischievous and happy, the speakeasy and musicians behind her.

"I think you look like her," Lucia said, between bites of lasagna.

"I don't know. Great-Aunt Lillian looks so young and fashionable here—it's hard to tell."

"You're young."

Pam snorted.

"Young enough."

Pam gave her a little kick under the table.

Lucia laughed in a merry, carefree way that struck Pam. She didn't think she'd heard the teenager laugh like that before. She hoped it meant she was settling in, feeling more at ease.

They both continued eating for a few minutes.

"We need to fix the glass in the frame," Lucia said. "Then we can hang it up and think of Great-Aunt Lillian as our guide."

"Our guide?"

"Our mentor?" Lucia wrinkled her nose. "Our inspiration! We could use some of that as we work on this place."

"I thought your inspiration was your wages," Pam said dryly.

"Oh, that's *my* inspiration, for sure. But I think you need some inspiration, too, and not just the kind where you want to be done with something. This old building is pretty special. It's fun to think of living here a hundred years ago."

"No internet," Pam pointed out.

"I could read books by candlelight."

"I didn't say there was no electricity!"

Lucia laughed.

Pam picked up the broken frame. Lucia was right—she wasn't feeling exactly inspired lately. Turning the brass frame over, she slid aside the tabs and removed the backing, hoping to measure the photo and buy a new frame.

But instead of just the front-facing photo of her aunt, there was another picture hidden behind, smaller, of a mixed-race infant, eyes closed as they peacefully slept. Tucked in beside it was a lock of dark hair, held together with a strand of silk thread.

"What did you find?" Lucia asked.

Pam handed the photo to her and set the lock of hair on the table between them. Lucia studied the photo for a long time, then glanced up at Pam uncertainly.

Pam shrugged. "I'm not sure what I'm supposed to think. Saving hair with the photo makes it seem pretty special. People used to do that after someone's death. There might have been an obituary saved here if he'd died young."

Lucia winced, then turned the photo over. "Daniel, 1927." She handed it back.

Pam studied the little face again, so perfect and innocent. "He feels...familiar."

"Really!" Lucia's eyes sparkled. "Now this is a mystery. It's not like there was much socializing between the races a hundred years ago."

"But if interracial dating was going on anywhere in the country, it was happening here. Think of all the people who went to Harlem to party back then."

"Do you think this was your aunt's baby?"

"I don't know. I never heard that. She married and had a couple kids, and from the pictures I remember seeing, they were a very White family." She pulled the first photo out of the broken frame and held them side by side. "She looks very young here. And there's something about the baby's nose and chin…I'm probably reading too much into this. But why would someone hide this photo behind one of my aunt?"

Lucia frowned. "This building is full of mysteries."

"You know, I saw the family Bible in a box around here someplace," Pam said. "We might find some answers there."

"Why?"

"That's where people used to record family births and deaths."

Lucia set down her fork. "I'm done eating. Let's go find it."

Pam smiled and shook her head. "It's not going anywhere. Finish your—"

But Lucia was already out of her chair, heading up to the apartment on the fourth floor where they'd stored all the furniture and boxes they didn't immediately need.

They found the Bible with all the other books and brought it back to their living room. It was larger than a normal hardcover, and the edges were bent.

Pam traced her finger along the names, written by many different hands. "Ah, here she is. Lillian Featherstone. Her first child wasn't born until 1930, the second 1933."

"Maybe she had another and no one knew."

"People would have known."

"Really?" Lucia asked. "People also know how to keep secrets, especially ones that might make the rest of the family ashamed. Have you ever used one of those DNA sites?"

Pam frowned. "No."

"You might want to think about it."

Pam looked at the Bible again, at the handwriting listing Lillian's grandchildren, her second cousins. She remembered family reunions that had ended long ago when too many people moved away. Her dad had worked so hard to persuade relatives, but to no avail. Had she met Lillian's grandchildren?

"I don't know about putting my DNA out for anyone to grab."

Lucia elbowed her. "Sounds like you just don't want to know."

"I want to know." She touched the photo of the baby gently.

"Maybe you could hire a private detective."

That broke up Pam's pensive mood, and the two shared a chuckle.

"I'm not sure I want to know *that* much. But I will make more of an effort to go through Dad's box of old photos when I get a chance. Maybe we'll find something interesting. In the meantime, I'll buy a new frame."

"I can buy one for you. I'll be heading out to do some shopping for college." She hesitated. "Would you like to come?"

Surprised, Pam studied Lucia and thought the girl seemed to be blushing as she didn't meet her eyes.

"You'd want an old lady's help shopping for *college*?" Pam asked doubtfully.

"You're not old," Lucia said. "But you've been to college, and you've probably shopped a lot, and I never have. I have a clothing allowance from social services, and I want to be smart about how I spend it."

Pam felt that familiar squeeze of sympathy and fondness when she remembered all that Lucia had lived through, her parents dying young, her foster family moving away. She cleared her throat. "I'd love to go shopping with you. We can make a day of it, have lunch out, everything."

Lucia grinned. "No take-out? I'm shocked!"

~oOo~

They spent a day in Soho together, and Pam found herself truly relaxing and enjoying herself. Lucia was an amazing young woman, focused on her future and ready to work hard to make it happen. Pam thought of all the advantages she herself had grown up with that she'd ignored in favor of dwelling on how much time her dad spent on the restaurant. And lately Pam had only been able to focus on her anger about her husband's death. Lucia had lost both her parents, and though she obviously missed them, she wasn't letting it stop her from achieving her goals.

It made Pam uncertain about her own goals—because she didn't have any except selling the building. After that, there seemed to be a yawning void. And was selling Harbor House what she really wanted? She didn't know anymore.

In the Uber on the way back to the Seaport, surrounded by shopping bags, Lucia rested her head on the back of the seat in contented exhaustion. "Did you like the frame we bought for your great-aunt's photo?"

"I do. Suitably old-fashioned."

"Should we buy one for the baby photo?"

"I'm not sure yet what we should do about it, since I don't know the truth."

"You could find out..." Lucia said, dragging out her words.

Pam sighed. "I know. I don't have any idea where to start. Contact cousins I barely know and get them worried or curious?"

"What about the private detective? Then you could approach your family with some facts."

"Hmm." Pam hesitated. "I actually know a private detective—well, I went to high school with him, and I heard about his job years later when someone mentioned it at a reunion."

"Have you seen him since high school?"

"No. And I'm blanking on his last name, too. I'll try a couple old friends and see what they've heard about him. Or I can always dig out a yearbook. But I'd have to go to my house on Long Island to find that."

By Friday, after Lucia kept bugging her, Pam admitted her few friends didn't remember his name either.

"Doesn't make him sound too memorable," Lucia teased, from where she lay on the couch reading the old Featherstone book.

"He was just a guy in some of my classes," Pam protested from the table, where she was trying to catalogue her dad's old family photos by date. Surely something here would help with her National Historic Register application. Dad was a packrat for family history, she thought fondly.

"Well do you want to hire someone you know—or have you given up finding clues about the baby photo?"

"*You* certainly never give up," Pam grumbled. "All right, I'll take a drive out to my house tomorrow. It's been a few weeks. It's probably good I check up on the place."

Lucia opened her mouth as if to say something, then sank back behind her book.

Pam sighed. "Did you want to come, too?"

Lucia's sparkling eyes appeared above the book as she nodded. "If we go tomorrow, I can get someone to take my shift at the restaurant."

Pam was starting to forget what it was like to be alone—and maybe that was a good thing for a while. She'd been in a dark place since Will had died.

~oOo~

Pam noticed that Lucia didn't talk much on the drive along the Long Island Expressway. As they left behind the city, and the highway became tree-lined or blocked by privacy walls, Lucia studied it all as if she could drink it in.

"Have you been out here before?" Pam asked as they exited the highway and drove through countryside interspersed with scattered homes and businesses.

Lucia shook her head. "I've never left the city at all. It's pretty cool out here. More rural than I thought, for just being an hour away."

Pam snorted. "Just give it a few more miles. We're heading north toward Manhasset Bay, with gorgeous houses along the Sound."

"Is that where you live?"

"Hardly. I just live in a normal Colonial a few streets off Plandome Road, our main street, and where our insurance brokerage used to be."

"The one you sold? Do you miss it?"

Pam didn't take her eyes off the road as she shook her head. "I thought I would, but it's been a few months, and nope, it's in my past."

"What's your future?"

Pam shot her a glance. "I don't know. Just waiting to see what happens."

"When you sell Harbor House."

Pam didn't say anything, just looked back at the road. She thought of hanging the picture of her aunt—was that something you did if you were making a place your home? No, she wasn't doing that. It would suck every bit of her retirement security to modernize it.

Wouldn't it?

This inability to make decisions since Will's death was

exhausting. She wasn't a person used to feeling overwhelmed. People had told her it would take time and patience to recover from Will's loss, but she hadn't believed the extent of it.

She turned up Plandome Road, past the cemetery and the small businesses in old houses, then to the quaint downtown with its one- and two-story brick buildings joined in rows. She didn't point out the insurance brokerage, now under another name. It was in her past, and she was surprised not to feel emotional about it.

After taking a turn and driving a few more blocks, she turned into her driveway. The house was small by some Long Island standards, a white four-bedroom Colonial with black shutters, but it had been perfect for two people who'd been more focused on growing their business than starting a family.

"Nice house," Lucia said.

"Thanks."

They went in through the front door, and Pam turned off the security system. The air smelled stale and unused, and she paused, as if she might catch a hint of her husband's aftershave. But then, it wasn't as if she truly associated the house with him —he was never there all that much. Neither of them were. It was all about the work.

As they went down the hall to the kitchen, every table was empty of clutter, as if no one lived there. The white cabinets were all closed, the stainless-steel appliances gleamed without fingerprints.

"There's probably a soda in the fridge," Pam said, tossing her keys and purse on the kitchen table. "I'm going to grab the high-school box from the basement."

When she came back upstairs and put the box on the table, she found Lucia wandering the first-floor rooms, where the dining room set had once hosted the occasional party, through the living room with white leather furniture accented in blue pillows. They were only a few blocks from Manhasset Bay, and

Pam had liked to decorate in sea greens and blues. Now it just seemed...sterile.

"You found the box that easily?" Lucia asked, following her into the kitchen. "So organized."

Pam shrugged. "Will liked it that way, and I grew to like it, too."

"So you were once as unorganized as your dad?"

She smiled. "I think I was."

From the box, Pam pulled out notebooks on biology and English and math, grimacing at her foolish hoarding. At the bottom, the heaviest books were the yearbooks. She spread open her senior yearbook and sat down to page through the couple hundred students she'd graduated with.

"Love everyone's big hair," Lucia said gleefully, looking over her shoulder.

Pam ignored her. Each photo brought back different memories: fondness, indifference, disdain. She was suddenly back there again, focusing hard on her studies, but ready to have a good time.

And suddenly she saw him. "Keith Eldridge. I *thought* his last name began with an E."

Lucia was already tapping away at her phone. "Found him. Office in Manhattan. Sounds like he's got a lot of clients. He'll be able to help us."

"Or maybe he'll be too busy. Our request sounds silly now—a hundred-year-old baby photo with just a first name on the back."

"Private detectives love a challenge."

"In books anyway. In real life, they just want to earn a living like the rest of us." She closed the book and started to put it back in the box.

"Wait—where's *your* picture?"

Pam handed over the book, and as she did a quick tour of the upstairs, heard Lucia chuckling.

Pam stood alone in her bedroom, the large king-size bed with the white duvet stretching out silently before her, wondering where the feeling of "home" had gone. Had it left with Will's death? She didn't open his closet, didn't look at the clothes she still hadn't donated. More decisions she couldn't make. She turned around and left.

Back in the kitchen, Lucia was working her way through the clubs and sports teams, leaning close to the yearbook to look at all the miniature faces.

She glanced up at Pam. "You were busy—soccer, lacrosse, school paper."

"It seems like a lifetime ago." Pam took the yearbook and put it back in the box. She should throw away all the notebooks —but then with a sigh she just repacked them.

"You don't seem happy to be here," Lucia said softly.

Pam continued to fold the box flaps. "I'm not *un*happy. I'm surprised by how little emotion I really feel here."

"Maybe it's the excitement of the city that feels like home to you."

Pam frowned and gave that a moment's intense thought. "I just don't know." She let out her breath. "Ready to go?"

~oOo~

Over the next few days, Pam turned her attention to the fourth-floor apartment. She occasionally hired a friend of Lucia's, Jason, to drag all the garbage and donation boxes to the first floor, and he pocketed the cash while giving her a grateful smile. She kept Lucia busy when she was there, but often the girl was at her other job, and Pam was able to avoid the "Have you called him yet?" questions.

She kept trying to tell herself it really didn't matter who the baby was. Wasn't it a lot of work—and money—just to satisfy her curiosity? But every time she walked by the photo of her great-aunt, looking happy and confident, those jazz musicians behind her, she found herself wondering if the baby wasn't even her aunt's. Perhaps she'd been good friends with one of the men behind her, and she had fond memories of the child.

But there was still the shape of the baby's nose and chin that seemed so familiar.

Frustrated with her inability to make a decision, to find some direction in her life, Pam dug even more into her father's old boxes, the ones she'd moved from the apartment they were now living in. She'd gotten them out of the way, but they were still there, boxes of memories that she had to face.

There were letters between her parents that brought back their youthful flirtation; it was strange to see them as young people just starting out in life, so hopeful for the future. Their letters were intimate as they told each other their dreams; once or twice Pam had to stop reading, as if she shouldn't know how her parents fell in love.

She found their high school diplomas, their wedding certificates, and eventually the crafts of her own childhood: paper mâché rocks, macaroni necklaces, blobs of painted pictures on which her mother had painstakingly written what they were supposed to be, like house or tree or dinosaur.

And Pam sometimes cried as the memories of her parents swamped her.

Needing to put aside her grief, she focused on older boxes of memorabilia that had obviously been passed on by her grandparents. Birth and death certificates, and so many letters. In the days before the cellphone, when long distance calls were expensive, letters proliferated. Apparently her parents hadn't felt they could part with any of them. When she found postmarks from the nineteenth century, she called Lucia's name.

The teenager ducked out of the bathroom in leggings and an oversize t-shirt, her hair wet from a shower after her restaurant shift. She always smelled like French fries when she came home, and though it didn't bother Pam, Lucia couldn't stand what she considered a greasy smell.

"Look!" Pam said, holding up a yellowed envelope. "It's from France, 1894."

Lucia's mouth dropped opened, and she took the paper gingerly. "It's so thin and delicate."

"Cheaper to cross the ocean, I'm sure."

"What kind of packrats are you descended from?" Lucia asked, staring at the envelopes scattered across the table.

Pam smiled as she imagined her father surrounded by these old boxes and the treasures within. "I haven't even gotten to the bottom of the box yet."

Lucia held up another envelope. "I can't read the date." She delicately opened it and removed a letter. Unfolding it, she gasped. "1842! Let's read it."

Pam felt like a treasure hunter. "But maybe we'll find an even older one. How did I not know about these?"

At the bottom of the box, they discovered several folded pieces of parchment paper tied together with a faded, ragged ribbon.

"Wow," Lucia breathed. "These are really old."

Pam carefully undid the ribbon and unfolded the top paper. The handwriting was legible, although cramped. She inhaled sharply. "1790."

"Wow!"

She scanned to the bottom of the page. "It's from Abigail Featherstone."

"Do you think she's related to Andrew, the one who wrote the book we've been reading? That was published in 1823, so thirty-three years later."

"I don't know. There are two letters here. Why don't we each try to read them?"

Pam handed one over, and knew by the reverential, gentle way Lucia opened her page that she didn't have to warn the teenager to be careful. She thought the girl was holding her breath.

"You can breathe, you know," Pam said dryly.

Lucia gave her a brief, distracted smile, as if she was already immersed in the world of 1790.

Pam grabbed a notebook and began to slowly write out what she was reading because it took her a while to decipher some of the handwriting. Though the cursive was slanted and precise, age had yellowed the paper, and smudges and stains had obliterated some words.

"This one is about guests at the Featherstone Tavern," Lucia said.

"You sound glum."

"Well, it's not very exciting."

"But it was written by my ancestor who's been dead around two hundred years or so."

"You're right. How's yours?"

"It's not about the tavern, but about memories of the war. I think she was writing it to a relative, perhaps a grandchild, letting them know some of the things that happened. And that relative saved the letters. But...something is niggling at me."

"Niggling?" Lucia laughed. "Is that a word still used in this century?"

"It is," Pam said, her nose in the air. Then she smiled. "Abigail is writing about housing British soldiers during the occupation."

"Cool source material for your application to the National Historic Register."

"True." But it was Pam's turn to feel distracted. "But there's something about the way she talks about the soldiers, how they behaved, that just seems familiar to me."

"How can they be familiar—unless you mean from the book by Abigail's son or grandson?"

Pam nodded. "Why don't you read this and see what you think. I'll go fix our salads for lunch."

When she returned twenty minutes later, Lucia had the book *One Woman's Story During the War of Independence* open beside the letter. While Pam ate, she watched with amusement as Lucia ignored her meal to frown over the letter, then page through the book, then go back to the letter.

"I see what you mean," Lucia said at last. She looked up, her eyes bright with excitement. "There are similarities, even in some of the phrases Abigail uses."

"Are you thinking what I'm thinking?"

"That Abigail wrote the novel?" Lucia asked. "You bet I am. And she mentions her son Andrew in this letter, so she's definitely related to him."

"It's by A.E. Featherstone. Abigail starts with A."

"But why hide?"

"Remember how many female authors wrote under a male pseudonym, like George Eliot? Women weren't taken seriously and were discriminated against by the business world."

"No!" Lucia said with exaggerated shock.

Pam shrugged. "Maybe it was just easier for her son to publish. Not that we can ever know the truth," she added with a sigh.

"But *we* know," Lucia said. "And they did house British soldiers, and there's the hidden closet. Maybe the reason Abigail writes the letter—and maybe the book—is because she knows everything firsthand."

"It's fun to think about," Pam said.

"This is such an incredible building, full of so many secrets, isn't it?"

"Hmm," was Pam's response. She was going to pretend she didn't hear the hint.

But that night, after Lucia had gone to bed, Pam found

herself wandering up to the fourth-floor apartment, her father's "attic" and now hers.

The letters and photos from her ancestors made the building *hers* in a way she'd never felt before, and it unsettled her. In the low light, she felt the ghosts of the past moving all around her, not in a threatening way. She thought of Great-Aunt Lillian running a speakeasy here, something women seldom did. She thought of Abigail Featherstone, quartering British soldiers against her will, and maybe spying on them. Abigail had no husband to support her, only her own wits to protect her children and survive an occupation. They were brave women, and here Pam was waffling about her future, full of self-pity when she was alive and safe.

The least she could do was honor her family legacy, and her father, by finding out about the mysterious baby photo, rather than let it wait another hundred years. And she could get off her butt, get on a genealogy website to find more relatives, and make an appointment with Keith Eldridge. She was digging around so much in the past, she might as well rediscover someone from her own past.

## 13

---

# LILLIAN

1926

Lillian was at the restaurant by ten the next morning, before midday dinner. Mr. Dabrowski walked her through the entire restaurant operation, and she admired the chef and his assistants preparing for the midday meal by meticulously chopping vegetables and making sauces. Later, after watching the host seat guests for several hours during the busiest part of the meal, mostly businessmen from the financial district, she took a turn herself, greeting customers with a smile, practicing the subtle art of near-flirtation that had always come naturally. She made it a point not to say her full name, to avoid reminding anyone of her father's fate.

After the restaurant closed for the mid-afternoon break, Lillian studied the supper preparation and discussed the ordering of supplies and food with Mr. Dabrowski. Toward the end of the supper service, which was steady if not completely full, Mr. Weinstein arrived, and Lillian followed him down to his office.

"Mr. Weinstein, have you given my proposals any thought?" she asked.

He chomped on his cigar and peered into several desk drawers as if looking for something. "And what was that?"

She gritted her teeth. "We need to liven up the place and make it appealing to young people, especially women. We need to redecorate, establish a menu, hire bands."

"I don't got time for that."

"Then you'll *make* time. We need to earn more, and that starts with spending more, even if that makes things difficult. How else do you expect to receive a raise, if we don't improve?"

"I ain't seen a raise in five years."

"Then let that be one of our goals."

He gave her another baleful look and opened an accounting book.

Lillian took a deep breath. "Did you wish to show me something?"

"Nope."

"Then I will discuss The Underground menu with the head chef. Please present your plans to me in the next day or two."

He didn't look at her.

Lillian marched out of the office and up two flights of stairs to Mr. Dabrowski's office. He looked up when she knocked on the open door.

Before he could say anything, she said, "That man has appalling manners and a bad head for business."

He sighed and sat back in his squeaky office chair. "If you mean Weinstein, I agree about the former, not so much about the latter. He has a good head for business when he's in charge. He's been complaining that he won't work for you."

"Then he can find another job. He hasn't quit, so that means he's reluctant to go. I told him to present me his plans for improvements."

Mr. Dabrowski arched a brow. "I will look forward to that. Keep pressuring him. He will understand that you're now the boss and you're not going anywhere."

She felt a stab of sadness over her father, and he must have read her expression.

"Any news?" he asked.

She shook her head. Her throat tight, she said, "I'm going to speak with Chef."

"Do you want me to come?"

She hesitated, realized she wanted his support a bit too much, and shook her head. "No, but thank you."

Chef Guardini was dramatically appalled at the extra work implied by the speakeasy's changes, and when she insisted he could plan the menu as he wished, and she'd hire other cooks to follow his plans through the night, he calmed down a bit. He was doubtful just anyone else could replicate whatever masterpieces he planned to create. Lillian listened patiently, finally offering to take it out of his hands completely.

And he was affronted again, saying that Featherstone's was *his* restaurant with *his* name associated with it. She arched a brow but did not correct him. She knew his menus brought repeat customers.

Though she was tired, she remained after midnight, during the opening hour of the club. Mr. Weinstein scowled a lot but mostly ignored her, which was so strange, since she now controlled his pay.

She saw a lot of the same customers drinking themselves into oblivion, defying the government and teetotalers and perhaps their boring lives with dogged determination that didn't seem enjoyable.

But things could be different—they could have fun, she silently told herself, determined to make it happen. It would improve her customers' lives, the financial stability of the restaurant, and her family.

When almost an hour had elapsed, Lillian was about ready to leave, bored by the lackluster piano music and the dearth of people her own age to talk to. Although she *had* been propositioned by a man old enough to be her grandfather.

As she was putting on her coat in Mr. Weinstein's office, she heard a burst of laughter and excited voices.

She peered out into the dimly lit, smoky club and found two couples coming down the stairs. To her surprise, she recognized several of them as college-aged friends. They still hadn't seen her, and she was tempted to remain hidden in Mr. Weinstein's office, but if she was going to lure younger, wealthier people, she should start immediately.

She shrugged off her coat, put on a smile, and went out into the club.

"Lillian!" cried Marlene Holmes.

Lillian waved and stepped toward her.

After glancing about, Marlene's smile briefly froze, and Lillian knew exactly what she was thinking. This was not a club anyone would return to a second time.

Lillian recognized the others, friends with whom she'd gone to high school, Frank, Wesley, and Hazel. They'd been part of the popular crowd, as Lillian once had, but she couldn't say she'd known them well except to drink and smoke together at parties.

"What are you doing here?" Marlene asked. "I know your family owns the restaurant above, of course, but I thought you were at Penn."

"I'm home to be with my family," Lillian said vaguely.

One of the young men, Wesley—she vaguely remembered English class together—met Marlene's gaze with a frown.

"In fact," Lillian continued, "I'm here because I've temporarily taken over management of the restaurant, and of course, The Underground."

Marlene looked around. "Not exactly the cat's meow."

"No, it's not," Lillian agreed. "In fact, I knew nothing about it before this week, but it obviously needs work." Smiling again, she offered, "Would you all like a drink?"

Soon the five of them were standing at the bar, discussing college life. Lillian couldn't miss the way her friends kept glancing around at the other patrons. When the piano player took a break, the silence was an eerie backdrop to the slurred voices of drunks bragging to each other.

But most depressing were the solitary drinkers who sat alone looking at their drinks. Lillian's friends began to give her sympathetic looks. Wesley elbowed Marlene.

Marlene turned to Lillian. "We're making a night of it, touring the city speakeasies up in Harlem. Would you like to come?"

Wesley gave a faint grimace, but he didn't speak up. She knew her presence wasn't necessarily wanted. She almost demurred to step back into Mr. Weinstein's office and hide.

But another part of her knew she might face these kinds of people for the rest of her life. She'd done nothing wrong and blaming her was just cruel.

She turned to Marlene with a smile. "I would love to go. I'm going to start renovating the club, and good examples will help."

Marlene clapped her hands together. "Perfect! Are you ready?"

"Let me get my purse and coat."

When she ducked back into Mr. Weinstein's office, he glowered at her. "Taking paying customers away, are we? Not sure how that helps The Underground."

"It's so deadly dull out there you can hear our conversations through the wall?" she countered.

He chomped his cigar to the other side of his mouth but said nothing.

"My friends are so disappointed by the entertainment that

they don't want to stay. That is *your* problem, and I've asked you to fix it. Please have your proposal to me by tomorrow night."

He opened his mouth, but she talked right over him.

"In the meantime, I will investigate the entertainment offerings of our competition and elaborate on my own ideas. I do believe we'll be able to compromise on a plan that will improve The Underground. We can be successful together, Mr. Weinstein."

"What if I don't want to?" he grumbled.

He sounded childish, but she didn't point it out. "Then I'll consider replacing you. I appreciate the work you've done. But I need this restaurant and club to be even more successful." She lowered her voice and spoke solemnly. "My family is depending on me. I cannot let them down, and I won't see them in reduced circumstances because of my father's choices and my inability to improve things. I need your help, Mr. Weinstein. I hope you'll rise to the occasion."

She didn't wait for him to answer, just put her coat over her arm, lifted her purse, and left the office.

The party was large enough that they had to take separate cars. Marlene rode with Lillian, and they filled the time with surface conversation about what their school friends were up to. Lillian sensed that Marlene wanted to ask more personal questions about her father, as if one of the others had finally informed her about Lillian's situation, but they'd never been close enough for that. She couldn't help feeling relieved.

Up in Harlem, the streets teemed with revelers; Whites and Negroes mingled in a way her parents' generation had never imagined. But the Great War and the Spanish Flu had changed everyone and everything. People wore their fanciest clothes, and the women glittered like birds in their finery, their heads decorated with hats and headbands elaborately adorned with feathers and paste jewels. They drank and partied together except at certain exclusive nightclubs like the Cotton Club, where Negroes performed but were not allowed in the audience. Lillian refused to attend such a place.

They headed for a smaller club off Fifth Avenue, where she was swept up in the press of people mingling at tables, crowding at the bar, or dancing the Black Bottom with everyone else on the burnished dance floor, a haze of smoke shimmering above them. She admired the shiny brass rail circling the perimeter, the potted trees scattered down each side, the mirrors lining an entire wall, which made the club look even bigger. She thought about what she might be able to do without spending too much money. New tables and chairs would be expensive, but it would have to be done.

They found a table near the bandstand, ordered drinks, then perused the menu. Canapes, oysters Rockefeller, and deviled eggs weren't too different from what her restaurant already offered, but could she afford to serve food all night in her small club? Once a waitress had taken their order, Lillian glanced up at the stage, where a Negro band was playing. The trumpet player was extraordinary, and after a solo, the crowd rewarded him with cheers and applause.

He flashed a charming smile. Lillian felt her breath catch, her face flush, and she stopped breathing altogether when his gaze met hers. A yearning moved through her, reminding her how alone she'd been since returning home. His smile faded a bit, his dark gaze intensified, and time seemed to stand still. His smile turned rueful, playful, until the trombonist nudged him, and then he brought up his trumpet and began to play again.

When their gazes broke, Lillian felt a little dazed. She glanced at her companions, but no one seemed to notice her behavior. The Waterman Jazz Band played incredibly well. There were only four of them, and she realized that her stage would be big enough.

Should she hire a Negro band? Others had, but it was still

risky. Yet all of the young people of New York came to Harlem to enjoy their music—surely the same customers would come to her club.

The band started a new song, and more people rose to dance.

Lillian leaned toward Marlene. "What do you think of them?"

"I've heard them before—they're marvelous."

"Do you know if they play other clubs?"

Marlene shrugged, then eyed her closely. "Why?"

"I need to hire entertainment—surely you noticed that," she added dryly.

"Well…" the other woman drew out her words, spreading her hands wide. "It wasn't my place to say anything."

"I've only just begun to be involved in the running of our family businesses," Lillian said. "I'd like to widen our entertainment, improve the facility, maybe add a menu."

Marlene frowned. "Won't you be going back to Penn?"

Lillian forced a smile. "Not for the moment, though I will eventually."

Marlene patted her hand, then turned back to watch the entertainment. Though they'd not been particularly close, Marlene now knew more about Lillian's predicament than her own best friend Grace did. It made her uncomfortable that she hadn't trusted her relationship with Grace—or maybe she was uncomfortable because she felt ashamed and diminished.

As Marlene and Frank leaned toward each other to talk, Lillian's gaze drifted once again to the trumpeter. He was dressed sharply in a navy pinstriped Jazz Suit, with its slim lines and high waist, his tie bright blue in the center of his white shirt. His skin was dusky against the white, his jaw square, his cheekbones sharp. His hair was close-cropped, with a side part.

He lowered his trumpet and grinned at her again. She felt

herself blushing, but she didn't look away. The last time she'd blushed around men, she'd been fourteen.

"Let's dance!" Frank said, taking her hand.

Wesley was already leading Marlene onto the dance floor. Hazel, leaning over the back of her chair to chat with the group at the next table, hardly seemed to notice.

They threaded through the warm, swaying mass of dancers until they found a large enough place to do the Charleston. Lillian forgot her cares, forgot her worries and fears, and let herself go. Frank's arm hugged her waist as they kicked to the side wildly. She laughed and swayed with abandon as the music moved through her. When it was over, she applauded with the rest, turning to the band to clap even louder in admiration. With a wave, the musicians set down their instruments and headed toward the bar. Another piano player went up onstage and began to play.

"I overheard you tell Marlene you're looking to book bands," Frank said in Lillian's ear.

She nodded, staring up at him quizzically. But all he did was take her hand and begin to pull her toward the bar.

She wanted to pull back, as they wove their way through the other dancers. The bar seemed to be rushing toward them. But she didn't say anything, just let herself be drawn toward the man she hadn't been able to stop staring at since she arrived.

"Ray!" Frank called.

The trumpeter turned around, a beer in his hand, and when he saw them approach, his gaze sharpened briefly on Lillian before he turned to her dance partner.

"Hey, Frank."

Ray's voice was low and smooth, but she heard it perfectly even in the crowded club.

"Ray, this little lady is Lillian Featherstone, and her family owns a club downtown."

"Nice to meet you, Miss Lillian," Ray said.

To her surprise, he reached out a hand. She took it and found his grip warm and firm. "Please, just Lillian."

"I'm Ray Waterman, and you've been listening to the Waterman Jazz Band."

"You play wonderfully," she said, finding herself reluctant to release his hand. "Your entire band does," she added quickly.

His grin was still captivating.

"Thank you. I saw you dancing. You know how to follow the beat."

"Thanks." She looked back at Frank, uncertain where this was supposed to go. He gave her an encouraging nod, and she found herself momentarily sad that she didn't know him better. He seemed like a decent man.

"I'll let you two talk," Frank said, backing up until he was swallowed into the crowd.

Before she could overthink it, Lillian found herself asking Ray, "Does your band accept work at other clubs or do you perform here exclusively?"

His eyes widened a bit, but that winning, confident smile never left.

"We like to work, and take it where we can get it," he answered.

She opened her purse and fished out a card. It just had her name, but she used a pencil to write the restaurant telephone number and address. "Perhaps you would consider booking some time with me—at my club, I mean."

He didn't take her card right away. "You're awfully young to be running a club, aren't you?"

She shrugged. "It's a family business and my father can't right now."

She held her breath, waiting for him to ask, wondering how she'd answer.

Ray nodded as if he understood without needing to pry.

She moved her card closer, and he took it with some obvious reluctance.

"Come see if you think the club would suit you," she said. "I'm making changes, redesigning the interior, adding a menu. It's not much right now, but I'd really like to have entertainment that would draw more customers, and I can tell your band certainly would."

His smile faded a bit. "You know I can't just come visit a White club, Miss Lillian."

He kept calling her by the formal title, an obvious attempt to distance himself. And suddenly her invitation seemed even more important. "It's Lillian. We all seem to mix just fine here —why should my club be any different?"

"This is *Harlem*."

At his emphasis, she wanted to flinch, wondering if he thought her ignorant. But she didn't get that impression. He was being kind, even gentle, as if they lived in two different worlds and he thought her too innocent to understand.

"This is New York City," she countered firmly. "I've seen Duke Ellington play in midtown clubs."

"He's Duke Ellington."

"You get my point."

He said nothing for a moment, then finally tucked her card into his breast pocket. "I'll discuss it with the band."

Now it was her turn to give him her winning smile. "Thank you. Will you still be playing tonight?"

He nodded.

"Good, I'm looking forward to it."

The piano player started another lively song.

"I'd ask you to dance," Ray said, "but if I book a gig with you, it wouldn't be right."

There were other reasons he might not want to dance with a White girl, she knew, but there were a few other mixed couples bravely dancing.

"You'll find I'm not too strict about old-fashioned rules," Lillian said.

One of his dark eyebrows rose, and he chuckled. "You're a brave girl."

"I'm a brave woman, Ray. And women can do anything." She turned away, then flashed him a smile over her shoulder.

**14**

---

# LILLIAN

1926

A few days later, Lillian woke up to insistent knocking. The sun was already high in her window, and she was still groggy, after having spent a late evening interviewing and hiring young waitresses for the club. Her sleep had also been disturbed by dreams of her father wasting away in jail, not helping himself nor letting his family help. It was like she didn't know him anymore. His arraignment had been delayed again due to overcrowding, leaving them uncertain of his fate. Mother said her visits were awkward as he continued to dodge any questions.

The knocking grew a little louder.

"Who is it?" Lillian pushed her hair out of her eyes and squinted at the clock.

"It's me!" Viola called. "May I come in?"

Lillian sank back into the pillow. "Very well."

Viola opened the door, stepped inside, and closed it behind her. "You never sleep this late."

"I never used to work late hours."

"The restaurant is open that late?"

Lillian made a show of untangling her hair with her fingers, not quite meeting her sister's eyes. "Sometimes. But last night, I was interviewing possible employees."

Viola sank down on the edge of the bed. "I can't believe you're managing the restaurant in Papa's place."

"I have to. Mr. Dabrowski advises me as I make decisions."

Viola heaved a dramatic sigh. "It must be nice not to have to go to school and see people staring at you, pitying you."

Lillian reached for her hand. "I actually miss school. But I'm sorry for what you've had to go through. I've encountered some of it myself."

Viola's gaze landed on the dress Lillian had worn last night and then thrown across an upholstered chair. It was blue silk, with a drop waist and layered rows of fringe. "Your clothes are so beautiful. Did you buy them in Philadelphia? Surely Mother didn't approve some of these."

Lillian gave a reluctant smile. "You're too smart for me."

"You probably should stick with one she bought when we attend the luncheon."

Lillian stiffened. "What luncheon?"

"Didn't she tell you? I just assumed..." Viola trailed off with a sigh. "It's at Mrs. Blackwell's house, one of the few ladies still speaking to us."

"What kind of people are so cruel when a family is obviously suffering something through no fault of their own?"

Viola shrugged. "Society people, the ones Mother most wants to impress."

"And the people we'd like to continue dining at our restaurant," Lillian said, admitting defeat. "Did your friend Pansy come around?"

Viola shook her head.

"I'm so sorry."

With a shrug, Viola stood up. "We're leaving at eleven. You have forty-five minutes. What are you going to wear?"

Without asking permission, Viola opened Lillian's closet

and looked inside. She made "oohs" of approval. "Some of these are so daring! You wore them at college parties?"

Lillian nodded.

"What a shame you can't wear them here."

"What do you mean? I've been wearing those clothes to the restaurant each night."

"I mean you can't wear them around Mother."

"And why not? They are perfectly fashionable."

"She won't think so."

"I'm not a child," Lillian said stiffly. "I'll wear what I want to."

Viola gave a little smirk. "I'll look forward to the results."

She sauntered out, and Lillian almost stuck her tongue out, but she caught herself. She was an adult, with adult responsibilities, including the welfare of her siblings. She *wanted* Viola to feel so secure that she could someday be carefree again, that she could tease with abandon. Maybe that was slowly happening.

Or maybe it was a temporary attempt to feel normal when everything was still so uncertain, especially concerning their father.

Forty-five minutes later, Lillian descended the front stairs to find Mother and Viola waiting for her. Viola's eyes widened with admiration when she took in Lillian's dark green robe de style dress with its full skirts ending at the knee, and wide shoulders straps which continued over her bodice into a point at her waist.

Mother gave an audible gasp. She was dressed in black as if someone had died—someone *had* died, Lillian remembered, wincing inwardly.

"What are you wearing?" Mother demanded. "You do know that this is a luncheon for decent women."

"I only heard about the invitation less than an hour ago and chose what I had available. It is a perfectly decent dress."

"Perhaps at an evening club, but not amongst our friends."

Mother hit close to the truth with "an evening club." "This dress is fashionable among young people. It will not embarrass you in front of your *friends*."

She regretted her emphasis on "friends" the moment it left her mouth. But instead of being angry, Mother looked stricken, her eyes wide, her lips trembling.

"Mother—" Lillian began.

"It's true I do not know if we have any friends remaining," Mother interrupted, her voice stiff and faint. "These women might just be gossips who want to see how we're surviving our scandal and laugh behind our backs."

"Let's not assume that," Lillian said, as Viola's eyes filled with tears. This confrontation wasn't going as Lillian had expected.

"I hope they don't ask about our living situation," Mother continued, her gaze distant. "Don't tell them we've had to release our maid and chauffeur."

"What?" Lillian demanded. "When did this happen? What about Mrs. Vickers?"

"Not Mrs. Vickers, of course," Mother snapped. "How cruel do you think I am?"

"I didn't think—"

"Mrs. Vickers is a part of our family, but she is elderly now and certainly can't do Bonny's chores along with her own. Lillian, you'll have to help keep the household functioning."

"I am already doing so," Lillian said patiently. "I work full-time at the restaurant to *pay* for our household. Viola and Julian can be assigned chores, and you can probably do your share as well."

Viola gasped, Mother drew her bosom up, and Lillian resisted rolling her eyes. But she didn't take back the words.

Through gritted teeth, Mother said, "We will continue to

discuss this. Right now, we're late. Lillian, you can drive our car."

*That* Lillian could do. Their Model T car wasn't as fun as the roadster, and when they passed her car on the street as they headed for the parking garage, Lillian saw Viola look longingly at it. But Mother was obviously still upset by Lillian's refusal to meekly agree to even more work.

Or she was upset about the luncheon.

Or Papa.

There was so much to be upset about, and Lillian couldn't blame her.

The drive took them across Central Park to the Upper West Side. The Blackwell family had servants who met each guest at the curb, ready to drive their car into a nearby garage so the guest didn't have to. It was a welcome courtesy. Lillian never admitted aloud that sometimes she grew tired of circling the same blocks over and over, looking for a parking spot.

When they entered the large foyer with its crystal chandelier high above, ten or so women and girls turned to look at them, the plumes of their hats and head gear fluttering like a flock of birds.

Many of the older women were like Mother in dress, stiff corsets holding up floor-length gowns of muted color but expensive fabric. Some of the younger ones were dressed more fashionably, corsets abandoned, dresses clinging to their lithesome figures.

Viola clutched her hand, and Lillian gave it a squeeze. Then Mother sailed forward, and they followed like ducklings in her wake. Lillian spotted Grace, who smiled. She looked adorable in white, her pregnancy still only a gentle swelling. But she didn't rush forward to hug them, as she once might have.

Lillian recognized Pansy Jameson and her mother, who took Pansy by the shoulder and held her in place. Pansy's dark hair was in braids, as if she was a child instead of almost an adult.

"It's not as if I don't see her in school all day," Viola whispered.

"Let's be patient," Lillian whispered back.

Their hostess, Mrs. Blackwell, stepped forward and took Mother's outstretched hands with a polite nod.

"Vivienne, how good to see you," Mother said.

Lillian couldn't tell if Mrs. Blackwell's smile was restrained or false.

"You, too, Cora. We've all been so worried about you."

*I bet you have,* Lillian thought unkindly.

But there were some nods in the group that might have been sympathetic, so perhaps she should assume the best about people until they proved otherwise.

Mrs. Blackwell drew Mother into the drawing room. Pansy, after dipping away from her mother, came to walk beside Viola, while Grace approached Lillian.

Lillian nodded distractedly at her friend, too worried about Viola and Pansy. But Pansy gave her mother a single glare then whispered something to Viola, whose smile was tremulous.

Lillian let out the breath she hadn't known she'd been holding and slid her arm through Grace's.

"Your mother looks well," Grace said softly.

"She's doing well enough."

They followed the other women into the large drawing room. Lillian was hoping that the older guests would gather together, and Lillian could relax with Grace and the other daughters, but instead the sofas and chairs were all gathered in one central area. She still felt as if she and her family were the center of attention—but that wasn't surprising.

"So how is the nursery redecorating proceeding?" she asked Grace.

Her friend blushed and opened her mouth to speak, when another of the younger women, Gladys, spoke over her.

"Lillian, are you really reduced to waiting tables at your family restaurant?"

Gladys's voice carried, and other burgeoning conversations faded away.

Lillian gave her a cool smile. "I am not waiting tables. I am overseeing the restaurant management."

Mother's face blanched white as she clasped her hands together but said nothing.

"It doesn't seem that different to me," Gladys said.

"Then I imagine you've never observed the running of a restaurant," Grace said. "I admire Lillian for helping to take care of her family."

Gladys shrugged.

"Many women work," Lillian said. "We have the vote now. I've always planned a career after college—before I married," she added, so as not to seem so different from other young women of their set. "Gladys, didn't you once consider becoming a teacher?"

"I did, but—" She broke off, looking at the older women. "But that's not the point."

"The point of what?" Lillian asked.

She knew she should keep quiet, that her mother's face had turned splotchy as she held back tears. But Lillian wasn't about to pretend her life hadn't drastically changed just to placate people like Gladys or Pansy's mother.

As if her thoughts had summoned the woman, Mrs. Jameson approached.

"Come, Pansy."

"What's wrong, Mrs. Jameson?" Lillian asked coldly. "Did my sister do something to offend you? She's the same person she was before this tragedy."

"It is definitely a tragedy," Mrs. Jameson said. "My daughter doesn't need to be around someone whose father is a murderer."

There were momentary gasps, and then a hush that was only disturbed when Mother pulled a handkerchief from her purse and sniffed into it.

Lillian squared her shoulders and spoke forcefully. "My father is not a murderer. He is innocent. But regardless of what happens, my sister shouldn't have to be punished for something she hasn't done. You should be ashamed of yourself."

"Lillian!" Mother said, her voice a shadow of itself.

Lillian didn't look at her.

"Our meal is about to be served," Mrs. Blackwell said above the murmuring voices. "Do come along to the dining room."

Lillian allowed the others to go on ahead. Viola gave her a brief look of appreciation, but her eyes were still shadowed with grief and confusion. Mrs. Jameson had pulled Pansy ahead of them. Mother stiffly followed her friends.

"Good for you," Grace whispered, taking her arm again and leading her forward.

"I shouldn't go in. I'll probably say something worse."

"Nonsense. You'll sit with me and Edna."

Edna was another school friend, but one who'd gone to college in Manhattan so they hadn't spoken much the last few years except for niceties at parties. But Edna gave a smile and nodded.

Lillian couldn't believe how grateful she felt for that. She sat at the end of the table with Gladys, Edna, and Grace, while Viola sat across from her. Pansy had been moved down the table. Viola didn't lift her gaze from her plate, and Lillian ached to take her away. But that would be cowardly. She glanced at her mother, who was talking to a friend, doing her best to pretend nothing had happened, even as the woman on the other side of her pointedly kept her back turned, eating awkwardly.

For a moment, Lillian could almost admire Mother for tolerating these women, for not hiding in their house. But had it been wise to bring Viola, who was suffering?

Lillian picked at her salad, telling herself she had to eat, as if that would prove something.

"There's a banquet this evening at the Plaza," Edna said to Grace. "Gladys is attending, aren't you?"

Gladys nodded, glancing uneasily at Lillian.

"I'll be there," Grace said. "What about you, Lillian?"

"I can't. I'm needed at the restaurant." She had to fight not to slump in dejection.

"Surely the manager could cover for you?" Grace asked.

"We're doing some renovations, and since they're my ideas, I want to be there to discuss them."

She didn't point out that she hadn't been invited to the banquet. She was worried that if she said too much, self-pity would make her spew the words that lingered deep in her mind, that she wished she was back in college, that she wanted to wear her favorite dresses and attend parties.

But she forced herself to remember how important it was to support her family, that she was no longer a woman who could work only if she chose, that she had no choice at all.

To keep herself from crying, she remembered the feeling of success, of winning over her managers, of giving her opinions on the wall décor, on choosing the waitresses, and of course, hiring a band. Ray Waterman had not called or visited. She'd lined up a new piano player to liven things up, but it wasn't the same as being so daring that customers would attend just to see how things were changing.

She wasn't giving up on Ray.

**15**

---

# ABIGAIL

1780

Abigail and Henry walked from the tavern to Bowling Green in silence. She had tried to convince him to stay home, not to risk seeing the British soldiers who'd beaten him only the day before just for being a Negro, but he limped at her side, resolved to do his part in the war. He'd given his leg, almost his life, and had brought her husband's body back to her—what else did he need to do?

But he saw it differently, that until they'd won, he would offer all the support he could. His wife, Pearl, had stood calmly at his side, agreeing with him. Pearl had taken over the running of the tavern for the day, since their part-time barkeep Jacob would not arrive until supper. Abigail knew what that cost her. Pearl's fear of White men made her pinch her lips tight to keep from trembling. But she was doing her part, too.

Even the children seemed to know something important was happening, because they did not protest when Pearl said it was time to practice on their slates: Lottie her words; Andrew, his multiplication.

Abigail and Henry had left them in the kitchen, all going about their work, while Abigail wore the finest gown she owned, feeling nervous, uneasy, her gaze darting about. Over the shame of her clothing that made her feel like a fraud, she wore a cloak because it wasn't safe to be noticed in the dangerous streets.

Those streets were crowded with British soldiers and the tradesmen who needed to sell their goods to anyone who would buy. In times of war, no one could be choosy. Just as she served the British with a forced smile, her neighbors the grocer and the cooper did the same. It gave her a simmering feeling of guilt that never went away, even though she was trying to strike a blow against the Redcoats.

The air reeked with the sewage piled along the center of the wide streets. It was the stink of neglect, of disregard, which was how the British treated them.

The pavilion erected on Bowling Green rose above the wagons and mounted soldiers. A military band would be playing a concert there, as if the city wasn't a disaster all around them.

As Abigail and Henry reached the outskirts of the grassy park, she remembered being there when the Declaration of Independence had been read, and she felt her resolve harden. Her husband had been proud and excited, ready to defend his new country. She'd been so very afraid, wondering what the British empire would do in retaliation, fearful of what would happen to her children, to her family. And then the mob had torn down the statue of King George the Third, male voices roaring, women cheering. The last she'd seen of it, they were dragging it up the paved stones of Broad Way on a wagon. Later, Edmund told her they'd melted it down in Connecticut for bullets to fight against the king's army. He had loved the irony. Edmund had been a thinker, a scholar, a man in whose tavern teachers and professors had once gathered to debate history. He'd seen himself as living through important history with the war, and it had killed him.

Was this her vengeance? Vowing to help bring down the empire that had taken her husband and left her alone to raise and protect their children? Or could her participation just be her attempt to contribute to the country's struggle?

She might never know.

The lawn was a sea of color, women in their best gowns, men in their uniforms. Besides the red-coated British, Hessians with their towering brass caps, mustaches colored with the same paste as their boots, mingled with Highlanders, their checkered bonnets at an angle, knees bare between their stockings and kilts. Women clung to the arms of their men. For the last few years, every time a ship docked from England, it disgorged wives of British soldiers. Even Loyalists were evicted so that British officers and their wives could be "comfortable."

Abigail found herself looking beyond Bowling Green, on the other side of Broad Way, where in the fire-scarred pits of Canvas Town, runaway slaves who'd flooded the city after British promises of freedom lived beneath tarps alongside the desperate poor. Often, the Negroes could only make their living hauling clean water from Collect Pond on the north side of town.

She thought again of the children she fed, White and Black, who went back to such a life.

But here in Bowling Green, was a scene of gaiety.

General Clinton, instead of his daily ride with his entourage from Kennedy House on Broad Way to the public houses above St. Paul's, was at the concert, flaunting his mistress on his arm. Abigail could see his powdered white wig bobbing as he spoke, holding court near the pavilion.

When her sister Rebecca spotted her and waved, Abigail waved back and took a deep, resigned breath.

"I'll leave you to your sister and brother-in-law," Henry said quietly. "I'll be nearby should you need me."

"Don't court trouble eavesdropping too openly," Abigail whispered.

"Me?" He smiled, but it lacked amusement.

She thought of the risks he took in public places with British soldiers who tried to lure him to their side with the promise of freedom, as if he was a slave. Yet he was here with her. Never were there truer friends or patriots than Henry and Pearl.

As Abigail approached Rebecca and Thomas through the throngs of revelers, she didn't see Lieutenant Rutherford at her brother-in-law's side until it was too late. He was giving her a faint smile which conveyed no emotion she could understand.

Rebecca, a parasol shading her face, pulled her close. "You'll ruin your complexion, Abigail. I knew you'd forget, so here is your own parasol."

She handed it over and Abigail opened it, smiling her gratitude. "Always taking care of your older sister."

"That is what sisters do."

That caused another stab of regret, but Abigail was getting used to ignoring the pain of her own betrayal.

The lieutenant asked, "Would you walk with me before the concert begins, Mistress Featherstone?"

Abigail glanced at Rebecca. "I only just arrived—"

"No worry about offending me," her sister said almost gleefully. "I'll keep a spot on the bench open for you."

Abigail turned to smile at the lieutenant. "A walk before the concert would be lovely, thank you."

He held out his arm, she took it without hesitation, and they walked in silence for several minutes. Officers nodded to him and sometimes arched a brow upon noticing her. Much as she was dressed in her best gown, she could never be a young, fresh-faced girl again, the kind that should be on a British officer's arm. She'd been married, borne children, been widowed—all of it had given her threads of gray in her hair, and lines of life marked her face before she'd turned thirty-five.

Her trepidation increased as he steered her out of the crowd on the green and toward the river. Soon, they were walking along the walls of the Battery, the wind warm and brisk, the Union Jack rippling. In the harbor she saw British frigates and ships of the line, their sails fluttering as they overwhelmed and crowded out local ferries. She felt a moment of bleak helplessness.

But no, she knew some of those ships were departing in a manner mysterious even to other British officers. Though it felt dangerous to be away from her family, she had to find out what the lieutenant knew.

"There are so many ships," she murmured, allowing a trace of awe in her voice. "To think some foolish people believe the British fleet can be defeated."

"It is not possible."

He sounded so certain, so contemptuous of any who would disagree with him. How could she persuade him to say more about the ships?

"Why did you join the army?" she asked. "I always felt the life of a naval officer must be so much more exciting."

He arched a brow. "You must never have been on a ship."

"When I was very young, my parents brought us to the colonies on a ship."

"Then you weren't born here. You could return to Britain."

She shook her head. "My children were born here. My business is here."

"You could sell it."

"During a war?" she asked dryly.

He gave a faint smirk. "That is a good point."

"Those ships," she said, taking a chance, "why are they here? Purchasing supplies? I'm given to understand that the war has shifted south."

"Are you asking if the British army and navy are about to abandon New York?"

She feigned shock. "Why would you do that? This city is so important, the center of shipping for the colonies. My tavern patrons come from all over the world—before the war made it too dangerous to travel, of course. That has been a hardship for some merchants."

"Some?"

"Many are just like me; we do business with either side. I certainly did not close down when General Washington held the city. My children would have starved."

"And who would house my friends now that we've returned? I hope they are being polite."

"My children or your friends?"

He actually chuckled.

More than once she'd heard the soldiers bring women to their rooms. They stole rum from the tavern and smashed empty bottles.

"They are young," she said evasively. "They'll learn."

"To be better behaved?"

"It is a war," she said simply. "Everyone does what they can to forget about the danger."

"That is surprisingly astute, Mistress Featherstone."

They had walked past the walls of Fort George and were heading toward the Lower Barracks. He steered her with pressure on her arm.

She wanted to turn around, didn't like heading where there were even more of the enemy, but how to do so without making him suspicious?

"Lieutenant Rutherford!" a man called.

They both turned around, the lieutenant not releasing her.

A soldier gave a salute. "The captain told me to fetch ye, sir," he said, his accent more common than the one spoken by officers Abigail was acquainted with. "The concert is about to begin, and Mistress Chambers is concerned about her sister."

Rebecca was concerned about her reputation alone with an unmarried officer, but Abigail was relieved, whatever the reason.

And suddenly she recognized the soldier's voice, even with the exaggerated London accent. It was Ben, her contact with the Culper Ring. She turned back to Lieutenant Rutherford, not wanting to reveal her surprise. For a moment, she thought she should be offended that Ben was following her, but she wasn't at all—she was grateful. And if that made her weak, then so be it. She had to protect herself so she could protect her children.

"Rebecca is overly worried," she said, twirling her parasol with girlish ease. "But I do want to hear the concert. It's not often I get to enjoy such entertainment with friends."

Let him think he was her friend, she thought. He hesitated a brief moment, then nodded.

"Thank you, Private," he said, not even glancing at Ben.

Abigail let out a shaky breath.

Ben nodded and went past them toward the Lower Barracks, not meeting her gaze. Abigail wanted to see if he was following them, but she didn't dare. She knew that he was attending the concert for the same reasons she was, attempting to uncover British secrets. But she'd had no idea he'd be so talented at pretending to be a Redcoat. She thought their conversation last night about his personal life had taught her much about him, but really, there was so much more to a person than a sad, failed courtship. Now she knew he was the sort of man who'd risk being called out as a spy and hanged for daring to wear the enemy's uniform.

By the time Abigail and Lieutenant Rutherford left the Battery, they could hear the concert, and it was more difficult to speak over the noise. She felt guilty that she wasn't very good at

using him for information. He frightened her, and she wasn't
certain why, since he'd never said or done anything threatening. But the way he looked at her, so intent, felt as if he were
trying to see into her soul.

Rebecca was waving as they worked their way through the
crowd, as if they needed her to guide them. She heard Lieutenant Rutherford give an impatient sigh and hid her
amusement.

"There you are!" Rebecca called. "It's been difficult to save a
seat for you, Abigail."

"I'm sorry," Abigail said, reaching her sister's side.

They sat down together, and the lieutenant stepped away to
say something to Thomas over the opening strains of a German
flute solo.

Abigail tried to appear interested in the musicians, a
Loyalist band gathered together to offset the lack of British
musicians the Crown hadn't wanted to fund. But her gaze kept
darting among the patrons, wondering who might have the
information she needed, and how dangerous it would be to get
it. She thought again of Ben's daring, and her admiration for
him grew.

After the first act, Rebecca gave a dramatic sigh.

Abigail saw her sister watching Thomas and Lieutenant
Rutherford moving toward another group of officers. "Don't let
me keep you from Thomas."

"It's not that," Rebecca said. "I had plans for another dinner
party, and I just found out that although Admiral Graves has
just arrived with six ships of the line, they don't plan to stay.
And I was so hoping that I could have an admiral at my table!"

Abigail swallowed and resisted the urge to gape at her sister.
This was information that could help her, and she heard it from
her *sister*?

Carefully, Abigail said, "I'm sorry to hear that."

"Of course you are," Rebecca said in a teasing voice. "Maybe you like naval officers more than army officers."

Abigail smiled. "And now I might never know." She leaned close to Rebecca, afraid to be overheard. "Where are they going?"

Rebecca was tapping her toes to the music, and Abigail didn't want to raise her voice. But to her relief, her sister finally looked at her.

"I don't know. It seems to be a big secret."

Abigail nodded and turned back to the concert. This was another clue that the British fleet had orders that weren't general knowledge. It was more proof, but was it confirmation?

**16**

———

# ABIGAIL

*1780*

Before the supper hour, Abigail departed with Henry, leaving Rebecca disappointed and cross that Abigail had obligations to her customers and her employees. Abigail, too, could have wished to remain and discover more information. Time was running out.

But she had her children to think about.

Pearl met them at the kitchen entrance, her grave eyes relaxing into relief. Abigail could see a cauldron hanging over the open fireplace, and a spit roasting meat below. Rowdy voices from the taproom rose and fell, muffled.

"Are we busy?" Abigail asked, pinning on an apron.

"Not too busy that you should serve customers in that lovely dress," Pearl said, eyeing her. "Henry can help me and Jacob while we wait for you."

Abigail put her arm around Pearl's shoulder with a brief squeeze. "Thank you."

"Any luck?" Pearl whispered.

"Not much, but it might help confirm...what we recently discussed," Abigail said in a quieter voicer, then continued in a normal tone. "The children were well-behaved, I hope?"

"They're playing in the keeping room. Earlier, the youngsters from Canvas Town stopped by."

"Did we have enough for them to take food home for their families?"

Pearl nodded. "Then Lottie and Andrew showed them the docks."

Abigail felt an inward wince but knew she couldn't keep her children cloistered inside all the time.

"Andrew knows the safest places to go," Pearl said reassuringly.

"And it's good for them to be with other children. This war is so difficult, and children suffer."

"I thought the same." Pearl hesitated. "Then it was all right to allow it?"

Abigail nodded. "I trust any decision you make."

Pearl's dark eyes glistened, but she only nodded and turned back to slicing lamb onto several pewter plates.

Abigail ran up the rear staircase to their room and changed. Even with the window open, it was humid and uncomfortable, and she was glad the children had escaped for a while.

When she returned to the kitchen, she saw Henry and Pearl exchange a glance.

Repinning her apron, Abigail said, "Go ahead and tell me."

"Lieutenant Rutherford is here," Henry said. "You can remain in the kitchen and not see him."

"No, I won't play the coward to the British."

"It's not cowardly to protect yourself," Pearl said quietly.

Too late, Abigail remembered Pearl's preference for the kitchen after the way she'd been treated by White men. "No, it's not. But I'm playing a part now, and he's important to my mission." She took a deep breath and said dryly, "Maybe I shouldn't have changed. Never mind, it's better that he knows the realities of what I am. He might be more careless around me."

Henry retreated to the storeroom and returned with a small cask of rum.

Pearl handed her a tray with a bowl of stew and two pieces of bread, saying, "For the hearth table."

Abigail gave her a nod, waited for Henry to open the door, and smoothly walked into the taproom wearing a polite smile. The ripe smell of sweating men and the yeasty tang of beer might be overpowering to some, but she was used to it. It meant her tavern had customers, which meant she could feed her children.

She saw Lieutenant Rutherford sitting at the bar, talking to one of her boarders—probably the friend he'd mentioned. The lieutenant gave her a brief bow of the head, and she nodded and let her smile broaden a bit, but continued toward the hearth table.

Her customer, a British seaman, thanked her and eyed the stew as if he hadn't seen food in months. And maybe his recent voyage had been so severe they hadn't been able to cook properly. He was looking thin. But then this was war. She took his payment and returned to the bar, smoothly opening the cash box, letting the coins drop, and closing it again. She felt Lieutenant Rutherford watching her, and at last she raised her gaze to meet his.

"Lieutenant, how good to see you again so soon," she said.

"I needed a meal after such a fine concert and thought I should see what my friend here praises so much."

Corporal Cavendish seemed a bit startled, as if his words were being distorted.

"Thank you, Corporal," she said. She glanced toward a table near the mullioned windows. "Lieutenant Rutherford, I might have a table open soon if you would like to sit comfortably for supper."

"The bar is fine," he said.

The better to keep an eye on her, she knew. Or to flirt with her. If only Abigail knew which it was.

She did her job as she'd always done, seeing to new or returning customers, chatting with both in a friendly manner, not discussing the war, although many customers did with each other. It was her normal policy—she wanted no fights breaking out at Featherstone's.

In between, she saw to Lieutenant Rutherford's meal, managing to smile and converse with him without showing eagerness that some might misinterpret. She couldn't decide if he was impressed by her hard work or just curious. After all, by his polished accent alone, she could tell he came from a class where women did not work unless they were destitute, and even then, ladies only worked as companions or governesses, both positions making them dependent on others.

Abigail depended on customers, true, but cleanliness, good service and food were enough to keep them happy. She wasn't dependent on the money of relatives but made her own way in the world.

Andrew came out of the kitchen, holding a tray of clean tankards and goblets. He carefully set it on the counter behind the bar, smiling briefly at Henry, who as usual, ruffled his hair. Andrew reddened, but didn't pull away, out of respect for a man he knew loved him.

"This is your son?" Lieutenant Rutherford asked.

Andrew's pleasant expression faded into one of fear. She put a hand on his shoulder as she nodded.

"How was he beaten?"

Abigail met the lieutenant's gaze. "British soldiers."

"Beat a child? I cannot believe that."

Andrew wisely remained silent, although beneath a lock of hair she could see his eyes blazing with hatred.

She touched Andrew's arm. "You can return to the kitchen."

Her son nodded, took another tray of dirty dishes, and disappeared through the rear door.

Abigail let out her breath as she turned to the lieutenant. "He was trying to defend Henry." She gestured with her head toward her barkeep.

Henry didn't let his gaze drop, but his expression remained neutral.

"Why was such a thing necessary?" Lieutenant Rutherford asked.

"Because they thought to have sport with him."

Rutherford frowned but didn't say anything. Henry nodded to her and moved out into the taproom to see what their customers needed.

"He could be lying to you," Rutherford said.

"He is not." She wanted to put it behind them, so she said, "It doesn't concern you. They were most likely drunk."

"It is not right to take out their frustration on a child." He hesitated. "Things happen in war that no one is proud of."

Was that a warning? She didn't know. Did he suspect her of something nefarious and wanted her to stop?

She wanted to stop. Surely it was enough to confirm that ships were mysteriously leaving harbor.

And then, as if he read her mind, Lieutenant Rutherford said, "The soldiers might be in a heightened state of battle preparation. We have word that another French fleet will be arriving soon."

"Is that so?" she asked, her voice so calm she surprised herself. "It feels like this war will never end."

"Have you not felt the awareness in the city, the tension?"

"My son experienced it," she said dryly. "But there was certainly an...uneasiness in the crowd at the concert today."

"Ships are being deployed to meet the French. Naval officers know it's only a matter of time before they engage a more sophisticated enemy than the simple privateers of the American navy."

Heart pounding, Abigail tried to pretend she was barely listening to him as her gaze scanned the busy tables. She knew British officers often felt so superior to their dull American subjects that they said things they shouldn't.

She just didn't believe Rutherford was one of them. But had she passed some kind of test, where he now felt he could speak freely around her? Or were his words such common knowledge to some in the army he didn't see the harm?

She didn't know what to believe. This was the final confirmation, she was sure of it. The British knew the French were arriving—or so it seemed. And they were mobilizing to meet them.

She would just have to give what she had to Ben, and he to General Washington, and let their military minds sort all the information.

"Mistress Featherstone—Abigail—did you hear me?"

She realized she had stopped listening, her mind awhirl. He regarded her closely.

"Forgive me, Lieutenant. I have to compute the sums in my head for my last customer, and it's so difficult for me..." She trailed off, willing herself to blush. "I lost track of our conversation."

He smiled. "I asked if you were attending the officers' play tomorrow with your sister."

"I—I don't know."

"Then attend with me, and I'll be the luckiest man there."

Instead of feeling flattered, she felt threatened. "Your invitation is very kind, but I feel I must attend with my sister. She did insist on escorting me. Shall I meet you there?"

His smile faded a bit, but he nodded.

What else could she do but bat her eyelashes and act pleased?

He knew her place of business, her employees—and now her son. And she was caught in the trap of his regard.

Or his suspicion.

# 17

## PAMELA

### 2023

Pam had another business meeting with Ikeem Trent of Manhattan Seaport Development Partners. He wined and dined her at lunch, trying to persuade her to sell, then casually threatened her with a deadline, or he'd buy some other property. She only laughed and shrugged, and he sighed as if he knew he couldn't rush her. She did promise to keep thinking about it, and that wasn't a lie.

She decided to talk to other business and building owners in the neighborhood to get a feel for their experiences.

The dry cleaner was the first to respond happily upon hearing who she was, and spoke about Pam's dad with warm affection, about how good he was with the kids in the neighborhood, passing out candy—with their parents' permission—and giving them jobs once they were old enough. The boutique owner echoed the fond memories, talking about how her daughter learned the value of hard work at Featherstone's.

A doorman at a ten-floor apartment building shared that he'd been taunted into stealing a box of vegetables from the rear entrance as her dad was getting a delivery. He remembered her dad's look of sadness rather than anger. The doorman had returned the box and soon he was working at Featherstone's, too.

A restaurant owner from her dad's generation knew him as a friend, rather than a mentor, and told her about how much Dad would talk about his wife and daughter.

Every time these neighbors went on too long about her dad, she had to steer the conversation back to being business owners in expensive Manhattan. They said things that didn't surprise her—how much everything cost, how hard it was to find good employees, how developers were turning their neighborhood into high-rise streets with no soul, but they always turned the conversation back to her dad.

Pam's memories were bittersweet. She'd been jealous of Harbor House and the restaurant for keeping her dad away from home. And she'd chosen to marry a man just like her dad, driven to succeed, to find worth in that success, to be the best.

She couldn't blame Will for their career-focused marriage. He'd always been driven, and she'd admired that. She had known what she was getting into—yet she continued to be angry that he was the man he always was, and she hadn't liked what it had done to him and their marriage—and to her.

But all these stories about her dad made her see the differences in him—it wasn't just career and ambition that mattered to Dad, but also helping the people in his neighborhood. Somehow she'd begun to carry on that tradition with the young people she'd met, without ever connecting it to her father. Had she ever really known him? Had she been jealous for all the wrong reasons?

~oOo~

The next week, Keith Eldridge, the private detective, came to visit. Pam had thought he wanted a business-like meeting, but he arrived dressed in jeans and a polo shirt. She'd scheduled the appointment for when Lucia could attend, knowing how excited the girl was about the mystery of baby Daniel.

Or had she wanted someone else there with her when she met a boy from her past? Not a boy, but a man. He still had a boyish grin, though, even though his hair had gone salt and pepper gray. There were laugh lines around his eyes, and he was rangy and lean.

She'd given him her married name over the phone, but when they came face to face in the dining room, he said, "Pamela Featherstone."

She arched a brow. "You recognized me so easily?"

"I researched you." He shrugged. "It's what I do."

They shook hands, and his grip was warm and firm.

Pam introduced Lucia, who added, "I help out here."

Keith shook her hand, too. "Nice to meet you."

"She's heading off to Syracuse University this fall," Pam said, feeling strangely proud.

Lucia blushed and elbowed her.

"And you're not excited at all," Keith said to the girl.

"Nope."

His smile widened. Then he turned back to Pam. "What have you been up to?"

"You don't want to hear more about the mysterious photo?" Pam asked.

"Well, it'd be good to hear about you, too. It's been a long time."

"Can I get you something to drink? Coffee, water, soda?"

"Water's good, thanks."

"Have a seat."

He sat down at the table they'd readied for him. Pam walked behind the bar, resisting the urge to look again. She hadn't given him much thought over the years. She didn't know if he had kids, or what led him into his career. Maybe she shouldn't even want to know those things—this was a business meeting, after all. But he was smiling, looking around at the old restaurant, and seemed truly intrigued.

When she returned with a bottle of cold water, she said, "Welcome to Featherstone's."

"I remember the place. Your dad closed the restaurant to the public just so we could have a class party before we graduated."

She blinked in surprise. "You're right. I'd forgotten." It all came flooding back, her mom decorating, her friends' excitement—how proud her dad was to do something for her at Harbor House. She blinked back tears, hoping her gratitude had shown sincerity rather than a teenager just taking things for granted.

"Looks like it hasn't been open in a while."

She told him about the hurricane damage, and then how Covid had taken her dad away from her and closed the restaurant for good.

Keith's smile faded. "I'm sorry to hear that."

"Thanks." She opened her own bottle and took a drink, feeling the sting of tears. They kept surprising her at the strangest times.

"Were you in business with him?"

"No, my husband Will and I owned an insurance brokerage out on Long Island. But after he died, I sold it, and now...I don't know what I'm doing. Except renovating the building so I can sell it."

She didn't look at Lucia as she spoke. She didn't know if the girl was disbelieving or disappointed.

"You've had a lot happen in the last few years," he said. "My life has been pretty typical. I was divorced about five years ago, and my ex and I have joint custody of our teenage son."

"Sounds challenging. And certainly your job can't be boring."

"You'd be surprised," he said dryly. "A lot of surveillance is for people who think their spouses are cheating on them, or companies who think their worker's comp employee is lying about the severity of their injury. Sadly, other people's trauma is my bread and butter. That's why I'm really looking forward to your request."

Lucia handed him both the newly framed photo of Great-Aunt Lillian and the unframed photo of the baby, then sat down at the table with them.

Keith took a pair of reading glasses out of his shirt pocket, gave Pam a light-hearted shrug as if they both knew a bit about getting older, and brought the speakeasy photo up close first.

"Where was this taken?" he asked. "Do you know?"

"Downstairs. What I always thought of as a basement storage room was an illegal speakeasy during the 1920s."

He glanced up at her in surprise over the rim of his glasses. "Really? That's cool."

She nodded, "I don't know a lot about it—I guess people didn't admit to running speakeasies, even once they were closed. My great-aunt Lillian, the woman at the center of the picture, looks pretty young there. I know she managed the restaurant, got married at some point, and had her first child in 1930."

He gave a low whistle. "When the Great Depression started getting bad."

Pam turned to Lucia as if to explain and was rewarded with the young girl's fake outrage.

"I know about the Great Depression!" Lucia said with exaggerated indignation.

Pam's gaze met Keith's and they both chuckled.

He turned his attention to the baby photo. "You say this was hidden behind Lillian's photo?"

She nodded. "We only found it because it fell off the wall and the frame broke."

"Like it wanted to be discovered." Keith elbowed Lucia.

She rolled her eyes but was still smiling.

"That was a dad joke," he said. "My son rolls his eyes just like you do."

Lucia continued to smile, but Pam felt a touch of sadness, wondering if Lucia's dad ever got the chance to tell her dad jokes.

Keith turned the baby photo over. "Daniel, 1927."

"I looked in the family Bible," Pam said, "and there wasn't a child of that age or birthdate. But I imagine at that time, if he *is* related, his birth might not have been welcomed by most in the family."

"Good point. Have you talked to any relatives?"

"Not yet. I probably met Great-Aunt Lillian's kids when I was younger, but we didn't keep in touch much, as everyone either moved away or became more centered on their own growing families. I admit, I was far too focused on my career. Maybe I drove family away." She blinked in surprise. "I'm sorry, forget I said that. It's not important. I'll reach out to cousins who I still have contact info for."

Lucia was glancing pointedly at her phone, but Keith didn't break eye contact, just nodded as if he understood. Who knows, maybe he did. He, too, was self-employed. It took drive and ambition to succeed at your own business.

And that wasn't a character flaw, she reminded herself, although it could be overdone—which she knew, because she'd done it. It hadn't been just Will working too much, although toward the end, she wanted to relax and enjoy their success more than he did.

"For my part," Keith said, "I can start by getting a copy of Lillian's will from public records. That might tell us something."

"About a secret baby?" Lucia said doubtfully.

Keith gave her a rueful smile. "Probably not, but sometimes

the heirs aren't always who you assume. For instance, your father owned the restaurant."

"His father, my grandfather, was Lillian's brother. He got involved in the restaurant as an adult, and I don't believe Lillian's family was interested. I think it was all legally done."

"I'm not disputing that," he said, "just looking for details. I can't help myself. The other thing to consider is that the will could be a Pandora's box. You might regret digging deep. Families can do bad things to each other. I speak from experience."

"I can't believe that of my relatives," Pam said, although inside she winced. "Surely I would have heard rumors."

He shrugged. "As for another detail…" He turned the baby picture over and pointed to the bottom. "That's some kind of identifying number and the name of the photographer, I'll bet."

Pam's mouth dropped open, and she bent over the photo. "It's so smudged I didn't even realize what it was!"

"Details," Keith said with a grin. "I can follow up on that. So am I hired? Now that I know a bit more about what I'll be doing, I can give you a quote. Then you could decide how much you're willing to pursue this, and you can stop whenever you've had enough."

"That sounds good." Pam smiled. "Will there be a waiting period before you're free?"

He shook his head. "I have people working for me, so I can choose what I want to work on. This seems fun and interesting. I've needed a break from serious and depressing."

*Me too,* Pam thought.

"I hope we find out the truth," Lucia said.

"I'll do my best," he said. He glanced at the fireplace. "Is that original?"

"I think so," Pam answered.

"I bet it's seen a lot in two hundred years."

"It's actually over two hundred and fifty years old," Pam

said. "A lot of things happened here—including quartering British soldiers during the American Revolution."

"And we think Pam's ancestors spied on them," Lucia added with excitement, standing up. "You should have a tour."

"This sounds worth exploring." He glanced at Pam. "Are you coming?"

Smiling, she got to her feet. "I guess you've become a part of the Scooby gang, solving the mysteries of one of New York's oldest buildings."

While Keith chuckled, Pam turned to Lucia and opened her mouth as if to explain.

Lucia threw her arms wide. "I know who Scooby Doo is!" She rolled her eyes and practically stomped toward the kitchen.

"She's so easy to tease," Pam said to Keith.

They shared a laugh, and it didn't feel forced. It felt kind of good. She realized she hadn't spent time with another adult in a while. She'd closed herself off, immersed in her grief and anger. That couldn't be healthy. She should reconnect with the friends she'd once made, even if they were on Long Island. She didn't have to be solitary for the rest of her life.

## 18

---

# LILLIAN

### 1926

When Lillian returned to the jail the day after the Blackwell party, she brought sandwiches, fruit, and cookies, fully expecting to have to share with Officer Riley. This time she gave him ten dollars, too. She had plans for how she was going to get her father to tell her the truth.

But when Papa was brought into the cell, separated from her side by strong metal bars, all she could think was that he looked paler, thinner, though rationally she knew it had been less than a week since she'd seen him. He'd been allowed to shave. He still wore the black-and-white prison uniform that made him look like a stranger.

But his eyes twinkled when he saw her. "My girl," he murmured.

"Twenty minutes," Officer Riley said, already unwrapping the paper from his sandwich.

This time he didn't tell them to stay seated, just banged the metal door shut.

Papa held her hands through the bars for a long moment, looking at her as if he needed to memorize her. It made her uncomfortable and deeply sad, so that she had to force a smile.

"Papa, I brought you something to eat." She opened her bag and brought out two sandwiches.

He took them but made no move to open them.

"Will someone take those from you if you eat them later?" she asked hesitantly.

He blinked, then reluctantly stepped away from the bars to sit down.

As he unwrapped the paper, Lillian asked, "I understand Mother came to visit you."

He didn't look at her as he took a bite. He closed his eyes as he chewed, and it was obvious that even a ham and cheese sandwich tasted better than whatever he was being fed. She tried to blink away her tears, thinking she would talk to Officer Riley about sending food from the restaurant.

"What did you and Mother discuss?" she prodded. She hadn't gotten much out of her mother except tears.

He swallowed a bite. "We discussed you children, how proud we are that you're helping at the restaurant."

Then he bit into the sandwich again, and she tried another tack. She told him about Viola and Julian, their work at school, then the luncheon the women had attended. He stopped chewing at that, even as she assured him that all went well. A minor lie, but worth it.

After he ate the second sandwich, she softly said, "Are you ready to tell me the truth now, Papa?"

He folded up the paper and held it awkwardly on his knees but said nothing.

"Papa, you are being stubborn. If you won't tell me why you insist on pleading guilty—"

"I don't want you involved," he said, his tone beseeching. "I don't want my beloved family caught up in my mistakes. We're finished discussing this."

"Finished?" she echoed in disbelief. "We haven't even

begun. Your staff tells me you ran out into the night, and the next thing they knew you were being arrested."

His eyes focused beyond her. "This is between me and my lawyer."

The lawyer who he'd never used before. "Did he convince you to say these things?"

"Of course not."

"How do you know he's any good? Who recommended him to you?"

When he didn't answer, she handed him an apple, and he bit into it gratefully.

Why would her father act this way? She tried not to let anger cloud her thoughts, but she was feeling overwhelmed.

And yet...the more she thought about it, the more she wondered if someone had framed him, and was now threatening him—threatening all of them. That's what made the most sense. And if he wouldn't talk to her about it, she would have to figure it out for herself, even if she had to involve his well-connected old friend Big Jim Russo. It wasn't as if the police cared about her father, now that they had a confession.

The sooner she could get her father out of jail, declared an innocent man, the sooner they could all go back to their normal lives.

"I've been working hard at the club, Papa," she whispered.

He opened his mouth to respond, but she handed him several cookies, and he focused on them. It seemed so pathetic that she rushed on.

"I'm expanding the stage, and I've hung new draperies. I added some columns along the walls to make it look more classical. I hired young waitresses, a new piano player, and I'm even going to interview a jazz band."

She hoped he'd be upset that she had to give up her plans for college and a different career. Would that motivate him to *do* something to help himself?

He swallowed his bite of cookie, then said, "I always knew you'd have a good head for business. College certainly brought out your confidence."

"I will go back someday, Papa," she said.

She spoke more forcefully than she meant to, but he seemed not to notice, focusing with delight on the cookie as if he was a toddler rewarded for good behavior.

What had happened to him? If he wasn't going to help himself, then it was time for her to meet his lawyer face-to-face.

~oOo~

Early that evening, it was the waiter Herbert who first alerted Lillian that something was wrong.

She was moving among tables of guests, smiling, chatting, trying to be the host her father had always been. There were several repeat customers, and she made it a point to greet them by name.

And then she practically ran into Herbert, who'd come to a dead stop in the middle of the dining room.

Lillian frowned and whispered, "Herbert, you're in the way."

She noticed that his face had gone pale, his eyes wide.

"What is wrong with you? Are you ill?"

"No, Miss Featherstone," he said hoarsely. "But that's Big Jim Russo."

Lillian followed his gaze to the door and saw that three well-dressed men had entered. They removed their hats and looked around as if inspecting the place. She saw several customers begin to whisper, and their gazes seemed as focused on the front door as hers was. The man in the center seemed about her father's age, slicked back brown hair only gray at the temples while the two on either side of him looked younger, their suits bulky with more than muscles.

"Mobsters?" Lillian hissed near Herbert's ear.

He jumped. "Yes, Miss Featherstone."

Jim Russo used to be her father's pal in youth, until Papa had realized the danger the family represented. Mr. Dabrowski had let her know they came for dinner once or twice every year, so she wouldn't be surprised.

Then why was her heart starting to hammer?

"I'll take care of them," she heard herself tell Herbert as if from a distance.

He hurried away from her and behind the safety of the bar.

Lillian walked toward the front entrance. It wasn't a long distance, and she wished she had more time to compose herself or plan what to say.

Instead, she donned a smile and said, "Welcome to Featherstone's, gentlemen."

When the older man's dark eyes settled on her, she expected to feel a chill, but then he put on a smile that was full of sympathy. The other two men didn't even look her way, just continued to examine every guest in the dining room, their expressions impassive.

"You must be Sam's daughter," Mr. Russo said. "I think I see a bit of him in your eyes. I'm a friend of his, Jim Russo."

"Nice to meet you, sir. Would you like a table for three or will more be joining your party?"

"We can't stay," Mr. Russo said. "I have business with my father."

There was something in his tone of voice that sounded grim at the prospect. Maybe mobster fathers and sons had the same problems regular people had. They just solved them violently.

But she was relieved they wouldn't be doing it at Featherstone's.

"I just wanted you to know that if there's anything I can do," he continued, "please let me know." He handed her a card she didn't dare look at. "Sam's been a friend to me, and I don't take that lightly. It's terrible what's happened to him."

He said "what's happened to him" as if he knew her father couldn't have murdered another man. It made her feel less afraid of him. Her father had warned her to stay away from this family, but maybe they were the only ones who believed him innocent!

"That is very kind of you, Mr. Russo," she murmured.

He donned his hat, and the two men took it as some kind of signal, one still watching the dinner guests while the other opened the door and peered out.

"I'll talk to my father about your predicament," he continued, lowering his voice. "Now is not the time to start collecting our fee—your family is suffering."

Her mouth dropped open.

Mr. Russo tipped his hat and went out the door, the other man following as he allowed one last glare to sweep the room in warning.

~oOo~

Lillian was on the doorstep of the office of Paul Webster, her father's lawyer, at nine o'clock the next morning, dressed in a slim jersey suit with a striped pullover beneath the jacket. A plump secretary, whose glasses hid some of the age lines around her eyes, didn't change expression when Lillian explained who she was. A plaque on the desk said MRS. O'NEILL.

"You don't have an appointment," Mrs. O'Neill said in a dismissive tone, as if she expected Lillian to turn around and walk away.

"I'll wait." Lillian sat down in one of two chairs in the nondescript waiting room opposite the secretary's desk. "Please let him know I'm here."

Mrs. O'Neill pressed her lips together in disapproval, then opened a door to an inner office, went in, and closed it firmly behind her. Lillian could only hear the murmur of conversation, but when Mrs. O'Neill emerged a minute later, her frown was even more ominous.

Lillian intended to march into the office regardless, when Mrs. O'Neill said, "Mr. Webster will see you now."

After a pause of surprise, Lillian rose to her feet, said "Thank you," and walked past Mrs. O'Neill through the doorway.

A man stood up behind his desk, and they looked at each other without saying a word. Lillian had expected an older, experienced lawyer, but Paul Webster wasn't even ten years her senior. He had dark blond hair, short above his ears, but longer on top, with a swoop above his forehead that might have been natural or deliberately styled. His hair stood out against his standard features of a clean-shaven face and light eyes. His suit was conservative rather than flashy.

After taking everything in—the neat office, the young man —she didn't know *what* to think. *This* was the lawyer her father had hired, recommended by someone her father wouldn't reveal? He had his own office, as if he'd struck out on his own, so perhaps he'd come cheaply, but was that what she wanted for her father's defense?

"Miss Featherstone," he said, coming around the desk. "Your father has spoken of you."

He stood there, hands clasped behind his back, serious and intent as he studied her. He made no attempt to shake her hand as if, being a woman, she didn't need that respect. She put out her hand and, after a beat of hesitation, he shook it. To his credit, he continued to look serious rather than amused.

"Mr. Webster," she said formally, "I'm sorry I did not make an appointment."

"I don't mind. We should talk." He gave a small smile and

gestured to a chair across the desk from his. "Please have a seat."

She did so, purse in her lap. Taking a deep breath, she said, "I'd like to discuss my father's case. I know he's innocent, but I can't get him to discuss it with me. All I know is that he ran from the scene of a murder and was arrested. Mother tells me you told her someone was threatening him, but Papa didn't mean to kill him. And now he tells me he's pleading guilty to manslaughter." She leaned forward and spoke forcefully. "This is completely wrong. He is not a murderer. If anything, it sounds like he acted in self-defense. Are you telling him to plead guilty?"

She thought Mr. Webster might look surprised or act defensive, but he simply folded his hands together on his desk blotter.

"I am here to guide and represent your father, that's all." He sighed. "And frankly, I shouldn't be discussing it with you, since you're not my client."

"But I'll be the one paying you since I'm running the restaurant," she pointed out. "Why is he pleading guilty?"

Mr. Webster hesitated, then his blue eyes met hers. "Because he tells me he committed the crime, and that it wasn't self-defense."

She crossed her arms over her chest with a snort of disgust. "He did not kill a man."

Mr. Webster shrugged his shoulders.

"Who is the man he supposedly killed? I read his name in the paper, but who is he to my father?"

"I don't know, but I've been told he's a criminal. Your father says he didn't mean to kill him, but it happened. He won't tell me any more than that."

"I don't know if I believe you, Mr. Webster," she said coolly.

"You have that right, miss, but I'm telling you what I can.

And I'm also reminding you that your father has asked you not to get involved."

"That is the most ridiculous thing I ever heard. Would you stand aside while your own father was railroaded?"

"Since my father abandoned my mother, leaving her to support two young children alone, I don't think your question applies."

She blinked at him for a long moment. His expression never veered from politeness, but she felt a pang of sadness and regret.

"I'm sorry," she said.

"No need to apologize for something that has nothing to do with you."

"Obviously your mother is a woman to admire, since you've done well for yourself. Would you stand aside while she goes to prison?"

"She did."

Lillian opened her mouth, but nothing came out.

"Miss Featherstone, I truly understand your dilemma. But I represent your father, and he wishes to protect you."

"Who is going to protect me from the mob?"

His eyes widened, and she could see that he was startled. "What are you talking about?"

"Mr. James Russo visited the restaurant last night to express his sympathies and offered to help if I needed it."

He gripped the edges of his desk. "And you are smart enough to refuse such an offer."

"I know what he is, Mr. Webster. I know he was a friend to my father when they were young, and then Papa distanced himself when he realized what the Russos were."

"Your father was being smart."

"And yet here he is, about to go to jail for something I *know* he didn't do. No one else is offering to help him, including you."

He pressed his lips together in a line, then said, "Mr. Russo offered to help get your father out of this predicament?"

"He said if there was anything he could do, to reach out to him."

"Then don't. It will tie you up in ways you'll never get out of."

For the first time he sounded sincere and human, rather than businesslike and distant. How did he know so much about the mob?

"He said something else I didn't understand," Lillian continued. "He said since we were suffering, he would speak to his father, that now was not the time to collect their fee. What does that mean, Mr. Webster?"

He laced his fingers together. "He means a protection fee."

He only confirmed what she'd suspected. "That doesn't sound good."

"It depends on how you look at it. If a business can afford it, it means they won't be troubled by crime. They think of it as an insurance payment."

"But that itself must be a crime. Why would someone pay criminals not to be criminals? Surely my father wasn't involved in such a scheme?"

"You'll have to ask him."

"It sounds like you don't disapprove," she said coldly.

"Oh, I disapprove, but I'm a realist. Such things happen in this fair city of ours, and one person can't stand against it."

"If everyone stood against it, or brought in the police, something might be done."

"You sound very young."

He didn't mean it as a compliment.

"Who else do you think has protection schemes?" he asked.

She thought of Officer Riley's bribery scheme. "You mean the police."

"They let a lot of crime continue, including speakeasies," he added, arching a dark blond brow at her.

She was disappointed to feel herself blushing. "That is not the same thing as violent crime. It's just people wanting to have a good time, to escape the drudgery of their lives."

"But it's still a crime."

"Did my father pay such a fee?"

He leaned back in his chair. "My conversations with your father are private."

"Am *I* supposed to pay this fee?" she demanded. "Is that what you're recommending?"

"You aren't my client, Miss Featherstone. But as a friend, I recommend you keep yourself and your business safe."

"So you want me to give in to the mob. That doesn't speak well for you." She stood up. "You are not my friend, especially if you won't help me convince my father he is making a mistake."

He got to his feet and came around the desk. She realized she had to look up a distance to meet his gaze. His eyes were suddenly full of sympathy.

"I do what's in my client's best interest, according to his wishes. That's all I can do."

"It's not enough," she said, her voice breaking. "It's as if no one cares but me."

"I'm sure your entire family cares." His words were soft. "And I know you'll do the best you can for them. It's what your father wants."

She spoke bitterly. "And you know better than me what my father wants."

He let out his breath. "I do. He wanted me to write to you, but your visit makes that unnecessary. Your father was arraigned today and pleaded guilty."

She gasped, feeling almost light-headed. "It's over?"

He shook his head. "The sentencing date hasn't been set yet.

After that, he'll most likely be sent to Sing Sing, thirty miles north of the city. It's not too far; you'll be able to visit regularly."

"But...he didn't want us there to support him?" she whispered.

"No, Miss Featherstone. He's ashamed."

She choked back a sob. "You probably won't even tell me when the sentencing is."

"I will if he lets me."

"That's unfair."

With a sigh, he said. "I know."

She turned around and marched out of his office, past his impassive secretary, and out into the city she thought she once understood so well.

**19**

---

## PAMELA

2023

When Keith Eldridge invited Pam for lunch to discuss her case, she almost asked, "May I bring Lucia?" and then realized the girl would think Pam needed a shield. But this was a business lunch, so she went alone.

They met at a restaurant in the financial district, with a narrow dining room framed with old brick walls, and clustered with small tables. After they ordered their meals, there was barely room for him to open his folder and show her a copy of Great-Aunt Lillian's will.

"It's pretty standard," Keith said. "Her heirs are the two children of her marriage, and no one else."

Frowning, she looked at the names, feeling the ghost of childhood memories. "These names are familiar. We used to have family reunions when I was a kid, but over the last twenty years they've dwindled. I told myself it was because more and more people moved away and didn't prioritize it. But I didn't live too far away, and I didn't prioritize it either. Old people can only do all the work for so long, yet none of us took over."

"It's not too late," Keith said. "I try to return to my July Fourth family reunion at least every couple years. It's fun. I'm a master at the balloon toss." He grinned. "Well, my son is really good at catching my bad throws."

She smiled. "That's a good kid."

"He is. I'll have to introduce you."

That felt weird—they were meeting for business, she reminded herself.

And then she heard her interior monologue, already falling back on old habits of business professionalism. But she'd once known Keith as a classmate, if not a close friend. She'd let too many friends fall by the wayside during the years she focused on her career. What had that gotten her but loneliness?

"Sure, I'd like to meet your son," she said.

They both sat back as their waiter brought their beef shawarma and rice. While they ate, they shared what they knew about old classmates and how they'd each fallen into their line of work. She thought it an amusing coincidence that he'd once worked in the insurance industry, too, investigating fraud claims, which had eventually led him to start his own agency.

When they were finished eating, she shared photos on her phone that her cousins had sent her, several of Great-Aunt Lillian at different stages of her life: managing the restaurant, posing with her children and husband, marching in the streets during the 1960s. She seemed like an impressive woman, but Pam couldn't have realized it when she was a little kid.

"Did you tell them what we suspect?" Keith asked.

"Not yet. We have no proof of anything."

"Speaking of photos," he continued, "I tracked down the information on the back of Baby Daniel's photo. It was definitely the mark of the studio, Griffin Photography."

She laughed. "It was so smudged, I thought it said 'Gifted' Photography."

"I tried that, too, but Griffin worked better. The studio has been closed for about thirty years, but I'm working on tracking down heirs of the owners to find out what might have happened to the company records."

"That's great to hear, thanks." She hesitated. "Anything else?"

"Not yet." He held up both hands. "I know I could have told you all this in a phone call, but I thought it would be fun to get reacquainted."

His warm gaze seemed to show admiration, and something in Pam just panicked. She'd barely talked to a man since Will's funeral, when she'd sold the business and started traveling. She hadn't thought of romance at all—and here was a nice man from her past just being friendly, and she didn't think she was ready to face that.

"I enjoyed lunch," she said, picking up the bill. "Since I've hired you, I'll pay this."

She heard herself practically emphasizing that this was business between them and inwardly winced, but that was what she wanted right now.

He didn't look surprised or disappointed, just nodded.

~oOo~

The following week, Pam stayed busy hauling boxes and bags of junk down to the first floor, ready to fill up the dumpster she'd ordered. The city wouldn't allow her to put it near either building entrance but had to settle for a block down the side street where she'd been granted a permit to take up a parking spot—for a sizable fee.

Lucia hauled another bag to the dining room, and they both stepped back to look at the mound before them.

"Wow," Lucia said. "Glad Jason helped with some of this. We're getting rid of a lot of stuff. So much broken furniture— you'll be ready to redecorate!"

Pam shot her a side-eye, and the teenager laughed.

"You're so easy to tease," Lucia said. "Yes, yes, you're selling Harbor House. You've said it over and over again. I think you're trying to convince yourself."

Pam just grunted as she pushed a box out of the aisle she'd created to walk through.

They both turned around when someone knocked on the outer door.

Pam glanced at the door camera app on her phone. "It's Keith."

"He didn't even call," Lucia said, peeking over her shoulder to look at the phone. "Probably didn't want to risk you turning him away."

"Stop that," Pam said mildly.

Lucia laughed and sauntered toward the kitchen.

"Where are you going?" Pam demanded. "He's bringing info you'll want to hear, Miss Future History Teacher."

Lucia did a one-eighty. "You're right."

Pam unlocked the front door and opened it, letting in daylight. She'd kept the windows and glass door boarded up for protection. Warm outdoor air flowed in around Keith, who stood there smiling.

Pam felt a momentary irritation—couldn't he have e-mailed her his next report?

And then she realized she was the one letting a business relationship become more important than it was.

She stepped back. "Hi, Keith. Come on in."

As she shut the door, he blinked, adjusting from sunlight to dim lighting. And then he noticed the pile of boxes.

"Wow, you guys have been busy," he said.

"Oh, this is nothing," Lucia told him. "There's even more on every level. But we've rented a dumpster so we can start hauling it out. Everything will look better then."

"Are you working on it now?" he asked.

Pam nodded and looked down at her old shorts and t-shirt. "Can't you tell we're dressed for it?"

"It occurred to me immediately," he answered with sincerity.

Pam just shook her head. "Did you have news for me?"

"I do. Not as much as I'd hoped, but we're getting there. I reached the photographer's heir and, surprisingly, she hadn't thrown away all the boxes of records from her grandfather's business. I wouldn't call her a hoarder, just a woman with a storage unit she could afford to pay for until she decided what to do. Frankly, she was thrilled to be of help."

Lucia drank from a bottle of water then said to Pam, "See, I'm not the only one who loves history."

Pam ignored the teasing. "And?" she asked Keith. "Don't keep us in suspense."

"There weren't any more photos, but the serial number led to an order placed by the Waterman family."

"How much digging did it take to find that out?"

He shrugged. "You can figure it out from my invoice."

Pam reluctantly laughed, then found herself sobering. "Hmm, the Waterman family. That's a name I've never heard of. Maybe the baby really is no relation."

"I don't believe it," Lucia said. "You don't keep a picture hidden like that for no reason."

"The baby could very well still be alive," Keith added. "It's a stretch, I'll admit, but you never know. Even if he's not alive, the family might be able to shed some light."

"Or we could be bringing up painful secrets they don't want to know about," Pam countered.

"It's been almost a hundred years," he said. "I don't think there's anyone left alive who'd be that affected." He hesitated, then quietly said, "It's almost like you don't want to find out."

"No, it's not that." Pam sighed. "Part of me wants Harbor House to just be a building, not a repository of secrets—"

"*Family* secrets," Lucia interrupted.

"Family secrets," Pam echoed. "In some ways, it's painful." When Keith watched her with sympathy, she lifted a hand. "Never mind. I've been overthinking everything this last year. It's good to be moving forward." She pointed to the pile of boxes and bags. "Moving forward and cleaning up."

Keith took off his jacket. "It's a good thing I haven't gone to the gym yet today. Let me help."

"I couldn't do that," Pam insisted. "This isn't your problem."

Lucia put her hands on her hips. "Are you really going to turn down an offer of help? How long would this have taken without Jason?"

Pam hesitated.

"Then it's settled," Keith said, picking up the heaviest looking box. "Point me to the dumpster. Let me know next time when you have a big mound ready to move. I can bring my son Dylan. He'd enjoy the workout."

"That's not necessary," Pam said, a little too quickly, too forcefully.

"Got it." Keith cheerfully started toward the door.

Lucia rolled her eyes at Pam and shook her head with obvious exasperation before following Keith. Pam picked up pieces of a broken chair, feeling hot with a blush.

# 20

# ABIGAIL

## 1780

Late the next afternoon, Abigail walked to her sister's home and was greeted at the door by Rebecca's husband Thomas. He gave a brief nod and opened the door wide.

Abigail smiled. "Good day, Thomas."

"And to you," he said, studying her after closing the door. "I did not quite believe it when Rebecca told me, but it does appear you are looking for a husband, if you're attending a play performed by British officers."

"Can companionship not be my goal? And missing my sister?"

"Hmm," he said, obviously not believing her.

Abigail couldn't blame him—she *was* lying, and he might have sensed that. He'd never trusted her, believing her husband's politics had surely swayed her. And they had.

Rebecca floated down the stairs, beautiful in a yellow gown embroidered with leaves and vines. Thomas's expression changed to love and admiration, and Abigail tried not to fault him his politics, when he so obviously loved her sister.

"I'm so glad you came!" Rebecca said, hugging her. "I know Lieutenant Rutherford wanted to see you again."

Abigail hoped her smile didn't seem forced.

The three of them took their horse-drawn coach up Broad Way to a large private home taken over by British officers. They'd opened the sliding doors between two drawing rooms, and one was set up as a stage, and the other had chairs for guests.

Several dozen people mingled on the "stage," drinking punch and nibbling raisin cakes. Thomas drew Rebecca away just as Abigail saw Lieutenant Rutherford speaking with another officer she didn't recognize. She didn't have long to wait for an introduction. As if the lieutenant had been waiting for her, a spider in his web, he advanced, bringing his friend, another red-coated officer in a powdered white wig.

"Mistress Featherstone, I am pleased you accepted my invitation," the lieutenant said. "May I present Major John André, recently stationed in Philadelphia, and now back home in New York, victorious after the southern offensive."

Like every colonist, she knew all about the siege of Charleston, South Carolina, where two British armies had squeezed the outnumbered defenders, burning the city, until at last the Americans were forced to surrender five thousand soldiers. It had felt as if the war might be lost—but the French could yet help them win.

Major André bowed, presenting a leg to her in an elegant bow, his expression flirtatiously jovial. "Mistress Featherstone, how lovely to make your acquaintance."

She curtsied.

"I'll have you know," Lieutenant Rutherford said, "that Major André is quite talented. He wrote the play we'll be seeing today."

Major André batted the lieutenant's arm as if such bragging were too much.

Abigail gave him her brightest smile. "I will look forward to seeing your writing skills so displayed," she said.

And then the party was asked to take their seats, and the farce began, with officers playing both men and women. The plot was about a naïve girl's entry into London society, and her adventures that sometimes hinted at the risqué. Men were dying on battlefields, and these British officers were safe in the city they controlled, caring so little about the people they said they ruled, even Loyalists, that they wasted time and money on something frivolous.

She noticed that her sister's smile seemed a bit forced as she glanced at her husband. Even Thomas looked uncomfortable as the play made sport of common working people. There was a silly romance where the female love interest made a fool of herself. All around Abigail, men and women laughed uproariously, needing such entertainment to help them forget the decrepit state of a once vibrant city that now stood in partial ruins.

At last it was over, and Abigail applauded with all the rest. She felt Lieutenant Rutherford's gaze on her, and she smiled at him, silently aiming her applause at Major André, who bowed, appearing amused.

Light refreshments were served and then the lieutenant insisted on showing her Major André's next trick, casting silhouettes on the wall with a candle and tracing them.

Abigail remained still while Lieutenant Rutherford held the candle and Major André meticulously worked, tracing her profile on paper affixed to the wall. He concentrated so thoroughly that she wanted to laugh. The lieutenant eyed her since he had little to do but hold the candle. She felt his gaze touch her hair, her neck, her decolletage, modest though it was. Every minute that ticked by, she was forced to hear the two men breathing until she thought she'd go mad with it.

"Your expression is so serious, my dear," the lieutenant said softly.

Before she could answer, Major André said, "She must be

tired of humoring me. I am finished." When she would have turned, he added, "No, indulge me. I still have some finishing touches before I cut it out."

"Then excuse me, gentlemen, as I retire for a moment," she murmured, and took her leave.

Out in the foyer, a maid showed her to a bedroom set aside for ladies. Thankfully, she was alone, so she sagged into a chair and rolled her stiff shoulders. She knew men could not work—or make war—all day long, but these choices for amusement made no sense to her. They supposedly raised funds for charities, but thought maybe the charity was the production itself.

After ten minutes' rest, she took a deep breath, plastered on a simpering smile, and went to find the two officers. Their backs were to her, and they were talking in low tones. She made a point of being silent—easy in a room full of people enjoying themselves—looking at the silhouette of herself laid on the table while eavesdropping.

"I'm going to have to let my quarry wait while this engagement happens," Major André said. "Eight thousand men are embarking at Whitestone to confront the French near Rhode Island and Clinton wants me with him. A traitor to the American cause is not a priority right now."

"But you've worked so hard to snare him," Lieutenant Rutherford said.

"True, but he's so desperate for coin and so overly confident in his worth to us that he will wait."

Abigail stood frozen, looking at their backs, afraid they would turn around and see her, so she gave a delighted cry. "Look at my silhouette!"

Both men turned, Major André smiling, as she could already tell was his wont. Was Lieutenant Rutherford trying to hide his suspicion or was she just panicking? Several ladies came at her call to admire Major André's sketch.

"I still have some work to do, Mistress Featherstone," Major André said, "and of course I'll have it framed for you."

"That is very kind." It was easier to smile and appear sincere, when she had gotten just what she needed from him. Confirmation that the British knew about the French fleet and had plans to meet it with force.

He was also recruiting a traitor to the Patriot cause, but she couldn't worry about that now. It wasn't her assignment.

This new information was useless until it got into the right hands. Ben would be returning to the tavern late that night. She would try her best to be patient, when all she wanted to do was search the city for his silversmith shop, desperate to finish her assignment and be done.

"I must show my sister your work," she gushed to Major André. She raised a hand and waved, "Oh, Rebecca!"

Her sister approached, smiling at both officers, then made the appropriate gasp of delight upon seeing the silhouette.

"It looks just like you, Abigail!" To Major André, Rebecca said, "First the play and now this. You are truly talented, sir."

More female guests came over to ogle and flirt. It was obvious that he was talented with the ladies as well—and with luring traitors to the wrong side.

More refreshments were served, someone started to play the pianoforte, and Abigail was so fidgety she thought her skin was shrinking.

An hour later, she pulled her sister aside. "I'm going to return home. I'm exhausted and I'll be serving breakfast early tomorrow."

"You have servants for that, surely."

"Yes, but I work alongside them. In these times, we all have to help each other. Would you mind if I borrowed your coach? I'll send it right back. Unless you think you'll be leaving sooner..."

They both spotted Thomas, laughing over glasses of port with their host.

"I think there's time," Rebecca said. She kissed Abigail's cheek and whispered, "I think you've made quite the impression on the lieutenant."

Abigail smiled while thinking, *I hope not.*

Out in the nearly empty foyer, a maid fetched her shawl and Abigail slipped out into the night. The air smelled almost refreshing, touched by the brine of the sea. The wind seemed to have wiped out the usual odor of charred wood and horse droppings. Dusk crept over the city, and she could hear the distant sounds of a fiddle and raised voices. Far in the distance a gunshot went off, but she'd long ago stopped flinching at those, for drunken British soldiers shot in the air for the sport of it.

She began to walk down the line of coaches, chaises, and sedan chairs, nodding politely when the occasional driver tipped his tricorn hat. She reached the end and didn't find the Chambers' coach. Frowning, she retraced her steps a second time, then asked the first driver if he'd seen anything. He confirmed that Thomas's driver had driven away for a pint of beer.

Frowning, Abigail stood in front of the opulent home as the twilight deepened. She was filled with nervous excitement at the information she'd gathered and the need to pass it to Ben. The thought of going back inside and risking it all with the suspicious Lieutenant Rutherford confronting her—she couldn't do it.

With determination, she squared her shoulders and looked for a sedan chair to hire, but after two blocks, she stopped even trying and just began briskly walking. Night had not yet descended, and there were plenty of people on the street. She walked south down Broad Way, light spilling from windows like beacons. She turned down Wall Street, toward the East River.

She realized the streets were more deserted, the decent folk home to suppers and their hearth. She pulled her shawl tighter, wishing she could disguise the extravagant gown she wore.

The back of her neck tingled, a breeze raised gooseflesh on her arms. Someone was following her, matching her steps, drifting into the alley shadows when she looked over her shoulder. She increased her pace, knowing she was only two blocks from home. She picked up her skirts, about to run, when someone grabbed her arm hard, and her momentum swung her around until with a gasp she slammed into a tall, hard body.

She looked up into the face of Lieutenant Rutherford.

**21**

---

# ABIGAIL

1780

Lieutenant Rutherford's smile was no different than what he'd shown Abigail in the fine drawing room of a Patriot's commandeered home an hour before.

But he gripped her arm hard enough that she knew she'd bruise.

"Why Mistress Featherstone, it is a dangerous time of the day for you to be walking alone."

She tried to give him the same smile she'd worn all evening but was worried she wasn't as successful as he was at appearing unperturbed. "When a party goes on this late, what choice does a woman have?"

He frowned as if in confusion. "I believe I saw you arrive with your sister and her husband, did I not?"

"You did." She wanted to shake off his hand but felt trapped in a role she no longer wanted.

"Then why not return home with them?"

"Because they planned to remain much later than I did. I have a tavern to open in the morning, Lieutenant. You can see my predicament."

"I believe I can," he murmured.

And then he began to walk, pulling her along with him. There were few people about—if she fought him, no one would help her against a British soldier.

"How kind of you to escort me home," she said. "But the tavern is just down that street."

And when he didn't answer, fear clenched her stomach. He led her toward a dark alley, and for the first time she tried to pull away. He gripped her harder, painfully.

"Lieutenant, what are you doing? I need to—"

He hit her across the face, a small movement for him, but enough to snap her head hard to the side. Pain in her cheek made her eyes water, and she couldn't help staring up at him in disbelief.

"I know what you're up to, Mistress Featherstone," he said, as pleasantly as if he was courting her.

"I—I don't know what you're talking about," she said, the bewilderment in her voice real enough.

"Of course you do."

The alley yawned like a dark mouth in the twilight. She tried to dig in her feet, catch a cobblestone with her toes, but he moved forward relentlessly.

Desperate now, she looked around but saw only a pair of soldiers heading the other way.

Fear threatened to overwhelm her. Worry for her children paralyzed her, drummed a refrain in her mind of *All of this for nothing*, over and over again.

He gave a pull that threatened to rip the skin of her arm apart, and she stumbled hard into the alley behind him. The smell was worse here, abandoned refuse, urine, and the rotting flesh of the tanyards nearby. Off in the distance, two shadows detached from the wall and scurried away. Normally she would have run from them, but now she wished she could call out for help.

She bit her lip to keep from whimpering as she said, "Let

me go." Then louder, "Let me go!"

He did, but only to slam her back up against a brick wall and hold her in place hard with his body against her until she felt the bricks imprinting on her back. Her arms flailed. He grabbed them easily, crushing both wrists together with one big glove-covered hand over her head while he clamped her jaw with the other.

"Who did you intend to give your information to?" he demanded. "I can take away your tavern, your livelihood—your life."

His face was darker than the shadows, his eyes gleaming ruthlessly.

"What information?" she cried loudly.

His hand covered her mouth and nose before she had a chance for a deep breath. Her eyes went wide when she couldn't inhale.

"Are you going to keep your voice ladylike?" he asked softly.

She nodded with desperation as her lungs began to strain for air.

He removed his hand, and she gasped in a breath.

"Now who did you intend to give your information to?" he repeated with mock patience.

She rammed her knee up hard between his legs. With a groan he stumbled back and hunched over.

She ran toward the mouth of the alley, screaming for help. He caught her gown from behind and yanked. She stumbled to her knees, her hands scrambling in the mud and filth for something she could defend herself with. Just as he gripped her hips, she found a cobblestone and swung it hard behind her, connecting with the side of his head.

He grunted and let her go, falling onto his backside. He could only be stunned. She scrambled on her hands and knees to get farther away from him.

Then the silhouette of another man blocked the dim lamplight from the street. She ducked as he seemed to launch himself over her and onto Rutherford. She thought she saw a gleam of light on metal. The two men rolled over one another, each trying for supremacy. She couldn't tell what was happening, told herself to flee, but her muscles seemed traumatized, unable to function.

One man grunted and fell to the side. The other man rose up, and then he, too, gave a guttural sound and went limp, falling sideways.

At last, no one moved, and only the sounds of heavy breathing disturbed the alley.

Gasping for air, Abigail began to crawl backward, afraid to call attention to herself. She couldn't see the victor's face in the shadows, but the width of his shoulders seemed wrong for the lieutenant. She couldn't let herself relax her guard, because this stranger might very well want her for himself.

"Abigail, are you injured?"

*Ben.*

Her entire body sagged as relief swept over her. She felt weak and giddy. "How did you find me?"

He moved toward her on his knees. "I was watching out for you, knowing where you'd gone. Your gown is like a beacon under lamplight. I saw you blocks away. So did Rutherford," he added grimly, looking over his shoulder.

She tensed. "We have to flee before he awakens. He'll tell someone about me..." Words dried in her throat as she remembered his threats.

"He won't be telling anyone anything. He's dead."

It was as if time slowed and retreated around them, and she couldn't hear, couldn't see. The man who knew what she'd done was dead, but that presented its own problems.

"What do we do with the body?" she whispered.

"We leave him. Many people in this city would attack a

British soldier, and not just the desperate. But we need to go now."

He rose to his feet, then staggered before righting himself.

"Ben?" she said hesitantly.

"My ribs deflected his blade. It is nothing." He reached down to her.

She put her hand in his and he pulled her to her feet.

"Wait," he murmured, then bent over the body, rifling through the pockets.

"What are you doing?" she demanded in a whisper.

"Taking his coin. It needs to look like robbery."

"Oh." She never would have thought of that on her own, so jumbled were her thoughts.

Ben slid something into his coat pocket. "I'm ready."

They peered out of the alley and found more people on the street, a desperate woman propositioning soldiers, two drunks, arm in arm, staggering.

"Let's go out the far side," he said.

They moved swiftly, doorways like darker portals to unfamiliar realms. Someone splashed the contents of a chamber pot from an upper story, just missing them.

It wouldn't even have mattered, she thought with grim hysteria, for she'd already rolled in all manner of vileness.

At the corner of the building, Ben held her back, peered out into the street, then gave a nod. He put his arm around her with familiarity, as if he'd just purchased her for the night. He staggered again and gave her more of his weight. She felt a warm wetness along her side.

"Ben, you must be losing blood," she whispered, gripping his hand at her shoulder.

"I'll survive. Keep moving."

As they neared the waterfront, there were more and more soldiers emerging from boarding houses and taverns, and she thought of the eight thousand Redcoats on the move to confront General Washington.

No one would know unless they informed Ben's contact.

At last they turned a corner and approached the tavern's kitchen entrance. Though British soldiers were quartered within, it still represented safety and home to her. She lifted the latch and pushed open the door.

Pearl was standing at the hearth, Henry beside her at the worktable. They both turned to stare, mouths agape.

"Abigail...?" Henry began.

Abigail pulled Ben into the kitchen, and he dropped heavily to his knees.

"Ben has been wounded. Please help him." She heard the desperation and fear trembling in her voice.

The Barlows rushed forward, each to a side, and lifted Ben back to his feet. He groaned, his head lolling back.

"Take him into our room," Pearl told her husband, and between them they maneuvered him into the small storage room just off the kitchen.

"Are the children abed?" Abigail called.

"They are," Pearl answered. "We'll deal with Ben. Take care of yourself." She tossed Abigail a robe.

With the immediate crisis handled, Abigail could smell the filth saturating her clothing. Unfolding the privacy screen used when bathing, she stepped behind it and began to remove her gown, untying the laces across her bodice and pulling it wide, then unpinning the triangular stomacher from her corset. She slid out of her petticoats and loosened her corset before dropping everything into a muddy pile, leaving on her chemise.

Her hands were smeared with muck. She wiped the worst of it off with rags, then used a clean rag to lift the cauldron of water kept heated over the fire. She dumped some into a pail, added cooler water, then set about soaping her hands and face, then her limbs. She took care with the bruises on her cheek and arm. She tossed her shoes and stockings onto her soiled clothing.

When the worst of the alley filth was gone, Abigail donned Pearl's robe and stepped into the doorway of the little storage room. It was barely large enough for a bed to sleep two. There were pegs on the wall hung with various clothing, and two stacked crates to serve as a bedside table. But to make it more like a home, Pearl had sewn beautiful curtains decorated in lace.

Those curtains were drawn closed now, hiding Ben's prone figure. He was breathing slowly and deeply, and Abigail thought it was an attempt to control his pain. Pearl had laid a sheet beneath him, over the bed linens, and had already removed the clothing from his upper body. His chest was smeared in blood.

Henry held a bucket of water close to his wife, who was trying to wipe the worst of the blood away.

"Can you tell how bad it is?" Abigail asked from the doorway. She longed to move closer, but there was simply no room.

"The blood makes it look worse than it is," Ben said through gritted teeth.

When he winced at Pearl's ministrations, Abigail winced too.

"Pearl?" she whispered.

Pearl briefly raised her head to meet her gaze. "It is a long slash along his ribs. It does not seem to have pierced deeper."

"I shall find a physician," Abigail said.

"No!" Ben raised his head. "You will not. You cannot trust the political inclinations of anyone. Just wash and bandage the wound, and I'll be fine."

Abigail knew he was right, knew she couldn't risk revealing their cause, not without harming her children, or Henry and Pearl. "I will fetch more bandages," she murmured.

"I have to return to the taproom," Henry said. "I will come

back as quickly as I can." He touched his wife's shoulder as he passed by.

Abigail crept up the back staircase. The children were asleep on their small cots at the foot of her bed, faint lantern light making their sweet faces glow. Lottie had been afraid of the dark ever since they'd been forced to quarter loud British soldiers four years before.

Once again Abigail was torn between duty to her children and duty to her country. She'd tried so hard to honor both. She prayed she would not regret her choices. She picked up her depleted basket of medicines and crept back downstairs.

From the kitchen, she could hear patrons conversing, singing, and shouting good-naturedly. She prayed Henry could keep everything under control by himself. At this time of night, most wanted libation, not food.

Abigail returned to the small storage room. Ben's eyes were closed, his tension gone.

"Pearl?" she whispered.

"He is unconscious," Pearl said. "I'm not being gentle with my scrubbing. The wound is filthy."

"We were rolling around in the alley," she said bitterly.

Pearl arched an eyebrow.

"Lieutenant Rutherford followed me from the party, intending to arrest me. Ben saw when the lieutenant pulled me into the alley." Abigail stared down at him and whispered, "He saved my life."

"Does Rutherford know about us?"

"He's dead. Ben killed him to protect me." Abigail set her basket on the makeshift bedside table and began to sort through it. She'd long ago used the last of the Peruvian Bark that might have helped him.

Pearl let out a long breath. "Then we are in no immediate danger?"

"No. We left his body in the alley, stripped of its coin as if he'd been attacked by thieves."

Abigail looked down at Ben. He lay so still, his face occasionally twitching at Pearl's ministrations.

"The reason Rutherford followed me," Abigail continued," was because I overheard that eight thousand men are embarking to meet the French."

Pearl glanced back up at her swiftly. "So they know about the fleet's arrival?"

Abigail nodded. "But we weren't able to pass along the information."

"Then we had better see to this man's welfare."

Between the two of them, they applied a salve of vinegar and honey to Ben's wound. It continued to seep blood even as they applied a bandage, then wrapped a longer strip around his ribs to hold it in place, lifting his upper body off the bed awkwardly.

They helped him back down gently.

"Should we cover him?" Pearl asked.

"It's still so warm; perhaps a light sheet." Then she noticed his filthy clothing. "Oh Pearl, your bed! Should we try to remove his stockings and breeches?"

"I put a sheet down to catch the worst of it," Pearl said. "He'll be fine until he wakes up. Help me remove his boots."

When there was nothing left to do, Abigail said, "I'll sit with him. You take my bed and rest. I'll come for you if I need help."

Pearl frowned, but she obviously saw the wisdom, for she answered, "Very well. Encourage him to drink beef broth if he awakens. I left some warming by the fire."

Abigail nodded. She prayed for Ben, but nothing changed for many hours. She wished he'd given her his contact with the army, because she knew he'd never forgive himself if the American and French troops were caught unawares.

Henry checked in on her after closing the tavern, then reluctantly went to bed.

Abigail told herself to sleep, as she sat in a stiff wooden chair next to the bed, but it was overly warm, and the banked fire in the kitchen nearby made it worse. She occasionally dipped a cloth in cool water to soothe Ben's hot brow.

For many hours, he didn't move, but eventually he began to twitch and mumble in his sleep. The cool water wasn't helping—his fever was rising.

Abigail clasped his hand, feeling helpless.

**22**

---

# LILLIAN

1926

Mid-afternoon, when Featherstone's had closed between lunch and dinner, Lillian was examining the ledgers, seeing incremental progress in The Underground profits. It wasn't happening fast enough.

"Miss Featherstone?"

She looked up to find one of the waiters standing in the open doorway.

She smiled. "Hello, Herbert, what can I do for you?"

"There's a man to see you at the delivery door. He brought a card you might have given him."

Herbert stepped from foot to foot, his gaze darting toward the stairs repeatedly.

Lillian stood up, her senses alert. "Is something wrong?"

"His kind usually don't come here, that's all."

She felt the first stirrings of excitement, an emotion she hadn't let herself feel since she'd discovered two days ago that her father would soon be sentenced to prison.

"Maybe I should talk to Mr. Dabrowski?" Herbert continued. "He'll give him the bum's rush."

"No need," she said, taking the card and moving past him to the stairs. "I'll handle this."

She went down to the kitchen, and her breath caught with amazement and also satisfaction. Ray Waterman, the trumpeter from the jazz band, stood near the side door. He was dressed smartly in a double-breasted suit with cuffed trousers, his fedora in his hands. His tense expression relaxed into a smile as she reached the bottom step.

"Good day, Miss Lillian," he said.

She held out her hand, and he stared at it briefly before shaking it. She knew the cooks and staff were staring at them both, but she didn't care.

"Hello, Ray. Please, it's just Lillian," she said.

He didn't look at their audience. "I'll keep trying, Miss—Lillian."

"Have you decided to play at my club?"

"Not yet. My bandmates sent me to inspect the place before we make a decision."

"Then let me show you around."

She opened the door and led the way down to The Underground. The lights were on as employees cleaned and prepared for the evening. Chairs perched on tables, and some of the curtains disguising the walls were drawn back. Lillian didn't think it looked elegant at all.

She turned to face Ray, whose gaze meandered around the room.

"It looks better with evening lighting," she said ruefully.

His dark eyes met hers, and he gave her that smile that made her insides reel. "The stage is right next to the tables—I always like to be a part of the crowd."

Her heart lightened a bit. "Does it look like somewhere you'd play? There's a room next to the office for entertainers to relax between sets. It's small, but I've tried to make it comfortable."

"I think it all seems fine."

"Then you'll perform here?" she asked, sounding too eager even to herself.

He regarded her for a long moment, his smile fading, his eyes searching hers. "Okay," he said quietly. "If you think your guests won't mind."

She clapped her hands together. "Mind? They'll be thrilled to have something different than just a piano player—not that he's bad. I hired someone new, and he's been appreciated. But some evenings, you just want to dance to a band."

Ray chuckled.

"Would you like to share a late lunch?" she asked spontaneously. "I haven't eaten yet."

"Lillian, I can't eat in the dining room."

He said it in a light tone of voice, as if he was amused, but she knew he couldn't be.

Though she wanted to protest, it was pointless—he was right. She'd lose customers, and that might cost her the family business.

"The dining room is closed, but why don't we eat in my office? My father's office," she amended, ashamed that she'd not given him a thought.

"Won't he mind?"

"He's not here. I'm managing the restaurant and the club."

He arched a brow. "A woman running the family business? You don't see that often."

She shrugged. "It's a long story. Come on upstairs and I'll ask Chef for a meal."

The chef grumbled, Ray hung back, but Lillian insisted on sandwiches, soup, and two pieces of apple pie.

"Herbert can bring it up when it's ready," Lillian said, giving Chef a sweet smile.

His answering smile seemed grudging, but then he looked over her shoulder at Ray, and his expression faded into worry.

Lillian turned away. "Ray, please follow me to my office. We'll discuss the contract for your band."

Chef's demeanor eased a bit, as if a Negro in entertainment was tolerable. Lillian bristled and opened her mouth to speak, although she didn't know what to say.

Ray spoke. "Thank you for lunch, sir." Then he turned toward the stairs.

Lillian hesitated, then moved past him and into the lead.

In her father's office, she gestured to the chair closest to the door. The only other one was the swivel chair, and it felt strange to seat herself across the desk from Ray, as if she were his boss—as if she were his superior.

"I'm sorry about Chef's behavior," she said earnestly, folding her hands together on the desk.

Ray's eyes widened. "Why apologize for someone else?"

"Because I'm ashamed of how he treated you."

He studied her for a long moment before saying mildly, "I'm used to it."

"You don't seem bitter."

"Then I would be bitter all the time, and I choose not to live like that."

She'd admired his talent, but now she could admire his attitude toward life. She herself was feeling pretty bitter much of the time.

"I first realized how bitterness was affecting me after I returned from the Great War," he continued. "In France, I was an American soldier, and that's all the French people cared about—I was there to defend them. I was treated like a hero, like an equal."

She thought his tone was more sad than bitter.

Ray sighed. "And then I came back here, and I was a second-class citizen again. All of my accomplishments didn't matter because of the color of my skin."

Lillian echoed his sigh. "People can be terrible to each other."

He shrugged.

"Your family—your wife—must have been happy to have you back"

One corner of his mouth turned up. "I'm not married."

She fought down a blush.

"But my family was happy," he continued smoothly. "My mama especially, and my sister. Mama hadn't wanted me to fight the White man's war, as she put it, but this is my country, and we'd vowed to help our allies. I thought it would improve our standing when Negro soldiers came home alongside White soldiers."

Since they both knew how that turned out, she only bit her lip and nodded.

They heard someone coming up the stairs, and both turned to watch Herbert enter with the lunch tray. He placed a complete meal before each of them, adding napkins and silverware. Lillian noticed he kept sneaking glances at Ray when he thought the musician wasn't looking. Once Ray caught the stare and gave him a friendly grin.

Herbert blushed and swiveled to face Lillian. "Would you like something to drink, Miss Featherstone?"

"Iced tea for me. Ray?"

"Same for me," Ray said. "Thank you."

Herbert hurried out of the office. By the time he returned, Lillian and Ray had already taken bites of their sandwiches and blown on spoons full of creamy potato soup.

After the waiter had gone, Lillian and Ray ate in companionable silence. He politely complimented the food, but other than that, they didn't speak again until their hunger was assuaged.

"Do you have other siblings besides a sister?" Lillian asked.

Ray wiped his mouth with the cloth napkin as he shook his

head. "Just my sister Florence, who's a few years younger than me. How about you?"

"I have a sister who's fifteen and a brother who's eight."

"Oh, so you're the fine example they need to follow," he teased.

"I was hoping to be the fine example they followed as a college graduate, but—" She stopped herself, surprised to be mentioning something so personal to a man she'd just met.

His eyes softened with sympathy. "You weren't allowed to attend?"

"No, I'm in my junior year, but...I had to return and help manage this place."

He must have guessed there was more to the story, but he didn't pry.

"My father," she began, then sighed.

"He died?" he asked gently.

Her gaze flew back to his. "No! Well..." She trailed off, feeling helpless. All of her family's friends knew the tragedy that had befallen them. For just this moment, it felt good to be with someone who wasn't pitying her or looking down on her.

He raised both hands. "It's your family business. I understand."

"Thank you," she murmured, taking another bite of her sandwich. And suddenly she felt like she was being a coward. This was her life now—a family scandal had changed everything. "It's worse than you think," she finally said. "You should know before you make a decision to play here. My father is in jail." The words felt scratchy in her throat.

"I'm sorry to hear that," he said.

She studied his face, but he didn't look taken aback or disgusted, just sympathetic, and it made her blink back tears of gratitude.

"Was it because of the speakeasy?" he said at last.

"No, or maybe, but we don't know. There might have been

someone pressuring him for protection money. Something happened and a man died."

He inhaled deeply and let out his breath.

"I would understand if you wanted to get far away from here," she continued. "I can't, you see. This place is supporting my family. I have to make it a success, and I was hoping with the updating and modern music, I could lure more customers."

"None of this is your fault," he said, "and you shouldn't be blamed. I can't believe my bandmates would have objections to playing here. Mobsters have done some terrible things in this town. They aren't...bothering you?"

She thought of Big Jim Russo's visit and shivered. "Not yet. Maybe never. I will make it work. I have to."

They let the silence enshroud them again as they finished their pie. Lillian was questioning everything she'd told him, her feelings of familiarity and ease—was she making the right decisions?

"Will you be able to return to college?" he asked.

"I don't know. I hope so."

"Did you enjoy it?"

"I truly did. I want to be in publishing someday." She sounded far more wistful than certain these days.

"I always wanted to go to college," he said. "There are Negro schools, of course, but it's expensive. And I do enjoy playing in the band."

She felt an ache of sympathy for him. "You're so very talented. I can't believe you're considering playing for us."

"Believe it. It won't take much for me to convince my friends. They've wanted to be as bold as Duke Ellington, and you're giving us that chance."

She smiled at him, and hoped it wasn't a risky chance.

~oOo~

After Ray had gone, Lillian returned to the second floor, passed her father's office, and knocked on Mr. Dabrowski's open door.

He looked up at her and smiled. "Miss Featherstone."

"You could call me Lillian," she said.

"Maybe, but you're practically my boss—it would seem rude."

She sank into the chair across the desk from his. Without giving it much thought, she said, "Tell me about my father and the mob."

His smile drained away.

"My father is in jail, Mr. Dabrowski. I need answers."

"Your father was always very careful to stay away from mobsters."

"Big Jim Russo was here, and he sounded very familiar with my father."

"Don't have anything to do with him—he's dangerous."

"Papa tried to stay away from him and is now in jail, so if that was your advice to him, it didn't work."

Mr. Dabrowski lit a cigarette, not meeting her gaze.

"In the newspaper," she began, "they finally released the name of the man my father supposedly—the man who died. Stanley Kellog. Did you know him?"

He hesitated. "I didn't know him personally, but I knew who he was."

"And?"

"He smuggled booze, but your father wouldn't buy from him."

"But others in the industry did."

Mr. Dabrowski nodded.

"Who?"

"What good will this do, Miss Featherstone?"

"Please tell me who his customers were."

He sighed, letting out a cloud of smoke. "I don't have a list, but I know he did business with the Italian place down the street."

"Lombardo's Restaurant?"

"That's the one."

"I remember the family—I went to school with the owner's daughter. Thank you for the information."

"Miss Featherstone, don't make trouble for yourself."

She smiled and left the office.

~oOo~

Once Ray confirmed his band would play at the club, Lillian focused on advertising their performance with a sign at the host station. They were becoming such a popular destination that they now needed a host to seat customers at tables. She moved among the patrons, chatting about the upcoming performance and the new menu.

Though the financial risk was scary, she had paid to upgrade the alcohol, including Scotch smuggled by way of the Bahamas, and new cocktails that masked the taste of moonshine with citrus or sugar or ginger ale.

She was feeling proud of herself, growing more and more hopeful that her plans would succeed, and occasionally manning the host station when her employee needed a break.

Her college friend Marlene returned, and this time she brought Johnny Coleridge and several of his friends. Flirting with him at the party she'd hosted on campus now seemed like years ago instead of a few weeks, but she kissed his cheek when he bent to give her a hug.

"Lillian," he said, "when Marlene told me what you were up to, I had to come see for myself."

Lillian gestured behind her to the club. "It's not a publishing career, but it's my family business. Are you home for the weekend?"

He nodded. "Thank God my parents finally went to bed so I can truly start to enjoy myself."

She forced a smile, thinking she'd give anything to just sit in the same room as her father. But Johnny was making a joke—probably—and she shouldn't start to take everything personally.

He re-introduced her to his three friends, two other men and a woman, all of whom she'd socialized with at Penn, although she didn't know any of them well. Johnny asked her to dance when the pianist's song turned lively, and she went along, remembering how attracted to him she'd been back when life had been simple.

Over the next couple dances, Johnny's friends took turns escorting her on the dance floor. Finally, she and his friend Betty ended up sitting at the table in happy exhaustion while the men went to the bar for the next round of drinks.

Betty lit a cigarette. "This place isn't too bad."

"It's getting there," Lillian said. "I have a new band playing this weekend. You should come if you're still in town."

"I'll be in town. I graduated last spring." Betty blew out a ring of smoke, then eyed Lillian. "I have more in mind than dancing. I'm a writer, and I've been looking for a place for my writing friends to relax and talk and work during the day. Would this place be open?"

Lillian sat back in astonishment. "You mean like a café rather than a club?"

"We'd be happy to buy food and drink, as long as you don't mind that we'd stay for hours." Betty tilted her head, squinting through the cigarette smoke. "Would this work?"

Lillian leaned forward with interest. "It would. I can't guarantee I can risk serving alcohol during the day…"

Betty shrugged. "Let's see what happens. We have work to do—it's not like we want to get drunk."

"Then let me talk to my managers." She thought about

uncovering the high windows for some daylight. They'd need a menu. "Why don't you come back next week, and I'll show you our ideas."

~oOo~

The next day, after presenting her café ideas to Mr. Dabrowski and Mr. Weinstein, she left them to talk things over, saying she had an errand to run. After she left the restaurant, she headed down the street to Lombardo's Restaurant. Unlike Featherstone's, they didn't close between lunch and dinner, although the place only had a few tables occupied. As she waited for the manager, she looked around at the décor, over-loaded with white columns and red draperies, accented with pottery from "the old world," she assumed. The aroma of Italian sauce made her inhale deeply as she briefly closed her eyes.

A tall skinny middle-aged man came toward her. "Miss Featherstone? I'm Vince Pacini, the general manager."

She reached out to shake his hand. "It's nice to meet you Mr. Pacini."

"I'm sorry the owner is out of town."

"That's fine. I only met Mr. Lombardo briefly. I went to school with his daughter."

"The whole family is away," he said with regret.

"That's not a problem. If you have a moment, can we speak privately somewhere?"

He frowned. "My office?"

"That would be fine."

He led her back down a hall that followed the length of the kitchen, until they reached several closed doors. He opened one and ushered her inside. It wasn't much different than Mr. Dabrowski's office, with its ledger books as well as restaurant industry catalogues. A window opened onto the view of a brick wall.

Lillian took a seat, and Mr. Pacini sat across his desk from her.

"What can I do for you?" he asked.

Seeing no need to meander, she got right to the point. "You know my father is in jail for manslaughter."

His smile faded. "I read that, and I'm sorry to hear it. Samuel is a good man."

"I think so, too, and I need to understand what happened."

"Shouldn't you be talking to your father rather than me?" he asked dryly.

His gaze shifted toward the door, but she refused to take the hint.

"I have and will continue to do so. But I need to understand who the victim is. His name was Stanley Kellog. Do you know him?"

"Uh...not personally."

"But you knew him."

"I knew *of* him."

"And he was involved with the mob."

"Look, Miss Featherstone," he said, leaning toward her, resting his elbows on the desk, "you seem like a nice girl. I don't want to talk to you about this."

"Why not?"

"Because it's dangerous. I would have assumed your father was proof of that."

"Why do you say that? Since my father is in jail, wouldn't *he* be the dangerous one?"

He pressed his lips together before standing and walking to the door. "It was good to meet you, Miss Featherstone. I'll tell Mr. Lombardo you stopped by. If you get the chance to speak with him, I wouldn't recommend bringing up this subject."

Though Lillian was shown to the door, she still wasn't going to give up. She tried two more restaurants, both friendly competitors of her father's, and received the same cool reception. No one wanted to talk about the man who'd probably been demanding protection money from all the local businesses. At the final restaurant, the manager took her arm and practically threw her onto the street.

She felt frustrated, sad, and scared. How was she supposed to help her father when no one—including Papa—would give her the facts?

## 23

## LILLIAN

### 1926

Friday night, the Waterman Jazz Band played at her club for the first time, and it was everything Lillian hoped it would be. There wasn't room for all the customers who wanted to attend. She'd hired three bartenders who could barely keep up with the demand. No one seemed to care that Ray and his fellow musicians were Negros. The evening was all about dancing and socializing. More than once, Lillian caught Mr. Weinstein's eye as he rotated cash boxes behind the bar because of the overflow. He chomped his cigar, arched a thick eyebrow, and shook his head as he walked back to his office. It was almost an apology, Lillian thought.

In between sets, the Waterman Jazz Band relaxed in the small room next to Mr. Weinstein's office that she'd set aside for entertainers. She tried to coax Ray out to the club floor for a drink, but he was insistent.

"Maybe next time, Lillian," he said from the doorway. "Please come inside and meet my sister."

She hadn't realized he had guests hidden away.

The room was small and overheated with bodies, the smell of hair pomade mixed with cigarette smoke. Ray's three bandmates turned to grin at her as if adding another person wasn't an imposition. Ray gestured to two young women, who came forward, their smiles shy and sweet.

"Lillian, this is Florence, my baby sister. I hope you don't mind that I brought her to meet you."

The shorter woman, with Ray's cheekbones beneath bobbed hair, gave her brother a shooing gesture with her hands. "None of that, Ray." She turned back to Lillian. "My brother forgets I'm a grown woman. It's nice to meet you, Miss Lillian. Your club seems quite successful."

"Thank you. Your brother and the band are a big part of that."

Ray turned to the other young woman. "I almost forgot, this is Anna."

The other young woman didn't seem upset at his forgetfulness. She gave Lillian a shy smile. She was taller than Florence, perhaps a few years older, with hair pulled back from her face. Unlike Florence, she wore a touch of make-up to highlight her wide pretty eyes—eyes which darted toward Ray regularly.

Lillian knew many girls who had had crushes on friends' older brothers.

While Ray introduced Lillian to the rest of the band, Florence continued to stare at her.

Ray finally noticed. "Florence," he said, a warning tone in his voice.

"But her dress is just so beautiful," Florence said,

Lillian looked down at her sleeveless red silk dress covered by sheer beaded netting. "It's one of my favorites."

"My sister makes all her own dresses," Ray said, "and sews for some of our friends."

"You're obviously quite talented," Lillian said, gesturing toward the young woman's black dress with white beading.

Florence blushed again, but before they could continue

speaking, Ray said in a louder tone, "Time to give the customers another show."

~oOo~

Lillian usually never stayed late, but she couldn't stop watching the band. Their presence overwhelmed her little stage, made the club pulse with energy and sound. Young and old, people were smiling and swaying or dancing. She saw even Mr. Weinstein tapping his foot to the music when he thought she wasn't watching.

The Underground was still going strong at three o'clock in the morning as the band played their last number. Lillian retreated up to her office and put the band's earnings in an envelope. Not long after, there was a quiet knock on her open door. She looked up from the ledgers.

Ray was leaning against the frame, his posture languid and tired, his smile soft with satisfaction. "I think it went well."

"I've never seen the place so full," Lillian said, beaming at him. "And all because of you—and your band," she added quickly, feeling herself redden. She hoped he didn't notice in the dim light.

"And all your improvements," he said.

"Thank you. It wasn't just me, of course."

"But you were the driving force."

There was a moment of silence as they just looked at each other.

Ray sat down across the desk from her. "Thanks for not minding that I brought along Florence and her friend."

"I didn't mind at all."

"Florence is training as a seamstress, and she's very focused on creating more fashionable dresses for our people to buy. If it wouldn't be too much of an imposition, she'd love to talk fashion with you sometime."

"A subject I enjoy," Lillian said with a smile. "She should come to my house, and we can look over my wardrobe."

Ray's eyes widened. "That's not possible."

"Why not?"

"Your mother wouldn't want a Colored girl in the house."

"Then I'll choose a time when my mother isn't there."

He looked at her for a long moment, until the silence grew thick with a tension she hadn't felt in a long time.

"I've never met anyone like you," he said softly.

She felt herself blushing again, like an innocent girl with her first crush.

"Would you consider having lunch with me?" he asked.

"I thought you said it wouldn't be proper."

"Not proper *here*," he admitted. "But we could meet uptown in Harlem."

She gave it some thought.

He seemed to stiffen. "I can't pick you up—too dangerous. If I'm being too forward, just tell me."

"I didn't say that. I'm flattered, and I would enjoy lunch. Just tell me where to meet."

His smile lit up his face again. She wanted to bask in its glow, to put her hands on him and bring him closer. Her heart picked up speed with excitement as he wrote down the name of the restaurant and the address.

He rested his hands on the desk, leaning toward her. "What are we doing?" he murmured, his gaze on her mouth.

"I don't know," she whispered, wishing he'd kiss her, knowing she wouldn't be brave enough—yet. "But I don't want it to stop."

He searched her eyes for a long moment, his smile fading. But whatever he saw seemed to reassure him.

He straightened. "Tomorrow."

"Tomorrow."

~oOo~

Lillian fussed with her hair and dress as if she'd never dated before. Viola sprawled on her stomach across Lillian's bed, chin propped on her hands as she watched. Lillian didn't tell her sister what she was doing, but Viola studied her curiously.

"Are you going to see Papa?" Viola finally asked.

Lillian shook her head.

Viola cocked her head. "Mother went today."

"I'm glad. He needs us."

"Then why can't I go?"

"Mother thinks you're too young."

Viola gave a mutinous glare.

"Then change her mind," Lillian said.

"You'll support me?"

"I will." Papa wouldn't tell Viola anything new, but maybe it would lift his spirits—or make him angry. There was no way to know.

But the topic distracted Viola, and Lillian was able to leave the house without revealing exactly where she was going. At the last moment, she saw Mrs. Vickers watching her from the hallway that led to the kitchen.

Lillian gave a little wave but didn't stop. She could still feel the housekeeper's eyes on her, and it was difficult to shake off the sensation. It was as if she knew Lillian was doing something her parents wouldn't approve of.

But would Mrs. Vickers?

And then she forgot her concerns as she drove uptown. Ray was waiting for her when she approached the restaurant, and he put out an elbow, eyebrows raised with defiance.

She slid her hand into the warm wool covering his arm and smiled up at him. She felt different and daring, and when they went into the restaurant, and she was one of only three White people there, it was as if she was in another world, where people could be equal. She wasn't blind, and noticed more than a few of the patrons looking at them askance, several in disapproval.

Mother often told her about the old days, when single men sat on the porch with the girl they were courting, sipping lemonade, knowing the girl's parents watched through the window. Now, Lillian was free to date any man she wanted— and she wanted to get to know Ray.

Once they sat down and started talking, everything felt so familiar and natural. There were no awkward silences, no wondering what to say next. He was curious about her college experiences; she was curious about his military service in Europe. She told him how hard it was to be accepted by the men she worked with at the restaurant, and he told her about the hours he picked up at the grocer's to supplement his musical career. Before she knew it, two hours had gone by.

"I need to get back to the restaurant," she said reluctantly, staring down at their hands, so near each other but not touching.

"Let's do this again," he said. "What about dinner at a club one evening before I perform?"

"Here in Harlem?" she asked, knowing the answer.

He arched an eyebrow. "Harlem is a playground for White people to spend money, isn't it?"

She winced, but knew it was true.

"Which means we can socialize more easily," he added.

"Is that what we're doing, socializing?" She felt bold and daring—brazen.

"What would you call it?"

"I think you're a born flirt."

He chuckled. "Call it what you want but say we can meet again."

"All right," she said softly.

He smiled and briefly squeezed her hand.

Over the next few weeks, they met at various places in Harlem, and sometimes they were alone. He didn't try to kiss her, although she was more than willing and couldn't hide it. But she let him take things at his own pace.

She got to know some of his friends and met up with his sister several times. Sometimes these encounters were awkward, but gradually people came to accept her.

Florence's friend Anna kept her distance though, and Lillian understood, because Anna just couldn't stop gazing with longing at Ray. But she was sweet, not the kind of person to try to take him away from another woman, and Lillian respected her for it.

The only mistake was finally accepting Ray's invitation for his mother's good cooking. Lillian had resisted, worried what the woman would think, but when even Florence started pressuring her to join them, she gave in.

And Mrs. Waterman took one look at her and started crying.

~oOo~

After the awkward dinner, Lillian drove back to Harbor House, knowing that if she went home, she couldn't hide her sadness from Viola.

In her office, she reviewed the ledgers Mr. Dabrowski had left out for her, because she didn't feel like she could relax and mingle pleasantly with her customers.

She jumped a little when she heard a knock on the door.

"Come in," she called.

Herbert opened the door and leaned in. "You have guests, Miss Featherstone," he said, wide eyes looking sideways.

"I'll be down soon," she said with a sigh.

Then someone else pushed the door open, and Big Jim Russo entered. Lillian slowly rose to her feet, swallowing hard.

The same two henchman stood in the hall and watched Herbert duck away, no doubt to escape down the stairs. She didn't blame him.

"Hello, Mr. Russo," Lillian said calmly.

"And hello to you, Miss Featherstone. May I call you Lillian?" he asked, as he took the chair opposite her desk.

As if she could say no. She gave a nod. "What brings you to Harbor House, Mr. Russo?"

"I heard you've made quite the improvement with The Underground."

"Thank you. We've all worked hard. I don't want to disappoint my father by losing everything he's built."

"I'm sure he's proud. I know I am."

She arched a brow but said nothing. He put his elbows on the desk and leaned toward her. She resisted moving away.

"Lillian, I wouldn't want to see anything happen to this great place. With New York City the way it is, you need help keeping the whole building protected."

He reached forward and patted her clenched hands like she was a child.

"I forgot that you probably don't know how this works," he continued. "I'm in the protection business. This can be an unsavory part of town, and you need someone like me to protect your interests."

"Isn't that what the police are for?" she asked coolly.

His smile faded a bit. "The police protect The Underground? My, my, Miss Featherstone, you work quickly."

"I didn't say that." But she'd allowed a certain policeman free drinks to keep quiet.

He studied her silently for a moment, and then the smile returned. "No, I can see that's not what you meant. Good girl."

She wanted to insist she was a grown woman but thought better of it. "I have insurance."

"That's for after something happens. I plan to make sure nothing happens to Harbor House."

"You're being kind, but why do I get the feeling that this will benefit you?" And then she held her breath in fear, realizing how he might take her forthrightness.

But Mr. Russo chuckled. "You're a smart girl. I like that about you. Shall we discuss your private insurance fee?"

"Private insurance?" she echoed, then bit back the word "blackmail." "Sir, I can't afford that."

"We can start easy and raise the rate the more success you have. I'll steer some clients here, too. That will help."

"No offense, Mr. Russo, but I don't want to be known as a place where your other clients gather."

He very slowly sat back, the smile leaving his eyes, though not his mouth, like a snake finally revealing itself.

"Okay, I get that," he said at last. "You're trying to stay above board—at least by day."

She bit her lower lip.

"But there's still a fee to keep your business safe."

Thoughts ran crazily through her brain, and she didn't know what to say. Finally, she whispered, "You're scaring me, Mr. Russo."

"Maybe you're not ready to run a business in this big scary city, Lillian."

"I am," she said without hesitation, "but I need to think about this. You've surprised me."

"Were you really surprised," he asked with a smirk, "a smart girl like you?"

She inhaled sharply, the tension in the room making her realize no one would come if she screamed.

And then he rose to his feet, and she let out her breath as he seemed to suddenly tower over her.

"You do some more thinking, Lillian," he said pleasantly. "Don't think too long."

## 24

---

# PAMELA

2023

It was mid-summer before Lucia brought a friend to the building to hang out. She occasionally mentioned names, so Pam knew she *had* friends, she just chose to socialize elsewhere—and who could blame her? Their apartment, though clean, was old-fashioned and sparse, except for the occasional framed family photo Pam hadn't bothered to pack away yet.

While she worked in the kitchen preparing Chicken Adobo for dinner, she listened to the cheerful chatter of Lucia and her friend Noah. He was a lanky kid who hadn't yet grown into his height. His blond hair was a shaggy seventies look that Pam was still amazed was back in style. The two teenagers sat side by side, laughing as they compared something on their screens and played a game together.

But when Pam invited him to dinner, he declined politely and took off soon after.

Lucia came upstairs after seeing him out, frowning. "I'm worried about him."

Surprised, Pam looked up from where she was setting the kitchen table. "Really? He seems like a good-natured, sunny kid."

"I know, but he's living in the group home and has been having a hard time finding a job. He's got no plans for college."

"Not everyone needs to go to college."

"I know, but I'm more worried about the fact that he's trying not to think about his future."

Pam hesitated. "Are you asking if I have some hours for him?"

"That seems like too big a favor."

"I don't mind, except I probably don't have that much to offer. Maybe ten hours a week? I do want to start painting some of the rooms."

"That's nice of you, thanks. Do you maybe have some friends with businesses looking to hire?"

Pam thought about the local business owners she'd been meeting. "I can reach out."

Lucia flashed her a high-wattage smile. "That would be great." She studied Pam for a moment, head cocked. "You know, if you opened the restaurant again, you'd need lots of employees."

Pam choked on the water she'd just sipped from her water bottle.

Lucia chuckled.

"Open the restaurant?" Pam finally said, her voice hoarse. "I hated the restaurant!"

"You hated serving," Lucia countered. "Being the owner is totally different."

"You think owning a restaurant is easy?"

"Of course not, but it seems to be a long family tradition."

"A tradition that takes one away from family."

Lucia didn't answer, and Pam realized Lucia didn't have any family. She wanted to take back her hasty, thoughtless words, but the girl just smiled at her.

"No speakeasy in the basement?" Lucia teased.

Pam put her hands over her ears as she walked back to the kitchen counter.

~oOo~

Keith scheduled an appointment to see Pam about his latest report. When she told Lucia, the girl conveniently made an excuse to be absent and ignored all of Pam's insistence that historical tidbits were going to be revealed.

Pam intended to meet Keith in the dining room of the old restaurant, but besides being swept clean, it was still dreary with boarded-up windows and another growing mound of things to be thrown away. When Keith arrived, Pam led him upstairs to her apartment instead and tried not to notice that he seemed pleased.

She gestured to the old kitchen table. "Would you like something to drink? Coffee? Soda? Water?"

He set his over-the-shoulder satchel near a chair and took a seat. "Water's fine."

She brought both of them glasses and a plate of chocolate chip cookies Lucia had made. Sitting down, she said, "I can't vouch for these. Lucia said they might or might not be vegan."

Keith chuckled and took a bite. "Tastes good."

Shaking her head, Pam smiled. "So, any more news about my ancestors?"

He finished his cookie, took a sip of his drink, then lifted his satchel onto the table.

"That looks pretty full," she said, trying not to be too excited.

"It's mostly my laptop," he said, pulling the device out. "But there's something you'll want to listen to."

He pulled a thumb drive out of his pocket and held it up like a magician proving the bird was real. She laughed in spite of herself.

He inserted the thumb drive into his laptop, then looked up at her with sincerity, his smile fading a bit. "I'm going to play you some mp3 files. The originals were cassettes recorded by the Waterman family, who gave me permission to make digital copies."

Pam froze with excitement, recognizing the name of the family who'd ordered the baby photos in the 1920s. "So you spoke with them? Are they related to Baby Daniel? Are they related to *me*?"

He held up his hand. "Hold your horses."

She was taken aback. Who said that old phrase anymore? Apparently Keith did. But her amusement subdued her panicked excitement, which was a good thing. "Go ahead," she said calmly.

"Baby Daniel is apparently the grandfather to the current oldest generation of Watermans. They recognized the photo as Daniel Waterman. Before you get too excited, he passed away about fifteen years ago."

Pam tried not to let her disappointment show. The odds hadn't been good that he'd still be alive at almost one hundred years old.

"But these are recordings the family made about fifty years ago, during the Roots craze—you remember the TV event the entire nation watched?"

"We were probably toddlers, but I heard about it."

"Well, that show made everyone interrogate their grandparents as if no one had ever realized their ancestors might have led fascinating lives."

She watched his face as he spoke, his amused exasperation that people didn't usually care about their family history, and how much he obviously did care. She told herself it was because he was an investigator, and solving mysteries was his purpose in life.

"And the Watermans were no different," he continued.

"Turns out, Grandpa Daniel had a lot to say that no one had ever taken the time to find out. I listened to the recordings—I hope you don't mind."

"Of course not. It's what I'm paying you to find out."

"He sounds like he was a pretty cool guy. I think you'll enjoy the recordings. He spent his childhood in Europe until World War II loomed because his father was a musician, a trumpet player for Josephine Baker."

Pam immediately thought of the musicians behind Great-Aunt Lillian in the photo.

"He and his parents escaped Vichy France to Africa, and eventually back to the States. Later in his life, a relative told him they thought there was something unusual about his birth. He didn't know if that meant he was adopted, but his parents were dead, and he couldn't ask them. It didn't matter to him, because they loved him, so he never pursued it, and it didn't come up in the conversation again. There's a lot more, filling four cassette tapes. The grandson is fascinated that you have a baby photo of Daniel, and he'd like to meet you. He's wondering if maybe you're a long lost relative."

Pam munched a cookie absently before saying, "Long lost relatives. Just because he thought he might be adopted, that seems a long leap to—to—"

"To what?" Keith asked gently.

"To assuming my great-aunt or someone else in the family had a child they gave away. I cannot even imagine the pain and desperation of such a thing." She thought of her aunt's sparkling eyes in the old photo, a young woman with her whole life ahead of her, and the Black musicians behind her.

Desperation might certainly be at play.

Then Keith clicked a button and soon she heard the gruff voice of an older man and the fresh inquisitiveness of a young boy explaining about the school project on his ancestors.

Pam closed her eyes, and it was as if she could hear her own grandfather. Could Grandpa and Daniel have been cousins?

**25**

## LILLIAN

1926

Winter teased New York City, blanketing Central Park with several inches of snow, decorating the tree branches with frost. Ice on the edges of the lake reached toward the center like frozen lacy fingers.

But Lillian, along with her mother and sister, were safe and warm inside, attending a garden party being given by Mrs. Arthur Manning, held in the mansion's iron-ribbed conservatory. Ferns and pink trumpet-shaped flowers on twisting vines reached toward the wan light of an overcast day, the glass foggy with the moisture of tropical plants and the conversation of twenty guests.

Mother had been pleased to be invited, and now talked to their neighbor Mrs. Yardley about a children's charity they both supported. It seemed an easy topic for Mother to ease herself another step back into Society.

Viola stood between Lillian and their mother, making no attempt to see her friend Pansy. Lillian hesitated to mingle, saddened by her sister's resignation.

"Go," Viola said, attempting a smile. "I know you want to talk to Grace."

"Then come with me."

Viola shook her head and glanced away.

Lillian squeezed her hand, then wandered among the guests, looking for her friend. She found Grace sitting on a wrought-iron bench next to a window overlooking Central Park. Birds of Paradise jutted from planters on either side of the bench, orange spikes resembling feathers.

Grace smiled and patted the seat beside her.

"Are you all right?" Lillian asked. "You look pale."

"Just tired. The baby keeps me awake at night with all his movements."

"'His'? So you think it's a boy?" Lillian grinned.

"William hopes so. I don't care either way."

Grace put her hand on her stomach with a sweet gentleness that made a small ache hug Lillian's heart, startling her. Now was not the time to think about marriage and babies, not for her.

"I wanted to tell you about something I'm doing at the restaurant," she began.

Grace nodded, but her focus was beyond Lillian.

Lillian turned her head to see their hostess's two youngest daughters, both barely old enough for school, taking turns smelling the roses that climbed a trellis along one glass wall. They nudged and tickled each other, making Grace chuckle.

"What were you saying?" Grace said absently.

"A group of writers is looking for a place to write, so I'm transforming the basement into a café." Lillian still couldn't get the words "speakeasy" out of her mouth.

"That's nice." She continued to be absorbed by the antics of the little girls.

Grace didn't ask for any details, and Lillian would have felt foolish offering them. The restaurant, her family business, was the most important thing in her life right now, but to Grace, wealthy and settled, only family and children seemed to matter.

Just then a newcomer stepped through the entrance to the conservatory, and Lillian caught her breath. She recognized Paul Webster, her father's lawyer. More than one woman looked his way, especially the unmarried ones. He was tall, his thick blond hair swooping above his forehead, and she suddenly realized he was attractive—something that hadn't even occurred to her the first time they met.

He wore a faint smile, his posture more relaxed than in his law office. Mrs. Manning intercepted him before he'd taken more than a couple steps, but by her cordial expression, she wasn't about to ask him to leave.

His acceptance was a mystery that made Lillian uneasy. He belonged to a different side of her life, where bad things happened to her father, and she was on her own trying to make sense of it all.

His gaze roamed the guests then focused on her. Lillian stiffened, nodding coolly.

"Who is that?" Grace whispered.

Lillian had almost forgotten her friend was there. "He is a lawyer, Paul Webster."

"A lawyer? I don't recognize his family name."

Lillian bit back a theory. It wasn't up to her to wonder how Mr. Webster had risen in the world—as if you could call being a lawyer to the mob, rising. She winced, knowing that was just a guess, but unable to stop her suspicions.

As the hostess introduced her oldest daughter to Mr. Webster, Lillian couldn't help noticing his elegant suit and expensive-looking tie clip. The mob paid well, she thought bitterly. And now she paid him, too.

"All the girls are quite giddy," Grace said, smiling. "But not you?"

Lillian realized she'd been frowning and relaxed her expression. "I—he's my father's lawyer."

Grace's eyes widened, and she put a gentle hand on Lillian's arm. "I'm sorry to bring up such a sensitive topic."

Lillian shrugged. "It's something I have to live with."

"There aren't any new developments?"

Now she had Grace's attention, and she told herself it was because her friend cared. But she hadn't cared when Lillian wanted to tell her about her new café.

Lillian sighed, frustrated at her own unsettled emotions. "Nothing new."

Grace leaned closer and lowered her voice. "He is still... pleading guilty?"

"He already did. His sentencing will be any day now."

"Oh, Lillian," Grace whispered.

Lillian might have said more, but then Mr. Webster was moving through the guests toward them, nodding at several hellos, seeming to ignore the occasional cool stare.

"Miss Featherstone," he said, giving a short nod.

Lillian rose, and so did Grace. "Mr. Webster," Lillian said, "may I present my friend, Mrs. William Nash."

Mr. Webster's smile was full of the charisma of a man at ease using it. Even Grace didn't seem immune.

"A pleasure, Mrs. Nash." He bowed.

"Good to meet you, Mr. Webster," Grace said, her eyes alight as she added, "I'll leave you two to talk."

Lillian almost called her back, but was distracted when she saw Mother recognize Papa's lawyer and turn away with a pinched expression.

Lillian didn't know what to say to the man. Guests were watching them, most surreptitiously, some with open curiosity. She glanced back up at Mr. Webster's face, having forgotten how far up she had to look. He seemed amused as he met other gazes with friendliness, and then he turned back to her, blue eyes still warm.

"What are you doing here?" she asked, then winced. "Forgive me, that was rude."

"But honest," he said, chuckling.

Where was his stern demeanor? She didn't know how to talk to him now, as if they'd both changed when they crossed to the Upper East Side.

He continued, "I've had business dealings with Mrs. Manning's husband and some of his partners."

Lillian's eyes widened.

"Very aboveboard dealings," he added. "I work for my income, and the money in his circles has been fulfilling."

"Still, they wouldn't normally invite a man of business for no reason."

Mr. Webster shrugged. "I can't explain it either."

She wasn't certain she believed him.

"But it does seem awkward to be here," he said. "I'm quite certain I'm the only person in the room who has experienced poverty in childhood."

She opened her mouth, but there was nothing to say to that.

"Yeah, I'm probably the awkward one," he said dryly. "Ignore me."

"But I don't want to ignore that. You told me things about your parents already. With such a difficult beginning, how did you get all the way to law school?"

"Growing up, my father worked in the household of someone quite wealthy—he ran errands, fixed carriages, then cars, and did repairs. He became friends with the son of the household, getting him what he needed, defending him in scrapes."

This sounded a bit like her father's situation with Big Jim Russo.

"In one particular scrape," Mr. Webster said, "my father was injured helping his friend. The family offered to fund my education as a reward to my dad, with the understanding that I would join the law firm they worked with."

"So the mob worked its wiles on you," she said.

His gaze never dropped. "I'm not ashamed of how I got here. I'm a good lawyer, and I now have a better life. I was able to help my mother after my dad left us. I even have my own practice. I can give things to my mother to make up for what she never had. And I don't do anything illegal."

She was tempted to roll her eyes, but his obvious sincerity stopped her. *She* was the one doing something illegal. But she had her reasons.

"How did you come to represent my father?" she asked.

He sighed. "That's between me and your father."

Mr. Webster had connections to the mob—did those criminals recommend him to Papa? She didn't know what to think, but her irritation soon spilled over into anger.

She turned her back on the other guests, pretending to look out on snowy Central Park. Between clenched teeth, she said, "If that man's death had something to do with the mob, do you plan to let my father rot in prison?"

"Miss Featherstone, I am treating your father as I do any client, trying to get him the best sentence possible. The written statements you and your mother provided might help. But he pled guilty."

"How long might his sentence be?" she whispered, fisting her hands to keep from trembling.

"With manslaughter, it could be anywhere from ten years to life. It all depends on the circumstances."

She didn't want to hear any more. She stalked away from him, trying to appear impassive. She could not think about this right now without running outside into the snow.

"Lillian!"

She turned when she heard Ruth calling her name. The

young woman was standing with other friends, including Grace. Lillian gratefully headed their way, hoping to forget about Paul Webster and his excuses.

Grace was giving her an odd look, her eyes full of worry and sadness. Before Lillian could speak, she noticed their other friends circling to gather around them, their expressions full of eagerness.

"Is it true?" Ruth whispered loudly. "Your family owns a speakeasy?"

Grace looked stricken, and Lillian realized she'd been cowardly to hide it from her best friend.

She tried to convey with just her eyes how sorry she was, even as she attempted a teasing smile to the other young women. "I don't have any idea what you're talking about."

They all laughed, whispering to each other excitedly. Grace winced as if she'd been pinched.

"Edna told me she'd been there last weekend and saw a"—Ruth leaned forward—"a Negro band!"

Lillian hadn't planned to promote her club to the residents of the Upper East Side. Too many people knew her and could make things difficult. But she'd grown up here and these women were future customers. She could hardly downplay what she'd been doing. But she had to be careful—her enterprise was still illegal, and the parents of these women could ruin everything.

Lillian felt a dose of cold fear, as if she'd brushed up against the iron ribs of the conservatory windows.

Society women had given her mother pitying looks and kept their distance. She was positive none of them went all the way downtown to eat at Featherstone's anyway. Many of them served alcohol at their parties—*serving* it wasn't illegal, only buying it, and the rich had certainly bought all the alcohol they could before Prohibition was enacted. Her father had complained about it to her once, that he couldn't sell it, while all their friends regularly enjoyed it in their homes.

It was average people who had had no access to alcohol except for speakeasies. And those average people were keeping the Featherstones in their home, with food on the table.

"Tell us all about it, Lillian." Vivienne looked at her with interest and admiration, something that hadn't happened in a long time.

"I can't confirm such things while at a garden party," Lillian said. "You'll just have to come to Featherstone's after midnight and find out."

"Is there a password?" Ruth asked.

"Seaport."

"I just don't understand, Lillian," Grace said quietly, but with enough force that their little circle of friends turned to look at her. "How will this help you find a husband?"

Every pair of eyes focused on Lillian.

Lillian stared at her best friend, feeling frustrated that Grace didn't seem to understand her dilemma—or maybe didn't *want* to understand it. "That's not what my family needs right now." She heard the coolness in her voice and regretted it.

"I didn't mean—" Grace winced, then took her arm and, with surprising force, led her out of the conservatory, through the foyer, and into a deserted parlor.

When Grace released her arm, Lillian stepped away, shoulders stiff.

"I apologize for how my words sounded," Grace said quietly. "I shouldn't have spoken at all. I was upset to find out that you hadn't told me about the speakeasy. I'm not proud of myself."

The tension left Lillian's shoulders. "I'm not proud of myself either. I'm sorry I didn't tell you. I tried when I last visited, but I didn't know how to tell you that my father's business was partly illegal, and I was going to keep it going. I worried you'd think me as bad as my father." The last came out in a whisper around a lump in her throat.

Grace hugged Lillian close, and the two women stood like that for a long moment.

"I can't know how you're feeling," Grace said, taking a step back even as she reached for both of Lillian's hands, "because I've never been in such a desperate situation. But I can imagine, and I can understand. You have to do what you have to do."

Lillian nodded. "This is all my family has. I didn't realize how little money a restaurant brought in without alcohol. But please don't tell my mother. I'm not sure what she'd do if she knew. It's the only thing keeping us afloat without draining Papa's savings. I don't want to have to do that."

Grace winced. "Many guests overheard—they might tell your mother."

"I know, but I'm hoping that young people aren't inclined to tell their parents where they're socializing."

"You may be right. So...tell me about Mr. Webster." Grace's curiosity changed into sadness. "Never mind. You don't need to be reminded of your family tragedy."

"It's not as if I can ever forget." Lillian sighed.

"You didn't look happy when you left him."

"He claims he cannot do anything to help, since my father pleaded guilty. I know Papa didn't do it," she added fiercely.

Grace enfolded her in another embrace.

~oOo~

After Lillian dropped her mother and sister off at the townhouse, she switched cars for her roadster and headed down to Manhattan to Harbor House. She found a parking spot, then walked to the side entrance, where there was now a sign advertising "Featherstone Café." Her spirits lifted at the evidence of her continuing effort to keep their family business afloat and disguise the speakeasy.

Once inside, she descended the stairs and entered the new café. The high narrow windows were uncovered and the draperies pulled back, emphasizing the many plants in large pots scattered through the space. The dark tablecloths were swapped out for floral patterns, and there were more little potted plants at every table. It was hard to make a basement seem ready for a garden party, but Lillian thought they hadn't done too badly.

At least the women writers seemed to agree. As Lillian passed the host station, she saw that several tables were occupied by women, some bent over their notebooks, others lounging and conversing. A victrola near the stage played jazz, with a stack of records nearby for inspiration as guests saw fit.

"Lillian!" Betty raised a languid hand, her cigarette trailing a stream of smoke. "You've been puttin' on the Ritz around here. I like it."

"Thank you." Lillian approached her table. "Sitting alone?"

"I need to finish this chapter. The girls understand."

All around them, several women nodded, wearing knowing smiles.

"Don't let me keep you," Lillian said.

"No, no, it's time for a break. Do sit down." She gestured toward the bartender, showing two fingers. "Your man is a dream. He makes the best mixed drinks—I forget I'm not drinking alcohol, and I'm certainly getting more work done."

Lillian smiled up at the bartender, who also did time in The Underground, as he set their drinks in front of them. He hovered while she sipped, then looked relieved when she grinned.

Lillian watched Betty's gaze drift to the notebook on the table. "Are you certain I'm not bothering you?"

Betty shook her head. "My brain doesn't leave the story when I'm actively writing it."

"Have you published?"

"Some short stories in the *New Yorker*."

Lillian's eyebrows rose. "How impressive." Though the magazine was new, it had quite the following.

Betty's lips quirked. "Perhaps, but that doesn't count the two manuscripts under my bed that no New York publisher would buy." She waved her cigarette again. "It's part of the process. I'm not giving up."

"You've chosen a different lifestyle for a woman."

Betty's gaze focused on her. "So have you."

"Not by choice," she said with faint sarcasm.

"No, but you were in college. That's not something every woman does."

"What do the women here do?"

"Two are married, others are nurses or waitresses, jobs with odd hours. Finding a place to meet during the day has been a rarity, which is why your offer of the café has been such a blessing."

"I'm glad."

"But living a different kind of life isn't easy," Betty said, watching her closely.

Lillian shrugged. "My mother doesn't understand why I spend so much time here—she doesn't *want* to understand how necessary it is to our survival." She thought of Mr. Russo's visit the previous week, another threat to their survival, and wondered how much longer she could delay her answer.

"It sounds like she's trying to pretend life doesn't change."

"Maybe. Or maybe I've changed."

"Maybe you have," Betty said with a knowing smile.

Lillian had changed in ways Betty couldn't understand. She thought about Ray and his dazzling grin, and the warm, dangerous way he made her feel. She wanted to be even more a part of his world—which made her feel more excited and happier than she had in a long time.

"Can you spare a piece of paper?" Lillian asked.

Betty tore a sheet out of her notebook and handed it over, along with a fountain pen.

Lillian bent over the paper and began a letter to Florence, Ray's sister. She'd promised the girl they would meet and discuss fashion. Neither of their mothers would like it, but Lillian was determined to stop reacting to what others did and live her life the way she wanted to.

**26**

---

# LILLIAN

1926

Lillian watched the band perform late that night—and she couldn't take her eyes off Ray. He played the trumpet like it was an extension of himself, full of soul and emotion. Most tunes were danceable, but a rare few held an ache of emotion, of repression and despair. Lillian saw some customers use those songs to relax between dances, to drink and converse. Whereas she felt the emotion like a clench to her heart.

Spending time with Ray these last few weeks had given a glimpse into the kind of man he was, one who had deep undercurrents of sadness and anger, as well as pride in his community, his family. She wanted him to unburden himself to her, so that she could support him, perhaps even love him.

But she was sensing a reserve within him where she was concerned, an almost intangible wall, as if she could never understand what he'd gone through, and he wasn't going to even try to explain.

Near the end of his set, Lillian went up to her office, knowing he'd join her to pick up the band's pay. An hour later, when he appeared in her door, he leaned against the frame, smiling that wide, endearing smile.

"Hello, Lillian."

"Hi, Ray."

She was around the desk before she knew it, facing him, her body eagerly leaning toward him. She wanted his embrace, but he didn't move from the doorway, just let his gaze sweep tenderly over her.

To cover the awkwardness, she reached behind her and retrieved the envelope on her desk. "Can you give this to your sister?"

His eyebrows drew together but he didn't lose his smile.

"It's an invitation to get together," she quickly added. "I've been trying to find a time to invite her to the townhouse, since she was so interested in my dresses."

His smile faded and his gaze, still tender, searched her face. Lillian had stopped breathing, as if that subtle sound might break this tension.

And then he leaned forward and softly kissed her.

Lillian wasn't a virgin, but for the first time she felt that old cliché about her knees getting weak. Somehow she moved toward him and slid her arms around his waist, kissing him back with all the passion she'd been trying to keep at bay.

At last, he lifted his head and gazed down at her with an expression she couldn't read. But she said nothing, trusting in what they shared.

After a moment, he caressed her cheek with the back of his hand. "That was unexpected."

"I liked it," she whispered.

"Me, too."

But he continued to stare at her as if he was almost puzzled. She wondered again about his time in France, if she somehow reminded him of kissing French ladies.

But she was just a woman, and he was just a man, regardless of the color of their skin. And if that made her an idealist, a dreamer, she was okay with that. She wouldn't believe she was some kind of substitute—their relationship meant more than that.

Whatever kind of relationship they had.

Ray slipped into his coat and retrieved his fedora. He held up the envelope for his sister with a nod, but they still kept looking at each other as if willing time to stand still. At last she made a shooing motion with her hands. He laughed, donned his hat at a jaunty angle, and strolled down the hall. She was tempted to run to the doorway and watch him walk away, but instead she sagged back to sit on the edge of the desk, shaking her head. Life finally seemed to be about more than the sorrow over her father, and desperation to save her family. She had hope.

To her surprise, Mr. Weinstein stepped in the doorway, startling her. She'd forgotten the club ledgers were in Mr. Dabrowski's office, and that he might be on this floor.

Gazing down the hall where Ray had disappeared, Mr. Weinstein chomped his cigar, face impassive, belly dipping over his suspender-held trousers.

Then he turned and looked at her. Lillian stiffened. Her life was none of his business, and she didn't need to be defensive.

"I saw Russo and his guys here earlier," he said.

Lillian stood up. "In The Underground? They were let in?"

"Who was going to stop them? They seemed way too interested in the band," Mr. Weinstein continued. "And not in a good way. What happens if they freeze our access to booze?"

"Why would they do that?"

He snorted. "To teach us a lesson. We're not exactly playing on the right side of the law down here."

If she refused to pay her protection fee, they might very well retaliate. It infuriated her. She clenched her hands into fists. "Why are they doing this? Is it because my father isn't here, and they think I'll just roll over? Papa worked hard to keep us away from them."

"And now he's in jail. Guess he didn't work hard enough."
Lillian flinched.

Mr. Weinstein studied her for another moment, shook his head, and walked away.

~oOo~

The next night, Saturday, brought many customers to The Underground to see the band. But when Lillian went downstairs to bask in Ray's talent, she found a different trumpeter in his place, one who was competent but without the ability to make one feel every emotion. Was Ray ill? He'd seemed fine the previous night.

The wait until the band's break seemed to stretch on forever, her stomach uneasy with nerves she couldn't explain. She followed them toward the small room, opposite Mr. Weinstein's office, where they relaxed. When she knocked on the open door, they all turned to look at her, several in the process of slipping off their jackets. Their usual welcoming smiles were gone.

"What's happened?" she asked quietly, tensely. "Where's Ray?"

Elijah, the pianist, put on a faint smile as he draped his jacket over a chair. "He's not feeling well, and Lenny here was good enough to stand in for him."

Lenny, the new trumpeter, nodded his head as he lit a cigarette, his eyes not quite meeting hers.

In fact, none of them were looking at her.

"I'll give him a call." She turned to go.

"Don't do that," Elijah said. "He needs his rest."

She faced them all again, trying not to panic. "I don't believe you."

Elijah arched a brow. "That he needs his rest?"

"That he's ill. Please tell me what's wrong?"

Although Lenny sank into a chair with a newspaper as if unconcerned, the other three musicians exchanged a silent glance. They all knew she was seeing Ray. She shouldn't have to beg for information.

Elijah sighed. "Someone beat him up. His lip is too swollen to play."

She gasped and briefly covered her mouth before asking weakly, "A robbery?"

They all nodded too quickly.

"You're lying." She looked pointedly at Elijah.

He gripped the back of a chair. "Mob guys."

She gasped, remembering that Mr. Weinstein had said they didn't seem happy about a Negro band—that she hadn't paid her protection money yet. "Is he okay?"

The pianist hesitated, then nodded.

Her insides clenched with fear, but she pushed it away. "I'm going to see him."

Wide-eyed, they looked at each other until Elijah said, "You don't need to risk that."

"I have to."

She turned away and headed into the little corridor, where Mr. Weinstein was standing in his office doorway. With a cool nod, she tried to move past him.

He caught her elbow. "We need to talk."

He pulled her gently but firmly into his office and shut the door.

"Hey!" She shrugged off his hand.

It was a small office, and he was too close to her, and his cigar breath was overpowering.

But he put his hands on his hips and leaned toward her. "You need to stop this."

"What are you talking about?"

"You're digging into things that aren't your business. It's probably your fault the trumpet player got beaten up."

She stiffened. "That's not true!" But was it?

"Let the mob alone, let the musician go. Be lucky we have this place that supports us all."

"This is none of your business." To her horror, her voice trembled.

"This place is my business. You're Sam's kid, and he's left you in this bad straight. Someone's gotta look out for you, because your family sure isn't. I'm kinda shocked it's me, but there you go."

Lillian fled back upstairs to her office, her breath coming too fast, her hands shaking as she sat down and flattened them on the desk blotter, pressing hard.

Ray's beating—was it her fault? Why would Mr. Russo go after the entertainment when it was her he was angry with?

Or was this because Ray had dared to come to a White neighborhood to entertain?

She had to know the truth. She dialed the four-digit number, listened while the operator connected her to Ray's apartment building, then waited patiently while the first person who answered the hall telephone went to knock on Ray's door.

Lillian covered her eyes with one hand, wondering if she was making a mistake.

But then she heard his deep voice saying "Hello," and tears stung her eyes. He mattered so much to her.

"Hi, Ray." Her voice wobbled, and she cleared her throat. "It's Lillian."

"Hi," he answered back, his tone mellowing into tenderness.

The tears she fought leaked down her cheeks. She didn't want him in the middle of her problems, but now he was, and it was all her fault.

"I heard what happened," she said.

He hesitated. "What happened? I'm just not feeling good."

"Stop. Someone beat you up. I want to come see you."

"No." His answer was swift and hard. "I won't have you coming up here right now. You could get hurt."

"I need to see you," she whispered.

"Then I'll come to you after the club closes."

She should tell him not to—she had no idea who'd hurt him, and he might be in danger. But he hung up before she could deny herself the comfort of his presence.

Hours later, as Mr. Weinstein closed the club, he kept giving Lillian suspicious looks, for she didn't usually stay this late. She didn't owe him an explanation. He walked away, shaking his head.

When she was alone in the building but for the tenants in the apartments upstairs, Lillian wandered into the kitchen, where the metal shelves dully reflected the light of the lamp she'd left on at the chef's desk. She was wondering how long she'd have to wait when she heard a soft knock.

She hurried back to the door Mr. Weinstein had left through and opened the speakeasy peep hole.

Ray gave her a nod, but didn't speak as he glanced over his shoulder.

She unlocked the door and opened it. He came in on a rush of cold air and early-season snowflakes. She only got a brief glimpse of his battered face before he closed the door behind him and took her into his embrace.

Her bare arms wrapped around his neck, the snow on his shoulders melting against her skin. For a long moment they clung to each other, and she thanked God that he was safe.

At last, she lifted her head from his shoulder and leaned back to get a good look at him in the dim light. There were dark bruises on his face, and his lower lip was twice its normal size. One eye was so puffy she didn't know how he could see out of it.

"Oh, Ray!"

"It's nothing," he said, trying to duck away. "I'll be right as rain in a few days."

She held his shoulders. "Don't minimize what's been done to you. Who did this?"

"It doesn't involve you."

This wasn't over, but she grabbed some ice wrapped in a thin cloth from the kitchen and led him up to her office, away from the chance of one of the tenants finding them. She pushed him into the chair in front of the desk.

"Lillian—"

"Stop." She held the ice pack up, not sure if it belonged on his eye or his lip.

His poor, battered face. Her heart ached for all he'd suffered —because of her?

Suddenly, he pulled her down onto his lap. She caught her breath, her eyes wide as she looked into his.

"Ray," she whispered, lifting up the ice pack helplessly. "Let me help. This is all my fault."

"It's not your fault," he said gently, tucking a strand of hair behind her ear. "This world was broke long before you and I got here."

She wanted to tell him about Big Jim Russo, but then he framed her face with his hands and gently kissed her.

After a long moment of forgetting herself, she tilted her head away from his. "Doesn't kissing hurt?"

"No. All that matters to me is how much you care." He kissed her again. "Can we shut the door?" he murmured against her mouth.

She gave a little gasp as a flush of heat swept up her body. They looked into each other's eyes for a long moment, and then they both smiled.

# 27

# ABIGAIL

## 1780

Ben slept so deeply from the trauma of his wound that Abigail feared for his life. A fever threatened to burn through him, and she kept bathing his forehead, arms, and chest in cool water.

In the darkest hour before dawn, she sat looking at him in exhaustion and fear when his only movement was the shallow rise and fall of his chest. Would this war take away another person she cared for? She'd tried so hard to avoid these vulnerable feelings. They had spoken of the intimate details of their lives but once. Yet he believed in the same cause she did and was risking his life just as she was.

And he'd risked himself twice now to protect her. How could a woman ignore that?

She must have drowsed in her chair, head hanging, when the sounds of movement in the kitchen woke her with a start. For a moment, she feared that officers had come to arrest them for Rutherford's death.

But the routine clinks of bowls and tableware at last settled her down, and she sagged wearily.

When she glanced again at Ben, he was watching her through heavy-lidded eyes.

"Ben," she whispered, leaning forward to put her palm on his forehead. It was still too hot.

He tried to readjust himself and winced. "I feel like I've been in the same position for hours."

"You have been. I feared—" She broke off.

"You feared for me?" he asked, wearing a faint smile.

"Of course." Before her emotions could be laid bare to him, she quickly added, "Only you can take my news to your contact."

His eyes widened. "You have news?"

She nodded. "I do. Rutherford and Major John André confirmed that the British are sending eight thousand troops to meet the French when they land. They must have boarded all those ships that mysteriously left the harbor."

"You did it," he breathed.

When he tried to sit up, he groaned and fell back, blood blooming through the bandage along his ribs.

"You need to lie still."

"I can't," he said between gritted teeth.

She rose and bent over him, putting her hands on his damp shoulders. "You have to."

"They need to know today. We've run out of time."

"Eat, and then we'll discuss. It's barely dawn. We have time." She went to the door and looked over her shoulder at him. "You will stay in bed, correct? I will return in but a moment."

He hesitated, then at last nodded.

"I'll send Pearl in to see you, as well."

Out in the kitchen, Pearl lifted her head when Abigail emerged and closed the door behind her.

"How is he?" Pearl asked.

"The fever hasn't broken, but he's awake."

"You should have come for me." She took off her apron and set it across a stool.

"You could do nothing I couldn't do. It was better one of us rested. I need to talk to Henry. Can you look in on Ben and see what he might be able to eat?"

Pearl nodded, patting Abigail's arm as she moved past. "Between us, we will help heal him, have no fear."

Was it so obvious how afraid Abigail was? She wanted to protest that Pearl was assuming a closer bond than she and Ben had, but protesting would certainly make Pearl think she was right.

Out in the tavern, Abigail felt suddenly conspicuous. There were British soldiers at the bar, several seated at various tables. One was just coming down the stairs from his rooms above.

And if they all knew how she'd helped bring about the death of one of their own, she would probably not last the day.

Her son Andrew carried a tray toward the kitchen, smiling when he saw her.

"You were awake long before me, Mother," he said.

Surely such innocent words couldn't endanger them. So she patted his head with love, and he rolled his eyes and headed toward the kitchen.

Henry was standing behind the bar, studying her face. Whatever he saw seemed to relieve him.

"How is he?" Henry asked quietly.

"He's awake but still feverish."

Henry nodded, then murmured. "I need to speak with you."

That was to have been her line, and now her worry ratcheted up another notch. "Once Jacob arrives, come find me."

She returned to the kitchen, heard the low voices of Ben and Pearl in the small bedroom, and didn't disturb them. She stirred the stew cooking in the cauldron over the fire in anticipation of noontime customers and tested the bread baking in the brick oven next to the hearth.

Henry came through the door and approached her, keeping his voice low as he said, "They've discovered Lieutenant Rutherford's body."

Abigail stiffened. "And?"

"They seem to believe it a robbery for now."

"For now?" she echoed.

"I only say that because there will probably be an investigation."

She nodded, her mind already putting aside that future issue. "I'll have to worry about that later. Right now, we have to focus on getting our information to the appropriate people."

"Do you know where?"

She shook her head. "Ben will tell me."

Abigail knocked softly on the bedroom door, and Pearl opened it. The other woman's expression seemed calm, but Abigail knew that Pearl's impassivity could hide much.

"How is he?" Abigail whispered.

"He's well," Ben called, his voice weak. "It's not as if there's room for private conversations here."

"The patient is being stubborn," Pearl said.

Ben rolled his eyes.

Abigail came closer to him. His face was shiny with perspiration, and the light sheet covering him also had splotches of dampness. He was bare above the waist, and the bandage tied around his ribs looked fresh and white.

"How is the bleeding?" Abigail asked Pearl.

"You could ask me," Ben said in a husky voice.

Pearl and Abigail exchanged a glance.

"He doesn't seem to be a very good patient," Abigail said.

"I am not. I need to leave, and this young woman is trying to stop me."

"You cannot leave," Pearl said briskly. "The bleeding will start again. Will you risk your life?"

Ben's gaze met Abigail's. "I must, or Abigail's work will be for naught."

"It won't be," Abigail said, "if you let me make contact with the spy ring and relay the news."

Ben frowned. "That is not how this works. We're all protected the less we know."

"No one is protected if the French, our only ally, are defeated."

Ben tried to sit up, getting one elbow beneath him. Blood soaked through his bandage almost immediately.

Abigail rushed to him and put her hands on his shoulders. "Stop this!" she said quietly, urgently. "Let Henry and me help. If you collapse on the way, we will all fail."

He seemed to search her gaze before slowly slumping back on the pillow.

Her heart pounding, she whispered, "What are your instructions?"

~oOo~

As Abigail and Henry walked along Water Street toward Townsend's dry goods store on Peck's Slip, she could not stop thinking about Ben and how pale he'd looked. Had it been a mistake not to find a physician, even though they might have to answer tough questions?

What if Ben died?

She'd faced devastating loss before, and if she could survive her husband's death, she could survive anything, including the demise of a friend.

But did she want to be alone forever? More than one man had pretended courtship for access to the ownership of the tavern, a proven commodity even during war. This had made her even more reluctant to trust anyone. Ben was the first man she'd found easy to talk to since she'd lost Edmund. She'd trusted him with her life—that must say something.

As they approached the dry goods store, Abigail and Henry stayed in the shadows of a nearby building, and she tried to get a sense of the place. Though they'd walked a sedate pace, her heartbeat was still rapid, and her skin rippled with gooseflesh at feeling watched.

There were soldiers, sailors, merchants, and dockworkers walking briskly past each other, along with the occasional woman dressed conservatively or flaunting her availability. Vendors hawked newspapers, shouting "Bloody news! Where are the rebels now?" Across the street, the piers jutted out, with ships of all sizes, from frigates to schooners to ferries, tied up, and masts rocked gently in the East River current. They reminded Abigail of tall trees in the wind, the edges of rolled-up masts flapping like leaves.

Abigail and Henry paused near a recessed doorway. On the next block, they saw customers coming in and out of the dry goods over the short time they watched.

"The owner of this place is one of us?" Henry said uncertainly. "I've heard of him, a Mr. Townsend. He writes for the Loyalist papers."

"What a good disguise for a spy." She realized she was biting her thumbnail and forced her hand to her side. Taking a deep breath, she said, "Let's go."

They walked down the cobblestone street, the basket on Abigail's arm lightly bumping her hip. Henry opened the door beneath the DRY GOODS sign and gestured her inside. Though several of the multi-paned windows were open, the room was overly warm and smelled of anise, probably from the goldenrod tea that had long since replaced the real thing. Shelves lined the walls above the occasional chest of drawers. A large counter had a scale at one end, next to the barrels of dry goods. The shelves were nowhere near as full as they'd been before the war, but there were bolts of fabric alongside hammers alongside pewter plates. The display of tea from across the empire was now replaced with local versions like strawberry leaf.

There were four customers at various displays, and one sitting on the stool at the counter being waited on by the grocer, a tall, dark-haired man, long in face, spectacles on his nose, his expression serious. Was this Mr. Townsend? He had to be several years younger than she was.

The door opened again, and two British officers entered, wearing the blue uniform of the navy with lapels held back with gold buttons. They doffed their dark tricorn hats to reveal shades of brown hair tied back in queues.

"Good day, Mr. Towsend," one of the officers said.

Mr. Townsend gave them a bow and a smile, as if he knew them, but continued on with his customer.

It was difficult for Abigail to turn her back and keep browsing, but she forced herself to do so, staring at a set of porcelain teacups as if she debated buying such an extravagance during wartime. She could feel the officers moving around, heard them discussing what tobacco to purchase.

How could she make contact with a fellow spy when the enemy was right before them? She was breathing too rapidly. She closed her eyes and forced herself to inhale deeply. She would do what she'd set out to do. It would save so many lives and aid the war effort.

When at last the customer at the counter left after paying for his gloves and smoking pipe, the grocer looked around at the first two customers still making their decision, then at the officers debating the tobacco merits, until his keen dark eyes landed on Abigail and Henry.

Abigail stepped to the counter, and Henry remained behind her. "Mr. Townsend?"

"Yes?"

She gave him a cordial smile and held up a piece of paper, surprised that her fingers weren't trembling. "I have a list of items needed by Mr. Bolton."

For an awkward moment, Mr. Townsend just stared at her, not even blinking behind his spectacles. She knew the risks they all took—she'd just used the code name Ben had given her, and it was very obvious she wasn't Ben.

And two naval officers were but a pace away.

Mr. Townsend reached out and took the list. "Very well, give me a moment to gather it for you."

Abigail pretended to browse as Mr. Townsend began to select items from the shelves behind him. Henry walked to the door to wait, arms folded across his chest, face impassive, like her bodyguard. What would she have done without him?

She stiffened. She would have done what she had to. But having him to share it with eased her soul.

The naval officers made their selection and set it on the counter but continued their conversation that had now veered to a disciplinary problem with the quartermaster's mate.

Without a glance at the officers, Mr. Townsend packed her basket with the few items she'd ordered for the tavern and Abigail paid him as Henry took the basket.

"Thank you, sir," she murmured.

Their gazes met for a moment too long, then with a nod, he turned to the next customer.

Outside, Abigail and Henry strolled down the waterfront then turned up the next alley as Ben had directed. Not five minutes later, they saw Mr. Townsend emerge from the back of his store ahead of them, then enter another door at the rear of the same building.

Abigail and Henry followed him, finding the door unlocked, and they let themselves into a hall with a closed door to the first floor and a cramped staircase winding up to the next floor. She went up first and found a single door on the landing illuminated by a polished four-paned window. Giving Henry a nervous look, she knocked quietly.

The door immediately opened. Mr. Townsend filled the doorway in an imposing manner, still wearing an apron over his shirt, waistcoat, and breeches.

"Who are you?" His voice was demanding but overly quiet.

"Ben sent us," she whispered.

He seemed to catch his breath. "Where is he?"

"Wounded."

He briefly closed his eyes, then stepped out of their way. Abigail and Henry filed into a small room, functional but sparse, with a neatly made narrow bed in one corner, no flowers on a table, no lace draped over the back of the matching chairs, no hand-made blankets that might have marked the presence of a woman.

"Ben was stabbed protecting me," Abigail said. "I was almost apprehended gathering information."

Mr. Townsend put his hands on his hips as he regarded her. "He mentioned you, but never said your name. Do not tell me."

She nodded. "I am sorry for confusing you, but we have important news that couldn't wait."

Mr. Townsend glanced at Henry, standing near the door. "What about him?"

Abigail gave a tight smile. "He has found you valuable information over the years, though you didn't know it."

Mr. Townsend let out his breath as if with impatience. "Just tell me."

"I eavesdropped on Lieutenant Rutherford and Major André, and the latter said that eight thousand men are embarking at Whitestone to confront the French at Rhode Island, along with nine ships of the line."

Mr. Townsend stiffened, his narrowed eyes studying her.

"Major Andrew said that Clinton wanted him with him, and to put off the recruiting of a potential traitor. That's all I know."

She found her shoulders sagging as if she hadn't realized how burdened she'd been by the weight of an important secret.

He hesitated, then nodded. "You have done well. Please tell me that Ben will continue in this role."

"I hope so. He's very ill."

Mr. Townsend's lips pressed into a thin line of what looked like disapproval. "He is good at what he does. I will pray for his recovery."

She blinked up at him in surprise.

He pointed to the door. "Now please go. And take care no one sees you leave this building."

~oOo~

Abigail spent the rest of the day taking turns caring for Ben and seeing to her customers. Ben seemed to rest easier once she'd safely delivered their information, though his fever still lingered.

Up in her room that evening, when the sun had only begun to set at her back, her relief at completing her assignment now warred with fear that it was too late. From her fourth-floor window, she could see the tall masts of the ships retreating from port one by one. She shivered with an eerie sensation of helplessness. If Washington's army didn't receive the information in time, the French might be set upon unawares and defeated as they landed.

And there would be no one left to stand with them against the might of the Crown.

What if Ben had been injured—perhaps died—for nothing?

**28**

---

# PAMELA

2023

The smell of fresh paint wafted down the hall as Pam entered her apartment. As usual, her gaze landed on the framed portrait of Great-Aunt Lillian with the jazz band behind her. The trumpeter drew her attention, since she'd devoured the cassettes of the man who was once Baby Daniel talking to his grandson. The stories of his life seemed to have imprinted on her brain, a glimpse of another time, when his father, Ray Waterman, served in Europe during World War I before coming home to be a professional musician.

Pam moved closer and studied the trumpeter. Was Ray Waterman Daniel's father? Was Lillian his mother? Daniel hadn't seemed to care if there was something mysterious about his birth.

But Pam found that *she* cared—she wanted to know the truth, as if the building's fate was somehow tied to the women who'd come before Pam, like Lillian, like Abigail, and all the others lost to history.

It was something Dad would have wanted, too.

She texted Keith to arrange a meeting with Daniel's grandson.

After leaving her phone on the coffee table, Pam passed through the living room and paused in the doorway to her bedroom, where sheets were thrown over the furniture as Lucia and her friend Noah painted. They didn't notice her immediately, and she remained quiet, enjoying their chatter about a musician they both liked.

Noah had been glad to help when Lucia asked, and he'd taken to it with ease. Painting was a skill Pam had learned because she'd always liked freshening up rooms back in Manhasset. Why hire out when it was something she enjoyed doing? The focus and attention to detail had been almost like a meditation to her, and Noah seemed to feel the same. He'd actually thanked her because no one had ever taught him to paint, telling her it was something he could do while he figured out what was next in his life. He even showed up to work when Lucia was at her other job. Pam felt glad she could be part of giving him a start in adulthood.

And when Lucia noticed her standing in the doorway and flashed that smile of happiness, Pam felt something inside her just soften into tender happiness.

Then she reminded herself that finishing the painting was another step closer to making a final decision about the building—about her own life.

~oOo~

Pam shook hands with Scott Waterman, baby Daniel's grandson, at a midtown restaurant, and it gave her a thrill of connection. Were they cousins? Scott seemed close to her own age, his short gray hair thinning on top, his complexion a shade darker than her own. His smile was wide with warmth beneath his wire-rimmed glasses.

"So glad to meet the woman who gave me a window into

the past," Scott said. "I've always been fascinated by my family history."

"Your fascination was the reason I was able to hear your grandfather's story in his own voice. I wish I'd thought to do that with my relatives." She felt a twinge of sorrow that she didn't have recordings of her parents or grandparents talking about their lives.

"I know it wasn't much help with your research into the picture's mystery."

"Maybe not, but you never know."

As they sat down, Scott continued, "When Keith showed me the baby picture and explained how you got it, I was fascinated. My grandfather loved his parents and wouldn't have said a word to challenge their family history—it was Grandpa's siblings who expressed their curiosity."

"Didn't they worry they'd be hurting him?"

"Oh, they never spoke in front of him. They said things to their children, who whispered of scandal to their cousin, my dad."

"I assume the siblings are long gone."

He nodded, then waited as the female server brought them glasses of ice water and menus. When they were alone again, he continued, "My first thought when hearing that the picture was hidden with a lock of hair, was the same as yours—a mixed-race baby would hardly be celebrated. If your aunt was the biological mother, she probably would have hidden that fact."

"I agree, at least in this case. I brought the photo that it was hidden behind. Would you like to see it?"

He leaned forward eagerly, and Pam handed him the framed photograph of her aunt and the musicians.

Scott gave a low whistle. "There's the trumpeter in the background, too far away to really see his face up close. Would you mind if I take a picture of it?"

"Of course—sorry I didn't think of having one made."

He carefully removed it from the frame and snapped a photo with his phone camera, then zoomed in on the screen, frowning. Pam gave him time to think as she put the photo back in its frame.

At last he shook his head. "I want to say the profile looks a little like my dad, but that might be wishful thinking."

"So we have the lock of hair," Pam said hesitantly, "but hair isn't a good candidate for DNA testing without the follicle, and this one was obviously cut. I was wondering..."

"If I'd agree to have my DNA tested with yours?" he asked, smiling.

She felt the last of her tension ease away. "If it wouldn't be too much trouble."

"Not at all. Let's see if we're cousins."

~oOo~

Pam was in her kitchen, deciding whether to order take-out or cook a meal, when she heard her name called. She'd left the door to her apartment open, the better to diffuse the paint fumes, so she ducked into the hall and came to a stop. Keith stood at the top of the stairs, baseball cap in one hand, hair mussed, his satchel dangling off one shoulder.

"Hi Keith."

"I know I didn't call," he said. "Lucia let me in. Hope that was okay. I was just too excited."

"Excited? What's happened?"

"I wanted to help you make an informed decision about Harbor House, and since you're obviously interested in the history of it, I decided to do some research. On my own time," he added quickly.

Instead of resenting his interference, she found herself

smiling. "That was nice of you. Come on in and tell me about it."

She turned and headed back into her apartment. At the kitchen table, she removed a couple of dirty coffee cups and the book Lucia was currently reading.

"Have a seat. Can I get you something to drink?"

"Water's fine."

He set his satchel on the table and began to open it as she grabbed two bottles from the fridge and put one near him. She didn't want to get in the way of whatever he was doing.

He brought out a manila envelope, then set the satchel beside him on the floor. "So I decided to check out the digitized collection from the Museum of the City of New York. They've inherited all kinds of items from the history of the city. Your family name has been around over two hundred years, so I thought maybe something ended up there."

Pam felt her own curiosity ratchet up with tension. "You've found something."

He nodded cheerfully, opened the manila envelope, and pulled out a stack of papers a quarter inch high. "Somewhere along the line, someone inherited a box of family papers and donated them to the museum. Among them was a very old journal written by Abigail Featherstone."

Pam caught her breath as she stared down at the scanned pages of the journal. The writing style jumped out at her. "It's really her," she said softly. "They match the handwriting in the letters we found."

Without even planning it, they sat down side by side and began to skim the pages together. Some of the words had faded or pages were stained. The formal style of writing added diffi-culty, but they worked their way through a section. At first Abigail wrote about her life as a tavern owner's wife, then raising her children. She wrote about remedies for illnesses her children had, and lists of goods she bought from merchants.

But the war changed everything. With her husband's death and the British occupation, soon she was housing British soldiers, and she wrote more detailed entries than she'd put in her letters, how she sometimes had to demand rent, as well as the damage some officers did to her rooms and her tavern.

"She writes nothing about spying," Pam said, "but I can't imagine she'd risk anyone finding out. The only way she could get the story out was by fictionalizing it, but so many of the descriptions are the same."

She glanced at Keith to see if he agreed and realized that in their shoulder-to-shoulder examination of the papers, they were unnaturally close together.

His smile had faded, and he looked into her eyes with a directness that was too disconcerting. She turned her focus back to the papers.

He cleared his throat. "All this time, history thought a man wrote this story, but it was a woman. You've discovered something else amazing about Harbor House. Does it make you change your mind about selling it?"

She stared down at the pages, all spread out before them on her father's old Formica table. "You sound like you want me to."

"It's not my decision, and I'd never presume. I'm just curious."

"All old buildings are full of stories—this one is no different."

"But they're the stories of *your* family," he said quietly.

"But I'd be taking such a risk," she cried. "My entire future is at stake. I have no husband, no children, and I'm fifty years old. I'd be jettisoning my financial security on this place! It's only ever given me heartache before now."

The feeling of indecision was like a twisting in her mind, a pulling toward two different goals—freedom from the past, from painful memories, and a pulling toward an unknown future of what might happen in this building if she wanted it to.

She'd had to make so many decisions since her husband's death that this more momentous one seemed impossible to make. She'd thought dealing with Harbor House was the challenge she needed to prove to herself that she'd gotten past the indecision, but so far, that hadn't been true. It made her feel like a failure.

She heard a sound and turned her head to see Lucia standing in the doorway, both hands on the frame as if she meant to stop herself from entering. Her expression was full of such compassion and sympathy that Pam felt overcome with the knowledge that this young woman, who'd suffered so much in her life, would feel compassion for *her*. It made her feel both foolish, angsting over problems, and blessed to have such a rare friendship at the same time.

What was she going to do?

**29**

---

# LILLIAN

### 1926

Lillian opened the door to the Webster law office and approached the secretary's desk.

Mrs. O'Neill gave her a cool stare before arching one eyebrow. "Miss Featherstone, you do not have an appointment."

"I know. I was hoping Mr. Webster could see me over his lunch break."

"You do not know how to work a telephone?"

A man's voice said, "It's all right, Mrs. O'Neill."

Lillian and the secretary turned their heads to see Paul Webster standing in the doorway to his inner office, dressed in shirt sleeves and vest over his trousers, his suit jacket absent. It made him look more approachable, and Lillian didn't like that.

Mrs. O'Neill sniffed. "You're setting a precedent, Mr. Webster. It's not how things should be done."

"Miss Featherstone won't take advantage." He stepped aside. "Please come in."

Lillian walked past him and sat down in the same uncomfortable chair, her purse on her lap, her lips pressed together in a firm line. He took a seat behind his desk and wore an impersonal, professional expression, as if he hadn't grinned at her on the upper East side a few days ago.

She got right to the point. "Is there any news about his sentencing hearing?"

"Not yet."

"Very well. The next thing I need is for you to speak to your other clients," she said.

"My other clients?"

"The ones you say you represent legally, but who do very illegal things."

He cocked his head and spoke impassively. "I don't know whom you mean."

She rolled her eyes. "They came to my restaurant! Big Jim Russo. They beat up a musician working at my club."

"You mean a musician working illegally for your illegal speakeasy?"

"Does that mean he deserves to be hurt?"

Mr. Webster frowned. "Of course not. Is he recovering?"

"He is. But his mouth is so swollen he can't play for a week or longer. This is how he earns his living," she insisted.

"Did you take my advice and let your questions drop?"

She thought about the restaurant owners she'd talked to and said nothing.

He pressed his hands flat on his desk blotter and leaned toward her. "You have to let this go. Your father knows what he's doing, and continuing to ask questions about what happened will only get other people hurt, not just your father."

"You don't think *I'm* hurt—that my entire family is hurt, because of whatever happened?"

He sat back, exhaling loudly as he shut his eyes.

"Look at me!" she cried.

He did so, and the sympathy in his expression made her eyes sting with tears she refused to shed.

"How can I abandon my father? How can I go on with my life with him unjustly in a jail cell for the rest of *his* life?"

"There is nothing you can do to help him. You need to tell me you're done with this, that you'll visit him like a good daughter, but let him deal with his own affairs. Maybe I can find a way to stop the reprisals."

"No!"

He abruptly stood up and leaned over the desk. "This is *dangerous,* Lillian! If you keep prying, not only will you be putting your family and friends in danger, but your father, too. It's how they work. I don't like it any more than you do."

"It's not about the prying—it's about Mr. Russo deciding he can take my hard-earned money!"

He slowly sat back down. "He came to you about the protection money?"

She nodded. "I told him I needed to think about it. But I don't want anything to do with him. You need to stop him!" Tears overflowed her eyes.

He pulled a handkerchief from his pocket and offered it to her. She wanted to refuse and stomp off, but she still had too much pride to show her defeat to Mrs. O'Neill. She took his offering, mopped her eyes, and blew her nose.

"Promise me you'll let this go," he said softly. "Let me talk to the Russos and try to protect you."

She glanced up at him.

"It's what your father would want."

Narrowing her eyes at his gall, she stood up, dropping the handkerchief on his desk, and left his office.

~oOo~

Two days later, Big Jim Russo was shown up to Lillian's office by the wide-eyed chef before the restaurant opened for dinner. She caught a glimpse of his two henchmen, who remained standing in the hall as the chef hurried back downstairs.

Mr. Russo shut the door and sat down across from her desk. Lillian slowly sank into her swivel chair, folding her hands on the desk blotter and trying not to grip them so hard her knuckles whitened. So much for Paul Webster's help.

She remembered Mr. Weinstein telling her about this man's visit to the club, and how he'd seemed unhappy about the Negro band. Then again, Mr. Weinstein was unhappy about them, too, so maybe he wasn't very objective.

"Lillian, what a pleasure to see you again."

As if she'd invited him to a party.

"Thank you, Mr. Russo. What can I do for you?" She almost winced at such foolish words.

He smirked. "You know what I want. It's time for you to start paying your fee."

He looked at her with such a kindly expression, as if he wasn't attempting to blackmail her, as if he hadn't ordered men to beat up Ray. She was outraged and angry and scared all at once.

"And I want you to keep being able to afford my fee, so take some advice. People like to be entertained by the right sort of people—our sort of people."

"Considering that your family is from Italy and mine is not, do you mean White people?" she asked.

He shrugged. "You want customers, don't you?"

"Mr. Russo, I have so many customers since I hired the Waterman Jazz Band that I have to turn them away at the door. People just want to be entertained, and talent matters more than skin color."

"I disagree," he said, his tone still paternally pleasant.

"Are you the reason the trumpeter couldn't play? Someone beat him."

Mr. Russo cocked his head. "I did no such thing."

But he probably ordered someone to do it. Not that she had proof.

"But I guess I'm not the only one who is not fond of Negro bands." He chuckled. "So are you ready to discuss terms, Miss Featherstone?"

"I need to speak with my father first. This is his restaurant."

Mr. Russo's smile faded again. "I have been very patient. I advise you not to see your father."

The coldness in his voice almost made her shiver. "Then that implies to me that what you're doing doesn't bear scrutiny."

He stood up. "If you refuse me, you'll have to live with the consequences."

"What consequences?" she demanded.

But without another word he strode out the door.

Lillian sank back in her chair and covered her face with both hands. Would she really tell her father about this? What was the point—it wasn't as if he could do anything from behind bars. Hadn't he forfeited any say in the business when he'd decided to plead guilty?

~oOo~

Not two days later, on Saturday night, while a crowd enjoyed Ray and his band performing, someone shouted "Fire!"

Lillian who'd been standing beside the bar meeting the playful gaze of Ray just minutes before, suddenly smelled smoke. She whirled and found it billowing from the offices.

Screams erupted all around her as people surged toward the exit.

For a frozen moment, time seemed to stop as all the possible scenarios rushed through her brain. She could lose everything, the entire building.

She caught a glimpse of Mr. Weinstein shouting into the phone, but she couldn't hear him above the noise of the panicking crowd. She was knocked sideways into the bar, her ribs taking the brunt of it. The stairs were narrow, and the crowd tried to force themselves past each other to get to freedom. She prayed her manager had been calling the fire department.

"Lillian!"

And then Ray had his arm around her, guiding her along with the crowd, his trumpet in his other hand.

"Wait!" She tried to turn toward Mr. Weinstein, but he'd run back through the smoke into his office. "What is he doing? We have to help him!"

"I'm getting you out of here first!" he shouted.

And then he tugged her along at the edge of the crowd, both of them beginning to cough.

Her lungs hurt, her eyes streamed tears when they finally made it to the bottom of the stairs. She looked over her shoulder, and to her relief saw Mr. Weinstein carrying a satchel and hurrying after them, a handkerchief tied over his lower face. She didn't think she'd ever seen him without a cigar clenched in his teeth, she thought, dazed.

When they finally burst out of the club doorway, a fire engine was already blocking the street, and helmeted firemen pushed past her carrying a hose. Most people fled down nearby avenues, shivering from the winter cold, but a few lingered, gaping. Smoke roiled through the open door.

Lillian found herself shivering hard, even with Ray's arm around her. Her frantic gaze kept moving along the narrow basement windows. She saw a flicker of fire in one and gasped, imagining her family's entire future burning up along with Harbor House.

But at last, the smoke coming out the door faded away, and the flame she'd glimpse died.

One by one, the firemen emerged, their strides no longer urgent, dragging their hose out with them. One of the firefighters approached Mr. Weinstein, and Lillian left Ray to hear what they had to say.

"—were lucky," the fireman was saying, his face dirty with soot, his helmet pushed back off his forehead. "The fire's out. It started in one of the small rooms and didn't spread far into the club. Some scorching on that carved bar, smoke and water damage. The room where it started will need to be gutted. But it didn't spread to the first floor." The man glanced with irritation at Lillian.

Mr. Weinstein said, "This is the owner's daughter, Miss Featherstone."

The fireman touched the brim of his helmet. "Sorry. You heard all that?"

She nodded. "Do you know what caused the fire?"

Squinting, he rubbed his neck. "Not for certain, but it looks like it started near a couch. It was pretty destroyed when we got in there."

"Cigarette?" Mr. Weinstein said brusquely.

The fireman hesitated. "Could be, but it seems more deliberate than that. I've seen it before," he added wearily.

"Then we'll call the police," Lillian said.

"I wouldn't, if I were you," the fireman said, exchanging a look with Mr. Weinstein.

Lillian felt as if he were silently telling Mr. Weinstein to keep her in line. "And why not?" she asked defensively.

"Usually this sort of thing is a punishment—or a warning. I can't say more than that."

Her relief turned back into the cold sweat of fear trickling down her back. Mr. Weinstein was looking at her impassively, but he might as well have shouted, *I warned you!*

Lillian clasped her shaking hands together. "Can we go back inside?"

"Sure. I have a man downstairs doing a final check, but he should be done soon."

She put her hand on his forearm. "Sir, I can't thank you enough for saving the building."

He shrugged. "Just take care of it so I don't have to come back again. So far you've been lucky."

He returned to his men, who were coiling their hoses, laughing and talking now that the emergency was over.

*Lucky?*

"Here," said a man from behind her.

She turned to find Mr. Weinstein shoving the satchel into her arms.

"Put this in the safe," he continued. "I'll tell the employees to go home, then see you tomorrow."

He walked away, shivering in his shirt sleeves. It dawned on her that he must have left his overcoat in his office.

Ray approached and put a hand on her shoulder before saying softly, "Are you all right?"

She nodded and turned back toward the door, the satchel awkward in her arms.

"May I come with you?" Ray asked.

"Of course, please come. I have to"—she raised the satchel —"deal with this."

As the firetruck drove away, the last gawkers left, and the pre-dawn stillness seemed frightening. She felt like someone was watching her from the shadowed doorways of other buildings. After drawing Ray inside, she shut and locked the door.

The smell hit her at once—wet smoke so strong she wanted to gag. She stared at the opening to her club, where the lights still lit the way down the stairs. "I need to go down there."

When Ray didn't protest, she put the satchel on a worktable and led the way, holding onto the railing to avoid slipping on the wet wood. When she reached the bottom, she stepped into several inches of water and cried out in dismay.

"Are you all right?" Ray asked, reaching out for her hand when he reached her side.

"Oh, Ray," she whispered,

Her beautiful nightclub. The carved wooden bar dripped water, and there were smashed liquor bottles glittering along the shelves and scattered across the wet floor like quartz stones at the beach. The beautiful draperies she'd bought to disguise the bare walls now hung in tatters on that side of the club, charred in a few places.

She walked into Mr. Weinstein's office, It had been blasted with water to keep it from burning, she assumed, which had worked. She hoped the files inside the filing cabinet could be dried.

Taking a deep breath, she turned to the entertainer's room. Everything inside was blackened by fire. The sofa was just a woodpile now.

Ray squeezed her waist. "This isn't too bad at all. You'll just have to close for a month or two of repairs, and the restaurant upstairs can continue to operate once you air the place out."

She knew he was right, but her stomach was still gripped by nausea at what had been done—and the fact that no one had died. She couldn't think about how much the restaurant's success—her family's future—had depended on the profits from The Underground. She shuddered.

She thought about Paul Webster's warning and could imagine him saying, "I told you so!" the next time they met.

She sloshed back toward the stairs. Ray followed her up and through the kitchen, where she picked up the satchel, then further up to her office. With a brief glimpse inside the satchel, she confirmed that it was the night's take, which she deposited in the safe before slamming the door shut again.

She turned and met Ray's sad, sympathetic gaze from where he stood beside the open doorway.

With his shoulders slumped, his hands deep in his pockets, he looked as defeated as she felt.

"Those mobsters don't want me and my band here," he said quietly.

She opened her mouth to disagree, but she didn't want to lie to him. "I didn't pay them their protection money. It's more about that."

He shook his head. "I can't be the reason you lose everything."

She gripped the edge of the desk. "What are you saying?"

"I've been offered a gig in France. Josephine Baker made a splash at the Folies Bergère last summer and I've been asked to join her band."

She just stared at him. His words were another body blow in a night of pain. She sank down in her chair, gripping her trembling hands together.

"I didn't plan to take it," he continued, "but since we can't play here anymore, I have to be sensible about this. It's a lot of money I can send home to my family."

She didn't try to talk him out of it. She knew how welcome he'd felt in France. "When do you leave?" she whispered.

"The ship departs in two days." Then he rushed around the desk to squat down in front of her, taking her hands. "Come with me. We can be together openly there."

She searched his dark eyes as her own filled with tears. Flashes of the life they could have together in France—marriage, children, success—brightened and then died away like the embers from a dying fire.

Squeezing his hands, she whispered, "I can't."

"Lillian—"

"Don't you see?" She pulled her hands away. "My mother and my siblings depend on me. How could I abandon them with my father in jail?"

"We could send money." But his words lacked force, and she

knew as well as he did there wouldn't be enough for both families.

"I can't leave them." She felt like she was memorizing his face, even as tears continued to dampen her own. She gave a shaky laugh. "And what would your mother say, after all? And mine. We would be destroying our families in so many ways. I just...can't."

He stood up, and to her surprise, he bent over and kissed her forehead. "I'll miss you."

The crack in her heart deepened painfully. "I'll miss you. But you'll have a wonderful time in France. It's for the best."

"I'll look you up when I come back."

She winced. "Don't do that, Ray. Let's each find our own happiness without second-guessing our decisions."

They were the right words, but they felt torn out of her throat.

Ray gave her a sad nod, bowed his head, then left her office.

Lillian sat limply in the chair for a long time, feeling like her entire life was a snow globe that someone had decided to shake again. But the snow was settling in her little world, leaving her cold and bereft as she turned and began to write a list of what she had to do to repair the fire-damaged club.

# 30

# LILLIAN

## 1926

Lillian had no choice but to tell her mother about the fire, since the cost to repair the damage might force the family to live frugally. They all insisted they wouldn't lose Mrs. Vickers, whatever it took. The old woman had continued to cook for them and take care of the kitchen while the rest of the family managed the household cleaning. To Lillian's surprise, Mother had already been working with a jeweler to sell some of the extravagant gifts Papa had bought her early in their marriage.

"I was a naïve young woman," Mother said with a sigh. "I had no idea we might be living above our means."

"Maybe you weren't," Lillian said, briefly touching her mother's arm.

"Regardless, this is the only way I can help, so I'll let you know the final amount. I've even been comparing prices at jewelers, so they can't cheat me."

Lillian blinked in surprise. "Thank you, Mother, that will help." Even if it only paid for the repairs, not the lost business of the next month, that would be better than nothing.

She drove down to Harbor House to see the progress of the

work crew she'd hired to clear out debris. As she entered through the dining room, she saw the sparse lunch crowd and wondered if the faint smell of smoke in the air was her imagination, or if it repulsed customers.

To Lillian's surprise, a man sitting alone at a small table stood up as she passed, and she recognized Mr. Webster immediately. She found herself irritated by his intimidating height, and worried there might be bad news.

"Mr. Webster," she said with a nod.

"It's Paul."

He didn't quite meet her eyes, as if he was embarrassed. It was too strange.

"Do you have news for me, Mr. Webster?"

"I do. The sentencing is tomorrow, and then the sheriff will immediately take your father to Sing Sing."

She covered her mouth with one hand. She shouldn't be surprised, yet the shock of it still landed like a punch to her stomach.

"I thought you'd like to see him, so may I escort you?"

Her shock plummeted through confusion to dread. Was there something he wasn't telling her?

"I can read every emotion on your face," Mr. Webster said softly. "You don't need to fear the worst."

A memory of his words echoed in her mind: *Let me try to protect you.*

Pressing her lips together, she gave a brief nod. She asked Herbert to tell Mr. Dabrowski she'd be back in a few hours. Mr. Webster gestured to the door, and she walked ahead of him.

"I'll drive," he said, once they were on the sidewalk. "My car is just down the block."

She clutched her coat together and hunched down in her fur collar against the winter wind. He opened the car door for her, and she sank inside, shivering.

The drive to the Tombs didn't take long. Lillian stared out the window and saved her questions for her father.

Once inside, Mr. Webster slipped money to Officer Riley and soon they were in the same private room in which she'd seen her father before, with a wall of bars dividing it, the stench of sweat and fear all around her.

The sounds of distant shouts, the smells of desperate, perspiring men still overwhelmed her. But she didn't have long to think about it, because Officer Riley escorted her father into the other side of the room. To her surprise, Papa had shaved and combed his hair. There was an air of resignation and calm about him.

"Lillian, my girl," he said.

They rushed together to the bars to grip hands.

Officer Riley, stationed outside the room, said nothing for once. Mr. Webster must have given a sizable tip.

"Papa, I'm so sorry to tell you bad news about the club," she began.

He waved a hand dismissively. "The fire, I know. Paul told me."

She looked over her shoulder at the lawyer and he shrugged, wearing a faint smile.

"It is a minor thing that can be repaired," Papa continued. "I'm glad no one was hurt. But I wanted you to know that you won't have to worry about such things anymore. You'll be safe from reprisals. Paul went to the Russos on your behalf, trying to protect you."

"Wait," Paul said. "They made no promises to me. I'm still working on them."

"And I don't need a stranger's interference!" Lillian quickly added.

"Don't you?" Papa countered, brows lowered. "I did my best to keep you safe, and I failed. You've been paying for my sins. And now that fire. I won't be able to bear it if you die."

"I'm not going to—"

"Just listen to me! You wanted my story, and now you're going to hear it. Sit down."

She wordlessly sank onto the hard metal chair.

Papa briefly sagged at the bars, arms supporting him, his head bowed as if bearing a weight for too long. Then after taking a deep breath, he met her gaze. "You know I was friends with Big Jim Russo when we were young. We were at school together, dated young women together—this was before I met your mother. Things changed when he angered his father, an immigrant from Italy, who briefly kicked him out. To support himself, Jim came to work for my father at Featherstone's. Jim was cocky and funny and smart. I didn't know that his father had established ties with the Mafia even before he left the old country, that he was gaining power outside the bounds of the law, that Jim became trapped and couldn't escape."

"You sound like you sympathize with a mobster," Lillian said.

She glanced at Paul, who was leaning against the wall, arms folded over his chest, watching her father closely.

"I did, at first," Papa said. "Jim knew too much to escape his father and that life."

She blew out her breath on a harsh laugh. "That's just an excuse." She leaned toward her father. "He's blackmailing me, and he almost killed some of our customers."

"Let me finish," Papa said. "I didn't know any of this at first. He was just a good friend who I sympathized with. And then we were visiting Coney Island one day, and though he was a weak swimmer, he went out too far. He started drowning, and I reached him before he went under the last time. He told his father I saved his life, and then I was golden in the Russo family. I was able to take over and improve the restaurant, and the Russos left me alone, even after I distanced myself from Big Jim. I couldn't risk becoming known as a mob restaurant. And then came the speakeasy. The Russos decided I was doing well enough that it was time to start paying for the protection I didn't realize I'd enjoyed. They didn't know that I was overextended with the townhouse on the Upper East Side, the social life it demanded, and even your college tuition."

She stiffened but said nothing.

"I couldn't pay—I didn't think it was fair that they wanted me to pay. I ignored them for a while, but the Russo men kept coming like clockwork every week. They didn't want to hear that I might lose my business or my home if I was forced to pay. So I did something that made everything worse. I leaked some information about what I knew to the DA, who was trying to make a name for himself against the mob."

Lillian couldn't help but gasp. Paul's expression remained impassive.

"They found out, of course," Papa said wearily, even as he dragged his chair closer to the bars and sat down. "And it made everything worse. They stopped threatening me and the business, and instead threatened my family. They threatened *you*," he added hoarsely, eyes wet. "And they only agreed to back off if I took the fall for the manslaughter charge."

She inhaled sharply. She'd *known* her father wasn't a killer. But relief didn't come. "Papa, why didn't you tell—"

"Stop. I didn't want you to know because it would put you in danger. I pleaded guilty because they promised no harm would come to our family. This deal kept you *alive*. I tried so hard not to get involved with them, tried to shake them off, and look what it got me."

Lillian felt helpless as she turned to Paul, who was watching her father with sympathetic eyes.

Then Paul looked at her, and when he spoke his voice was gentle. "I tried to get you to just agree to pay them—with the success of your club, you could have, easily, and no one would have been hurt."

She thought of Ray's battered face, of the fire that could have destroyed her family's only means of support. She'd resisted all she could, and suddenly it seemed like everything that had happened since she refused them was her fault.

She was too tired to think. Ray was gone, her club was in shambles, her restaurant was teetering without that extra support.

She turned to the door, jiggled the handle, then banged on it. "Let me out."

"Lillian!" Papa cried. "You need to take care of yourself, to understand how my experiences could become yours."

She felt Paul try to take her upper arm, and she shrank away. Thankfully the door opened, and she pushed past Officer Riley and marched down the hall, tears stinging her eyes even as she willed them not to fall. Ray had abandoned her, her father might as well have. She was sick of being manipulated when all she wanted was to make an honest living and protect her family.

And suddenly those thoughts sounded just like what her father had said he'd been trying to do. She gasped on a sob as she rushed out into the snowy street and looked for the nearest trolley.

When she arrived home that night, she told her mother about her father's sentencing. To her surprise, Mother contacted Paul to ask what time the sentencing was, something Lillian hadn't even thought to do, she realized with shame, and the two of them were in the courtroom the next day when Papa was sentenced to fifteen years. Mother cried out, Papa sent them one last agonized glance, and the sheriff led him away to be transported to Sing Sing.

She dragged herself through several weeks at the restaurant, waiting for the Russos to return. She made decisions about the club repairs, but it was difficult to focus on anything but her dilemma if she became complicit with the mob. They celebrated a quiet Christmas, visiting Papa in prison as a family. He kept giving her furtive looks which she ignored.

And then, two mornings in a row, she threw up. And everything got even worse.

# 31

# ABIGAIL

### 1780

Ben continued to sleep in the Barlows' bed, mildly feverish. Abigail thought part of it was that he was just exhausted from the intensity and short duration of their assignment. Though relieved and tired, she couldn't let herself feel at peace, when she didn't know if they'd been successful.

It was hard to keep her children away from the kitchen, but Lottie could be distracted with toys or schoolwork. Andrew had seen too much—his poor face was still covered in fading bruises—and he worried about Ben, who'd been so nice to him. Though Abigail reassured him that Ben would be fine, she thought it would be a long time until Andrew felt safe again. And maybe that would only happen with the end of the war.

Two days later, as Abigail walked to the market and home early in the day, she was surprised at the number of British soldiers and sailors on the street, rushing about, looking grim. She took a quick walk to Water Street and counted how many ships had returned. Almost a dozen. She tried not to let excitement cloud her thinking, but if the British fleet had returned, disgorging thousands of apparently uninjured soldiers, then surely they hadn't engaged the French.

She spent the afternoon waiting on every customer in a uniform, trying to pick up conversations without appearing too suspicious. She knew Henry was doing the same. No patron lingered over their food. There were hushed conversations, orders given, citizens looking fearful. Much as she tried, Abigail could not overhear enough detail to know what was going on. When Henry gestured toward the kitchen, she followed him in.

"I think I know what is happening," Henry said.

Then they heard Ben's voice. "Please speak louder so I can eavesdrop."

Abigail smiled at Henry, then opened bedroom door wider. "We didn't want to disturb your sleep."

Pearl nodded to them from the far side of the bed where she poured cider from a pitcher and handed it to Ben.

"I'm not tired." He was sitting propped up on pillows, wearing a shirt over bandages that no longer seeped blood. His pale complexion and exhausted eyes belied his comment. When he took a sip of his drink, his hand shook. "What's happening? I can hear troop movement on the streets."

"I think I know," Henry said, then explained, "The British speak far too freely in front of me, as if I can't understand their lofty language."

Abigail winced. "I'm sorry."

"Do not fret—it aids our cause. General Clinton has ordered the troops to defend the city. They believe General Washington is planning to invade."

A feeling of excitement seemed to move from person to person in the small room.

As Abigail met their gazes, she found herself afraid to hope. She took a deep breath. "All of this military maneuvering means our intelligence reached General Washington in time."

Pearl stepped to her husband's side, and he slid his arm around her. Ben dropped his head back on the pillows, his grin crooked yet relieved. Without planning it, Abigail sat down on the small stool at his bedside and put her hand over his.

He turned his palm up and squeezed her hand before saying soberly, "We cannot celebrate yet. Our news may have saved the French—which we can't confirm yet—but it also might have brought about a battle that could decimate our city."

"Would Washington attempt an invasion after they'd been overwhelmed and lost the city several years ago?" Abigail asked.

Ben shrugged, then winced at the movement. "We won't know until it happens. But until then, you should think about hiding away food and fuel for your family. I gave my apprentice instructions to prepare the shop as best he can."

"But the soldiers live with us," Pearl said. "The fighting could come right here."

They were all silent for a long moment.

Ben sighed. "I think the fighting, if it happens, will be north of the city, across land. I can't imagine the Patriots could successfully confront the Redcoats by rowing over on small boats from New Jersey."

"Should I go north to reconnoiter the British troop placement?" Henry asked.

"No," Ben said. "The city will be locked down, stopping our contacts from getting out word, so any information you gather will go to waste. Let's just wait."

For the rest of the day, the city remained abnormally quiet, as if its citizens were listening for the first cannon fire of battle as Patriots tried to retake the city they'd lost. Customers ate quickly and left. When Abigail ventured outside, the streets were almost deserted but for a few soldiers, as if everyone huddled indoors under the illusion of safety at their hearths.

When another day passed, and then another, New Yorkers began to emerge from their homes again. British officers resumed their nightly entertainments—Abigail even received an invitation from her sister for the following week.

In the tavern kitchen, she showed it to Ben, who was sitting on a stool, eating a slice of pumpkin bread, and looking healthier than he had in days. She found herself watching him with relief.

Ben read the note then smiled at her. "This shows that General Washington is a master at understanding what the British will do. Clinton couldn't bear to lose New York City again, and the thought of Washington besting him was too much. Clinton fell back to defend the city from the illusion of an attack. The French have surely landed by now and are safe. With such strong allies, the Patriots are bound to succeed in freeing the colonies from the yoke of Britain."

"I hope you're right. But I don't think it will happen quickly."

He gave a solemn nod.

But at least the days of intense worry that they couldn't deliver on their assignment were at last in the past. She wasn't sure if future assignments would come her way, but as long as the war lasted, she would help however she could.

Andrew and Lottie came banging through the door, laughing, as Pearl gave chase. Andrew ran around the far side of Ben, using him as a shield.

"Children," she began, "we don't want to risk injuring Mr. —" She broke off awkwardly.

"Mr. Gibbs," Ben said, his gaze not leaving hers. "And I'm doing much better. Let them enjoy themselves."

He'd offered his last name. Abigail felt herself blushing, even as the children gave a shriek of laughter when Lottie almost caught Andrew. Abigail turned away knowing that she would think about the trust Ben had placed in her later when she was alone.

They'd shared so much, experiencing danger as well as the

triumph of success. With all that had happened these last few days, Abigail considered someday writing down what she'd accomplished for General Washington in the journal where she recorded each day's market purchases, her tavern expenses, and the children's education progress.

But no, she could never tell anyone what she'd done; she had to keep her children safe. And for just this moment, they *were* safe in their house by the harbor—their Harbor House, she thought suddenly. Maybe the building that protected her family and supplied their livelihood deserved a name, a mark of recognition.

And as the children chased each other around the worktable, Ben met her gaze with warm laughter in his eyes. And the last of her resistance to him ebbed away.

**32**

———

# LILLIAN

1926

Lillian's queasy stomach followed her through the next week as a stark reminder of how things could truly go from bad to worse. She almost felt outside herself, working, reaching out to recommended contractors, all with a sense of detachment and unreality.

She certainly couldn't confide in her mother or sister. Other friends were away at school or, in Grace's case, waiting for the arrival of a baby any day now. She could hardly confess her sins.

Would Lillian soon be waiting for a baby to arrive, except without a husband or money or respectability? Her thoughts veered wildly from disbelief to dread.

She didn't even know if she really was expecting—maybe she was only making herself sick by imagining it?

And then she thought of one person she could talk to, and called Betty Tompkins, her writer friend, who surprised Lillian by agreeing to come within the hour.

After being shown up, Betty gently closed the door in Herbert's face, then turned to face Lillian, her hands on her hips.

"Thank you so much for coming," Lillian began, gesturing to the chair across from her desk.

"Since I'm not in business with you, why don't you bring your chair around so we can talk face to face."

Biting her lip, Lillian nodded and dragged her rolling office chair around to sit beside her friend. Betty was giving her an appraising, curious look.

"Are you going to say anything?" Betty asked as the silence dragged on.

"It's hard to know where to begin."

"Start where something in your life changes. That's where my stories always start, and it's good advice."

Lillian leaned closer and lowered her voice. "I'm worried I might be pregnant."

Betty exhaled, but her expression only became sympathetic rather than appalled. Lillian suppressed the tears that threatened to overflow.

"Are you having symptoms?" Betty asked.

"I've been sick almost every morning this week. I'm telling myself maybe I'm fighting an illness, but it doesn't feel that way."

"Sounds like you're pregnant." Betty sighed. "I have friends who've tried douching with Lysol or taking quinine, but that's very dangerous."

Lillian shuddered. "I can't leave my family defenseless."

"Against...?"

But Lillian couldn't explain about the mob. "I mean without me to support and take care of them. You know the situation with my father."

"What about the *baby's* father? Have you told him?"

"He left the country before I could."

"Then send a telegram."

Lillian hesitated. "He's a Negro. We can't legally marry."

"Oh, Lillian." Betty put a hand on hers where it rested in her lap. "Would you marry him if you could?"

Lillian nodded. "He wanted me to come to France with him, but who will take care of my family?"

"You're in quite the mess," Betty said. "But the first thing you need to do is make sure you're really pregnant." She reached for a pad of paper on the desk and started writing. "Here's the name of a doctor who'll at least confirm your suspicions and won't tell your parents. He believes women have the right to make their own decisions—now there's a revelation," she added dryly.

~oOo~

The doctor confirmed Lillian's pregnancy, and although she wasn't surprised, it still suddenly felt very real, very overwhelming. She spent too much time alone in her office, paralyzed over what decision to make, knowing if she was at home, she wouldn't be able to hide her emotions from her family. There'd be time enough to face them after she made a decision.

She spent hours deliberating, seeing herself holding a precious child in her arms, then imagining her family shunned by the disgrace, unable to feed themselves when people stopped dining at Featherstone's. She truly couldn't see any other course of action. So she made an appointment with Paul Webster.

His secretary, Mrs. O'Neill, made a subtly snide comment on Lillian's ability to actually schedule an appointment, but all Lillian did was nod at her and enter through Mr. Webster's open door.

He stood up behind the desk and smiled at her. "Lillian."

"Mr. Webster," she said with a nod.

"It's Paul."

She hesitated. "Paul."

His smile grew into a grin.

She told herself he'd gone to the Russos, trying to help her. Maybe it was working, since she'd had no other threats. But she still couldn't smile back.

"What can I do for you?" he asked.

She closed the door behind her and sat down stiffly across from him. "I'm pregnant."

He stared at her impassively for a long moment. She couldn't read his expression. He didn't show disgust or disappointment, but he seemed...sad and, strangely, resigned.

He sighed. "So when is the wedding?"

"I'm not getting married." She tried not to show the sorrow that seemed to be engulfing her these days—when she wasn't running to the bathroom to be sick.

He straightened, wearing a confused frown. "What kind of man doesn't propose?" he demanded, as if he was angry on her behalf.

That was...sweet of him.

"He has his own life now in France, and I can't move there and leave my family." Not the whole truth, but that wasn't his business.

She couldn't read the expression on his face—he must be very good in a courtroom.

"So if he's out of the picture, how do you plan to take care of a baby?" Paul leaned toward her. "If you're unmarried, who will come to the restaurant? Right now, people feel sorry for you because of your father's imprisonment. But eventually they'll forget, and you'll probably recover most of your social standing. Certainly your restaurant clientele have stayed with you. But when you raise a baby without any means of support? How will you make that work?"

Lillian felt as stiff and bloodless as a marble statue, except that his words landed like body blows. Nausea climbed up her throat.

But he wasn't saying anything she hadn't thought before. Still, the words were difficult to say. "I'm giving up the baby."

He moved his hand toward her, then seemed to change his mind and rubbed it across his face. Had he meant to touch her in sympathy?

"I'm sorry if my words were harsh," Paul said. "Making this decision has to be one of the hardest things any woman can go through. What can I do to help?"

She squeezed her eyes to hold back the tears, surprised at how much his kindness meant to her. "I would like your help with the adoption. I'll pay your fee, of course."

"You've paid enough. Don't worry about that."

She pressed her lips together and tried to give him a smile, but it was shaky. She realized she hadn't had much reason to smile lately.

"Let me do some research on the laws involved and who might specialize in—what you're doing."

*Giving up my child,* she thought, her throat tight. "I have heard there are places where women can go to...wait."

"I've heard about those, too. Give me two days and then let's talk again."

"Paul, this means a lot to me," she said in a low voice, unable to meet his eyes. If she saw sympathy, she'd crack apart. "I have not been kind to you."

"You've been in a tough situation. I knew that. And I saw how brave you were when other women might have fainted or had hysterics."

"You don't seem to have known the right women," she said dryly.

A corner of his mouth tilted up. "Maybe you're right. And that's a shame."

~oOo~

Two days later, Paul escorted her to another lawyer, who grimly talked about the legal aspects of her decision, looking at her as if she was a shameful woman who now had to live with the results of her sin. He told them he had several clients interested in adopting her baby.

And she realized he thought it was a White baby. Would such a lawyer even represent a Colored couple? Should she tell Paul the truth?

The lawyer gave them the name of two homes for women in her condition, and they left quickly.

"What an ass," Paul said when they were out on the sidewalk.

Clutching her coat tight against the winter chill, Lillian tried to smile. "It's all right."

"It's not all right. Wait for me here. I'm going back to talk to him."

She caught his arm. "No, please let it go."

He hesitated, and she felt the tension in his body. She removed her hand.

"All right," he said with obvious reluctance.

She took a deep breath. "Let's visit the homes."

But they didn't seem like "home" at all. At the first one, they saw pregnant women acting as household servants, while the matron in charge talked about the women paying for their sins and learning a lesson. The second place was little better. Although the young women didn't seem to be endlessly cleaning, they were listlessly looking out windows as if waiting for rescue, or sitting with books closed in their laps, their gazes unfocused. All glanced away from Paul and Lillian hastily, so ashamed that some of them ran out of the room. But then again, maybe they thought Paul was like the other lawyers who were condemning of their "sin."

Back outside, Paul angrily said, "I don't imagine the babies' fathers are treated this way." Then he gave her a startled glance. "I wasn't including your baby's father."

"I know." She let out a breath. "Thank you for your help. It's time for me to make my decision."

"Not yet. There's a park nearby we can walk in. I know it's chilly, but the sun's out."

She should refuse but she was so tired of being alone with her sad thoughts. "All right."

Though the small park was in the center of a bustling city, just walking along winding paths between trees was a relief. The leaves were gone, and the cold was enough to keep people away. It suited her. She turned up her fur collar. They didn't speak for two turns around the park, and he seemed to be deep in thought.

He suddenly stopped, and she turned around to face him.

"Marry me," he said.

Her mouth fell open in surprise. "Paul—"

"I know this is sudden," he said. "We don't know each other well."

"No, we don't," she said firmly. "You're just feeling sorry for me. But this is my mess, and I will clean it up. You're certainly not going to ruin your chances at a happy marriage because of me."

"The thing is, you'd be helping me, too."

She watched him warily. "I don't understand."

With a heavy sigh, he sat down on a bench. Heart pounding, mouth dry, she joined him.

"Big Jim Russo has a daughter," Paul began, not looking at her. "I don't like to socialize with them, but sometimes I have no choice. She's always flirted with me, and I've ignored it, but now Big Jim seems to be looking for the right husband for her and eyeing me for the position."

"You don't want to marry into the family you work for?"

"No!" He looked directly at her. "I represent him in court,

but I don't want anything to do with that family. I could leave New York, but my practice is here, my mother is in a home here, and who knows if I could even escape."

No wonder he had seemed so sympathetic to her problem. He was feeling as trapped as she was. But how do you build a marriage on that?

"Why choose me?" she asked bitterly. "There are many young women who'd be glad to marry you. Oh, wait, a pregnant fiancée proves to Mr. Russo that you have no choice—you *have* to marry someone other than his daughter."

"That's part of it, yes. I won't lie to you."

"And a mobster would let this engagement stand in the way of giving his daughter what she wants?"

"Most wouldn't, it's true. But Big Jim has been fair with me, on account of my father. I don't think he'd stand in our way. Besides, your father saved his life, and he hasn't forgotten it."

"Even as he put him in jail," she responded incredulously.

"Even then. But we're not talking about them—we're talking about us. And I *am* choosing you. There's the fact that you know the truth about me. I don't have to hide any aspect of my life from you," Paul said simply. "You understand what it's like to live in this city and have no illusions of how difficult it can be."

She stared at him in disbelief before finally saying, "This is crazy."

"Maybe. But maybe not." He spread his hands, as if helpless. "I don't know what else to say. I think a marriage between us could benefit us both." He glanced at her stomach. "And benefit that baby. I'd raise it as my own."

She covered her mouth and looked away, blinking back hot tears. For one moment, she thought of having her own household, her own family, of keeping the child that was now tucked so safely in her womb.

This child who would probably not look anything like the blond lawyer.

She spoke before she could change her mind. "There's more I haven't told you. The father is a Negro." She waited for his disgust, his quick retraction of the proposal. She'd gone against White society and found love in the arms of a man who didn't look like them. Would this be what finally turned Paul against her? His frown made her stomach clench in preparation.

"And he's not returning from France?"

Shocked at his practical question, she found her voice again. "I wasn't lying about that. Let's just forget this ever happened and you can take me home." She stood up, clutching her purse, feeling defiant and defeated all at the same time.

"Don't go, Lillian," he said softly, catching her hand. "We can make this work."

She looked down at their joined fingers. "You really must be desperate."

"And so are you." He hesitated. "Maybe the baby will look like you. It might not be so obvious.

Even if that were so, she couldn't imagine living her whole life waiting for the truth to come out. But this wasn't just about her and Paul—it was about the baby. What would it be like to grow up with people's suspicions? How could that be fair?

If she went through with the adoption, what would it feel like to wonder if her baby's new family could ever truly love him like she would?

But there was one person who would love the baby unconditionally.

She sank back down on the bench and closed her eyes. Paul said nothing, but he didn't release her hand.

"I think," she began softly, then had to stop and swallow past her tight throat, "I think the baby deserves a chance to be with his father." Tears overflowed and streamed down her cheeks.

Paul took a deep breath and squeezed her hand. "I didn't know if that was possible."

"Ray wanted to be with me, to raise our own family. How can I keep his child from him? I'm ashamed I didn't consider his feelings from the beginning, but I was so scared, so confused."

"I'll pay to have the baby escorted to France."

She gaped at him, but he never dropped his gaze, nor did he release her hand.

"I mean it. I want you to be at peace with this decision."

Lillian wiped her wet face with both hands and closed her eyes, feeling sick with more than nausea. She imagined Ray welcoming both her and the baby with open arms, but that was a dream she could never have.

At last she looked up at Paul, who shockingly got down on one knee.

"Would you still marry me?" he asked. "You're certainly smart and beautiful, but mostly I like how you want more from life than attending the right parties. I won't stop you from running the restaurant or your club, but I do want kids, and I want them to be raised in a better environment than I was."

She knew part of his motive was selfish, that he needed to marry, but her own motives weren't much better—she valued that he knew everything about her, and was a lawyer with financial security. She'd been so alone in the world, and sharing this secret with him had made her feel supported these last few days.

And he wanted children. She couldn't replace this tiny child she'd never raise, but she wanted the chance to be a mother.

"I don't mean this to sound like a bribe," he said, when she still hadn't found the words to answer. "But I'm also hoping I can do more for your father when the pressure dies down."

Was that a lie? Or an exaggeration? She didn't know

anymore. She felt lost, sad—but deep down, something eased inside her.

"I'll marry you," she said.

~oOo~

The next few weeks seemed like someone else's life. Paul started dropping by as if to court Lillian and found a way to make her mother laugh.

Lillian didn't let herself think of the baby as hers. She wrote to Florence Waterman and requested her brother's address in France. When she had that, she wrote the most difficult letter of her life to Ray, explaining that although she would love their baby forever, the child would have a hard life with her, and asking him to raise it. She thought of sending a telegram, but how could she condense such a complicated request down to a couple sentences? And that method was hardly private, with operators possibly gossiping over her message. She knew the letter would take several weeks to arrive, and then several more weeks before she'd hear a reply, so she kept the pregnancy from her family. It was even harder to keep from blurting the truth to Mrs. Vickers, who seemed to watch her far too closely.

To her surprise, a reply came via Ray's sister, who wrote briskly and with little emotion that all had been settled, that her friend Anna would accompany the baby to France. Lillian remembered the adoring way Anna had looked at Ray and knew she should be glad the baby would be taken care of by someone close to the family, someone who had Ray's best interests at heart.

But as winter darkness descended on the city, and Lillian sat alone in her bedroom window seat, she cried with her face in a pillow, deep sobs for what she was losing. Did Ray even plan to write to her? Or was he disgusted that she wouldn't come to France and be with him, even with a child to raise?

Lillian broke the pregnancy news to her mother, along with news of her engagement—and that the baby wasn't Paul's, explaining that he did know about it, and they'd both agreed she'd relinquish her rights to the father. Her mother seemed to reel back in her chair, her complexion fading to white, then back to red before she burst into tears. Lillian didn't blame her one bit and tried to find a way to explain her mistakes.

To her surprise, though Mother was initially disappointed and angry with Lillian's behavior, Mother blamed Papa more for what he'd done to destroy their family. Lillian let her blame someone else because she couldn't bear to lose even her mother's companionship.

Lillian and Paul were married in city hall with just her family. His mother wasn't well enough to attend, although Lillian did visit and sit by her bedside chatting.

They had a restaurant meal alone and went home to a quiet apartment. It was a small one-bedroom, but he seemed eager for her to do anything she wanted to make it her home. He didn't insist on a wedding night, saying they should get to know each other better first.

But she wondered if he wanted to wait until she was no longer pregnant with another man's baby.

It was strange to tell friends about her sudden marriage, and everyone certainly knew she was expecting because of the haste. Grace's smile was wobbly with tears, but she hugged Lillian and whispered that she'd be a wonderful mother.

Lillian couldn't even tell Grace the whole truth, and it made her feel like she plunged a knife of betrayal into their friendship. But maybe someday, she could explain everything.

As the months went by, and she grew to love the baby even more as it stirred within her, the inevitable ending was like a death coming ever closer. She was glad to distract herself with the restaurant and the reopening of The Underground. Big Jim Russo visited once, but all he did was congratulate her on her marriage. He didn't even ask about the protection money. Lillian knew she should find out what Paul had negotiated, but it just didn't seem as important as focusing on her last moments mothering the child she'd never know.

When Lillian was seven months along, she, her family, and Mrs. Vickers went upstate as if they were on summer vacation to a beautiful home on the Hudson that Paul had rented.

Paul visited every weekend, getting to know her siblings and her mother. Viola seemed enamored of him, as if he'd saved Lillian's life. And maybe he had. Mrs. Vickers began to have his favorite cookies ready every visit.

Paul liked to take Lillian on long walks about the property, telling her of his plans to find a better apartment, but that he'd wait until she could choose it with him.

When at last it was time for the baby to arrive, Lillian was determined not to dwell on her sadness. She was giving this baby life, a father, a good man full of love.

Her labor lasted more than a day, and she was exhausted and drenched with perspiration when the nurse allowed her to briefly hold her baby, a little boy. He cried loudly at emerging into an unfamiliar world, and she kissed his little cheek, his dark, damp hair, and touched his miraculously tiny fingers.

And then he was taken away, leaving her shaking with sobs. She knew Paul had hired a nurse to drive the baby back to the city, to care for him for a few weeks until doctors deemed him old enough to travel by steamer across the Atlantic with Anna. Lillian had begged to be allowed to care for him before he departed, but Paul had refused, gently telling her she'd never want to let him go.

And he was right. Her arms, her heart, felt horribly empty, even as her mind was tormented by guilt.

And then her mother rushed in to hold her like Lillian had been holding her own child. Lillian clung to her, the rocking and shushing not soothing her as she cried and cried for the life she'd given away.

~oOo~

The following weekend, Paul came back upstate. He'd had the terrible task of lying to all their friends that they'd lost the baby. Lillian knew it must have been hard, but it seemed like such a distant concern compared to the grief that swamped her every waking hour. She lay awake at night with painful, leaking breasts, missing her child, her heart.

She was at their temporary home, sitting on the covered porch, staring at the view of the Hudson at the far end of a manicured lawn, when Paul was announced by the maid. For a moment, Lillian wanted to refuse, to let herself sink ever deeper into this feeling that nothing mattered anymore. She knew she was frightening her family, that her brother Julian, who was told she truly had lost the baby, seemed almost afraid of her, but she couldn't find a reason to do something about it.

Paul smiled as he entered the porch from inside the house. Lillian thought she saw her mother peering at her through the screen, but Lillian turned her head away. Paul leaned over and kissed her cheek. She was aware of his unobtrusive cologne, the soft press of his lips, but it was as if she was far away, observing rather than participating.

"Hello, my dear." He sat down in the chair beside her.

She closed her eyes and focused on the scent of the dying autumn leaves drifting to the ground outside the porch.

"Pretending I'm not here won't make me go away," he said.

A breeze carried the faintest tinge of smoke, as if someone was burning a pile of leaves, destroying the evidence of their existence.

"You don't have any questions for me about how the baby is doing?"

She froze. "My mother said it's best not to mention the baby anymore."

"Is that what you want?"

When a tear fell down her cheek, she was mortified at her lack of control.

"It's still very fresh for you," he said. "I don't expect you to pretend it never happened. Although your mother is right that after a while, it will be best to let the memories be."

"What memories?" she whispered. "I only held him for five minutes."

"I'm not a woman, but I imagine carrying a baby inside you makes you...attached."

She almost snorted at his awkwardness. Was that nearly a laugh? She hadn't laughed in...she didn't remember when.

"Since you can't articulate your questions," he continued, "I'll tell you that the nurse is taking fine care of the baby. Anna is visiting regularly, so that he is comfortable with her when it's time to leave."

"Stop." Every word was harder and harder to hear, as if someone scraped the edge of a knife along her skin.

"I don't know much more than that, but I'd be happy to answer any questions now. But after this, once he's gone to be with his father, we should try not to talk about him. It isn't healthy for you, Lillian. You don't look well."

"I just had a baby," she said dully.

"You know what I mean. Your family is very worried. *I'm* worried. I think you need to find something else to focus on while you recover, like maybe looking for our new apartment?"

He said it so hopefully that she winced. He'd been so patient with her these last few months. It hadn't been the kind of marriage a man might expect.

She closed her eyes again.

"I've waited for you so we can make our plans together," he said.

"You didn't have to." Even she knew how ridiculous that sounded.

"We haven't had the most auspicious start to our life together, but it doesn't have to be this way. Perhaps we should spend a week in Niagara Falls for our honeymoon? Not that we need to rush any of our plans."

She shrugged.

"I'd also like to make a regular donation to one of the homes for unwed mothers that we visited. I've been trying to find something that would have meaning for us, and perhaps helping other girls who aren't as lucky as we are would be a good thing."

*Lucky.* She didn't feel lucky, but compared to those sad young women they'd seen, she had family, a career to return to, a man who helped her out of a bad situation and offered a future. Could she forget how it had all happened?

Lillian turned her head and looked at Paul. He too seemed to be inhaling the scents of autumn, a time of change. Then he met her gaze and reached to squeeze her hand.

She didn't pull away.

**33**

---

**PAMELA**

2023

"Guess what!" Lucia called, bounding into the apartment with the exuberance of youth.

Pam smiled, her heart twisting painfully with the sweetness of love for this brave young woman and the ache of knowing that Lucia was leaving for college in just a few days. She would no longer regularly burst into whatever room Pam was in.

Lucia grinned. "Noah found a job with a painting company! It's non-union, but he plans to apply for union apprenticeships soon. Isn't that great? It's all because of you that he found something he enjoyed."

Pam felt a flush heat her skin. "That's wonderful!"

And it was as if a lightbulb went on in Pam's head. It had given her great satisfaction to help Lucia out this summer, as she transitioned from foster care to full-time adulthood. Now there was Noah, who Lucia had brought to her, looking for help. Somehow, Pam had stumbled upon something that inspired him.

It gave her such an intense feeling of satisfaction, a hope for the future with this new generation of young people, knowing she'd had some small part in making it happen. During the year after Will's death, she'd felt nothing in her life that made her look forward to the future, until now.

And she wanted to keep doing it—helping young people who felt abandoned, just like her father had done. Harbor House, which she'd hated in her childhood, had been helping people for a long time, even back to her ancestor fighting against the British during the American Revolution.

Sure, if she sold the building, she'd have more than enough money for the future, but she had money now—it hadn't made her any happier.

"You have a strange look on your face," Lucia said.

"Strange? I was hoping I looked happy." Pam crossed the room and gave Lucia a hug.

Lucia was eyeing her with confusion when Pam stepped away. "Well, okay, happy," Lucia added, "but something else, too."

"It's hope," Pam said softly but with conviction. "I want to be hopeful. And I want you and your friends to be hopeful, too. So I'm not selling the building."

Lucia's brow wrinkled. "What? You've decided?"

Pam nodded.

"I don't understand the hopeful part."

"The best way to help kids is to give them jobs, which gives them hope. So okay, I'll reopen the restaurant."

Lucia took a deep breath and briefly closed her eyes. "I knew you'd change your mind about the restaurant."

"It'll take time," Pam warned. "And maybe we can create a network of business owners who want to help, too. I think this can be bigger than one restaurant."

Lucia shook her head, just staring at Pam with wide, glistening eyes. Then she rubbed her hands over them quickly. "Never mind me. I'm just...happy for you."

"Me, too. Would you help me out when you're home from college?"

Nodding, Lucia gave her a big hug.

~oOo~

The drive to Syracuse seemed short, as Lucia chatted away about what courses she'd signed up for, how she and her room-mate had connected, the first dorm party that was happening that night.

And then, as a sign for the university grew larger, Lucia got quiet.

"It's hard to believe this is finally happening," Lucia said. "I can't thank you enough for all you've done for me."

"Stop, you'll make me cry," Pam said, blinking hard. "Let's get back to talking about SU. I can't wait for Parents' Weekend when you can show me around."

Lucia swallowed and stared at her with wide eyes.

Pam gave a wobbly grin. "You know you're coming back at Christmas and next summer, right? Your room will be waiting for you."

"I—You don't have to do that, Pam," she said uncertainly. "The school said they can make arrangements for me if I don't have anywhere to go."

"Is that what you want?" Pam asked.

"No. I just didn't dare to hope…"

"We're going to be all about hope, you and I."

Pam reached across the console and took Lucia's hand. Pam didn't speak, just kept glancing at the teenager, who was trying to pretend she wasn't crying.

How had Pam gotten so lucky? Working on Harbor House had taught her so many lessons from the past. From that, she was going to make a future for herself. She had a new purpose in life, a man to date—and a daughter to cherish.

**34**

---

**EPILOGUE**

2024

When Featherstone's reopened the next year, Pam tried to incorporate the building's history, some colonial touches of pewter lanterns to match the prized family tankard on the main level, and then a harkening back to the speakeasy days down below with a new ornately carved bar and patterned tin ceiling. Dad would have loved it all—even her acceptance by the National Register of Historic Places and the grants she had access to.

She hired kids in the foster system as much as she could, hosting a weekly training program to prep kids to become more hirable in the restaurant industry. She coordinated with the foster care department to place other kids in the network of businesses she continued to expand. The storerooms on the fourth floor teemed with donated professional clothes, gently used furniture for apartments, and a comfy sitting area for groups to meet to learn interview and resumé prep.

One of the best parts was that Baby Daniel's grandson Scott was indeed her cousin. He and his kids regularly volunteered with her organization.

And then there was Keith, her own PI, who regularly

stopped in for dinner and often stayed the night. His son Dylan worked in the restaurant. Pam wasn't sure she wanted to marry again, but she felt blessed to have Keith in her life. Life wasn't all about work and volunteering—she'd learned that the hard way. She would never forget the lesson that life was something to explore, to experiment with, to enjoy.

Whenever school wasn't in session, Lucia was working at her side. The young woman had brought her back to life, and Pam couldn't wait to present her with the adoption papers next time she was back home at Harbor House.

# AUTHOR NOTE:

Hello Readers!

Thank you for taking the time to read my new book! If you enjoyed it, please consider telling your friends or posting a short review wherever you purchased the book. Word of mouth is an author's best friend and much appreciated.

In my previous book, The Daring Girls of Guernsey, a grandmother's story tied together two time periods, the 1990s and World War II. I wanted to do something different this time, and my good friend and critique buddy Laura Lee Guhrke (read her books, she's great!) suggested I use a building to tie all the time periods together. I loved this idea! I settled on New York City because two of my kids live there and can help me with research. I visited the Seaport area, walked its cobblestone streets, and found some very old buildings still in existence from the post-Revolutionary war era. One was from the 1790s and had been serving food for over two hundred years until Hurricane Sandy. Voila, the thread of the story in my head had begun.

I'd done plenty of American Revolution research from an early book I never published. It's been wonderful revisiting the time period. The Culper Spy Ring is historically true, as is the plot to uncover the British plans for the French landing. It was so enjoyable to insert my fictional characters into real history. And one other fun fact: Major André, who traced a silhouette of Abigail, was the real head of British intelligence. The American he was trying to turn traitor was Benedict Arnold. During his negotiations with Arnold only a few months later, when Arnold secretly offered to turn over West Point, NY, Major André was discovered trying to return to British lines and hung as a spy.

The Roaring Twenties was a fascinating time period. Flappers were the first modern women who wanted careers and a say in their lives, who dated instead of letting men court them. Prohibition encouraged men and women to socialize together, as well as Black and White Americans. It was an early step into equality, even though there was a long way to go.

I took some liberties with the legal timeline for Lillian's father. His fate probably would have been decided faster, but I'm hoping you won't mind that I delayed his arraignment and sentencing. It worked better for the story.

As for what I'm up to next, I'm writing a novella for an anthology called **What Happens in Brighton**, which will be published Valentine's Day 2026. I'm also starting to research an idea I have for another historical fiction novel. We'll see where it leads...

Please sign up for my newsletter if you'd like notice when the next book will be published.

Thank you so much for reading this book! And if you liked it, please leave a review wherever you purchased it. Reviews help authors find new readers!

Happy reading!
*Gayle*

# RESEARCH BIBLIOGRAPHY


*Washington's Spies: The Story of America's First Spy Ring*, by Alexander Rose

*The Battle for New York*, by Barnet Schecter

*Liberty's Daughters: The Revolutionary Experience of American Women, 1750–1800*, by Mary Beth Norton

*America Walks into a Bar: A Spirited History of Taverns and Saloons, Speakeasies and Grog Shops*, by Christine Sismondo

*Flapper: A Madcap Story of Sex, Style, Celebrity, and the Women Who Made America*, by Joshua Zeitz

*Last Call: The Rise and Fall of Prohibition*, by Daniel Okrent

# BOOKS BY GAYLE CALLEN

**Daring Women**

The Daring Girls of Guernsey: a Novel of World War II

The Daring Women of New York: a Novel

**Sons of Scandal**

Never Trust a Scoundrel

Never Dare a Duke

Never Marry a Stranger

In Pursuit of a Scandalous Lady

A Most Scandalous Engagement

Every Scandalous Secret

**Secrets and Vows Series**

You Only Marry Once

On Her Warrior's Secret Mission

The Knight Who Loved Me

The Bodyguard Who Came in from the Cold

**The Brides Trilogy**

Almost a Bride

Never a Bride

Suddenly a Bride

**Spies and Lovers Trilogy**

No Ordinary Groom

The Beauty and the Spy

A Woman's Innocence

**Sisters of Willow Pond Trilogy**

The Lord Next Door

The Duke in Disguise

The Viscount in her Bedroom


**Highland Weddings Trilogy**

The Wrong Bride

The Groom Wore Plaid

Love with a Scottish Outlaw


**Brides of Redemption Trilogy**

Return of the Viscount

Surrender to the Earl

Redemption of the Duke

# ABOUT THE AUTHOR

After a detour through fitness instructing and computer programming, GAYLE CALLEN found the life she'd always dreamed of as a writer. This *USA Today* bestselling author has written more than twenty-five novels of historical romance and historical fiction. She has won the Holt Medallion, the Laurel Wreath Award, the Booksellers' Best Award, the National Readers' Choice Award, and has been a nominee for RT Book Reviews Reviewers' Choice Award. Her books have been translated into thirteen different languages.

The mother of three grown children, an avid crafter, singer, and outdoor enthusiast, Gayle lives in Central New York with her husband, Jim the Romance Hero. She also writes contemporary romances as Emma Cane. To follow Gayle on social media or subscribe to her newsletter, visit her website at www.-GayleCallen.com.